"If those relics are extraterrestrial, I want them."

"You think there's something inherent in their properties that you can use?" Annja asked.

"Perhaps. But I do know that with my money and resources, I can get them examined faster than the bureaucrats in charge. And if there's power to be had, then I want it for myself, yes."

"Such a humanitarian," Annja said.

"Not a chance. Five hundred years can do a lot to make you rather self-centered, Annja. I'm horribly selfish, I admit it."

Annja smiled. "I didn't want to say anything, but—"

Garin held up his hand. "Get back to your shelter and stay there. If anyone stops you, tell them I said you're to stay there until I say it's okay to come out."

"So, I'm grounded?"

Garin frowned. "Get to work, Annja. Lives just might depend on it."

Annja opened the door. As she did, one of the medical team soldiers came in and reported to Garin. The medic shook his head. "We did all we could. Colonel Thomson is dead."

Titles in this series:

ROGUE Angel™

Alex Archer

POLAR QUEST

A GOLD EAGLE BOOK FROM
WORLDWIDE®

TORONTO • NEW YORK • LONDON
AMSTERDAM • PARIS • SYDNEY • HAMBURG
STOCKHOLM • ATHENS • TOKYO • MILAN
MADRID • WARSAW • BUDAPEST • AUCKLAND

Recycling programs
for this product may
not exist in your area.

First edition January 2009

ISBN-13: 978-0-373-62134-7
ISBN-10:   0-373-62134-5

POLAR QUEST

Special thanks and acknowledgment to
Jon Merz for her contribution to this work.

Copyright © 2009 by Worldwide Library.

Printed in U.S.A.

The
LEGEND

...THE ENGLISH COMMANDER TOOK
JOAN'S SWORD AND RAISED IT HIGH.
The broadsword, plain and unadorned,
gleamed in the firelight. He put the tip against
the ground and his foot at the center of the blade.
The broadsword shattered, fragments falling
into the mud. The crowd surged forward,
peasant and soldier, and snatched the shards
from the trampled mud. The commander tossed
the hilt deep into the crowd.
Smoke almost obscured Joan, but she continued
praying till the end, until finally the flames climbed
her body and she sagged against the restraints.

Joan of Arc died that fateful day in France,
but her legend and sword are reborn....

1

The LC-130 Hercules turboprop plane jumped and dropped as the turbulence buffeted it about the sky. Annja Creed, dressed in extreme-cold-weather gear issued to her by the U.S. military, clutched at the armrests on her seat. She felt as if her stomach were on a roller-coaster ride and had forgotten to inform her.

She swallowed the rising bile in her throat and felt the plane lurch again. "This is getting ridiculous," she said. She unclasped her seat belt and tried to stand, bumping her head against the interior bulkhead in the process.

"Damn."

If the plane was going to crash, she at least wanted to see it coming rather than sit trapped in her seat. Annja clawed her way forward toward the cockpit.

She passed one of the crew on her way. "Is it always like this?"

He grinned. "Yup. This time of year, it's always stormy down in these parts. You get used to it after a few trips."

"Wonderful," she said, not feeling any better about the turbulence.

She made her way to the flight deck. "Hi."

The pilot turned. "You're supposed to be strapped in, Miss Creed. It's not exactly safe for you to be roaming around."

Annja smiled. "I got the distinct impression that it wasn't safe sitting in my seat, either."

"We're totally fine," the pilot said. "This is run-of-the-mill updrafts, turbulence and assorted atmospheric anomalies."

"Anomalies?" Annja asked.

He shrugged. "We don't really know what to call them. But they come with the territory of flying near the bottom of the world."

The copilot glanced at her. "You're in no danger."

Annja smirked. "Guess I figured if the end was coming, I wanted to see it rather than hide from it."

The pilot nodded. "Understandable sentiment. I'd be the same way. If you want to, you can stay as we make our approach."

"How much longer?" she asked.

"Maybe fifteen minutes. We come in low and fast, so make sure you hold on to something when we hit."

"Hit? You guys sure do have a great way of putting things."

"Well, we don't so much land as we skip and slide to an eventual stop. Those skis underneath our wheels are there for a reason," the copilot said.

Annja nodded. When they'd taken off from the Air National Guard base in New York, she'd noticed the long skis on the underside of the plane. Without the benefit of a proper runway, aircraft going to Antarctica sometimes had to land on skis.

It was the first time Annja had ever done this and she wasn't quite sure what to expect.

The flight to New Zealand had been a long one with three in-flight aerial refuelings supplied by KC-130 supertankers. Annja had watched the experienced crew guide the plane to within a quarter mile of the flying gas station, take on a full tank of gas and then continue on its way.

She looked out of the cockpit glass and could see snow falling. The pilot pointed to the instrument console. "Wipers, please."

"Wipers." The copilot switched them on and they flicked the flakes from the glass.

The plane felt as if it was starting to descend. Annja could hear flaps grinding in the cold blasts of air outside. The pilot kept the throttle up. Suddenly, Annja felt very much out of place.

Best just to let these guys get done what they need to get done, she thought. She turned and headed back to her seat.

She passed more crew members. One of them was drinking a tumbler of coffee. "Can I get you some?" he asked.

Annja shook her head. "No, thanks. Not sure my stomach will let it settle right now."

He grinned. "We'll be down in about ten minutes. You can have all you want then."

Annja sat down and secured her seat belt. As she glanced around the dimly lit interior of the plane, she thought back to the letter she'd received in her mailbox shortly after returning from her latest dig. The letter had been sent from a colleague she'd once worked with: Zachary Guilfoyle. Zach had always been obsessed with prehistory on the planet, and his quest for the strange had made him something of an untouchable among other members of the more conservative scientific community.

But Annja had loved hanging out with him. Zach, while a sucker for any bit of the mythical, was also a mean card shark and could spin a tale that often left you wondering what was truth and what was fantasy.

His letter had asked Annja to come down to the research station in Antarctica. He was currently there, studying something that he would only describe as "very interesting."

Annja had put the letter away intrigued but with no real thought toward going. She had reports to file for *Chasing History's Monsters,* after all. And she had some very overdue bills to pay.

She was all set to send Zach an e-mail telling him she couldn't go when a pair of men in dark suits, bad haircuts and disposable sunglasses had shown up outside her loft one afternoon as she returned from a jog.

"Are you Annja Creed?" one of the strangers asked.

She glanced at them, knowing immediately they were with the government. "You're telling me that with all the technology you guys have at your disposal these days, you really have to ask if I'm who you're looking for? What is that, some sort of leftover ritual you still follow from the Cold War?" she said.

It got a smirk out of one of them. "Well, you were out jogging."

"Ah, so it's more a comment on how crappy I look right now. Well, as long as I know," she said, wondering what she was in trouble for now.

Annja started up the steps. "What can I do for you?"

The Fed leaned against the railing. "You got a letter recently from a Mr. Guilfoyle."

"Are you asking me or telling me?" Annja said.

He looked over the top of his glasses at her. Annja smiled. "Right, of course. Yes, I got the letter from Zach. So what?"

"He's requested your presence at the research center in Antarctica."

Annja sighed. "If you already know about the letter, I'm assuming you know all about the contents of the letter. So how about we don't waste any more of each other's time—me being the sweaty, stinky creature in need of a shower—and you guys tell me exactly what it is you want and then go back to scaring little kids with those costumes. Okay?"

"We need you to go to Antarctica," the man said.

"Why?" Annja asked.

"Because Guilfoyle needs your help. He says you're the only one he can trust. The only one he'll work with."

Annja felt the sweat rolling down her back. It tickled a bit whenever it did that and she really wanted that shower. "What's the big deal in Antarctica?" she asked.

"It's classified."

"Of course. All that snow and ice. No wonder you guys want to keep a lid on it."

The Feds said nothing, but just looked at her.

Annja cleared her throat. "You guys aren't leaving until I agree to go—is that what I'm seeing here?"

"Something like that."

"Right." Annja took a breath and sighed. "All right. I'll need a day or so to get my things in order and let my boss know that I won't be in to do that work on the reports I'm supposed to be filing," Annja said, stalling for time to figure out what was going on.

"That's already been taken care of," one of the men said.

Annja frowned. "Excuse me?"

"Your boss. He's already been called. He knows not to expect you for about ten days."

"Ten days?"

One of the Feds shrugged. "Well, it's not like they run daily flights into the research station. Especially this time of year. Weather's a lot worse than usual."

"Oh. Great."

"We need to get you to New Zealand, Miss Creed."

"New Zealand?"

"And then on to Antarctica."

Annja nodded. "Did you guys already take a shower for me, as well?"

"Not quite."

Annja started up the steps. "Good. In that case, I'm going to soak my tired muscles. I'd invite you guys up, but I know what habitual snoops you are. There's no telling what kind of trouble you'd get into up there."

The lead Fed grinned. "That's okay. We've already seen the place."

Annja started to laugh, but something about the way he said it told her he wasn't joking. The slimy bastards had been into her place.

She stalked into the building and slammed the door shut behind her. What the hell had Guilfoyle gotten himself mixed up with this time?

The plane jerked again and seemed to turn slightly. Annja felt as if she'd just been jarred awake.

They must be starting to come in now, she realized.

One of the crew members moved past her. "Won't be long now. Sit tight. We'll be on the ground shortly."

"Thanks," she said.

He moved off and Annja closed her eyes. The propellers seemed to be groaning now. She could hear them straining against the Antarctic gales. It sounded like frozen pellets of snow pummeling the plane outside.

She could imagine the pilot and copilot going through their loading routine. They'd lower the flaps, decrease the throttle and line up the nose of the plane with the point on the ground where they'd be landing the plane.

Did they have runway lights strung out down here? Annja didn't know what to expect. All she knew was that two days ago she'd been standing on her front stoop back in Brooklyn sweating profusely while two Feds spoke to her. She'd gone upstairs, showered, tossed a few items into a bag and then been whisked off to the 109th Airlift Wing of the New York Air National Guard based outside Schenectady. From there, she'd been hustled aboard a big military plane and then flown across the world to Christchurch, New Zealand.

In Christchurch, the weather was seventy degrees and pleasant. She could have lounged there in jeans and a T-shirt. Instead, the flight crew made her clamber into thermal underwear and extreme-cold-weather survival gear.

"In case we go down, you have to be clothed already in survival gear," the loadmaster told her matter-of-factly.

"You ever go down?" Annja asked nervously.

He grinned. "Once we pass the boomerang, we either land or crash."

"The boomerang?"

"The point at which we can't come back here." He zipped up her parka. "But I wouldn't worry about it. It's only bad if we have a whiteout landing."

"I don't think I want to know about that," Annja said. By that point, the two Feds who'd flown down with her from New York City had maneuvered her onto the plane and then waved goodbye to her. They'd never told her why she was heading to Antarctica and she'd given up asking.

"I hardly even got to know you guys," Annja said.

"And that's how it should be," one said. Then they were gone. Back to the shadow world they lived in. Annja shook her head and focused on trying to keep herself in the moment.

Her ears popped as the plane descended. It banked again and then leveled off.

The propellers strained further and the entire cabin filled with a kind of metal grinding noise. Annja hoped the skin wasn't about to tear itself free from the framework.

"Stand by!" One of the crew shouted over the din, and Annja clutched the armrests of her chair, willing herself to breathe normally while her heart did its best imitation of a jackhammer.

She could almost hear the wind.

She could almost feel the cold.

And somewhere below her, Zach Guilfoyle and his desperate need for her assistance waited.

The plane touched down with a bump and then a skip, followed by another bump and then it was nose down into a screaming, skidding slide that seemed to last utterly forever while Annja kept her eyes closed and her mind focused on her breathing.

And then, everything was still.

"You okay?"

Annja opened her eyes and saw the crewman with the coffee tumbler standing over her.

Annja released her hand rests. "Yeah. I think so."

He nodded. "Great. Well, we're here."

"We are?"

"Yep. Welcome to Antarctica, Miss Creed."

2

As Annja stepped off the plane, she took in the vast scene before her. She saw snow and ice everywhere, but also the look of an entire town some distance away.

"That's McMurdo," the pilot said. "Most of the folks who come down here stop by there first. Last chance at a decent watering hole, too."

"It's big," Annja said. "Much larger than I expected any of the outposts down here to be."

"During the Antarctic summer, there are between eleven hundred and fifteen hundred people at the station. With over one hundred and fifty buildings, they've pretty much got something for everyone," he said.

"What about now?"

The pilot pointed overhead, where a distinct lack of sun sent howling winds across the barren ice runway. "When it gets dark like this? Maybe two hundred altogether."

"Cozy," Annja said.

The pilot laughed over a gale. "We don't usually fly this time of year."

"How come you did this time?"

He looked at her. "Orders, Miss Creed. Our orders were to get you down here whatever the risk."

Annja frowned. "I appreciate the chance you and your crew took on me. I don't know what the big deal is, but I'll try not to let you guys down."

He shook her hand and then headed off to oversee the refueling procedure. Annja knew that once the plane's tanks were topped off, they'd be flying back to New Zealand.

She felt remarkably warm despite the frigid temperatures outside. The extreme-cold-weather gear she wore had certainly proved itself capable of keeping the harsh conditions at bay, but she wondered how long it might last in a survival situation. She shuddered at the thought of freezing to death out here, but her thoughts were broken by the sound of a vehicle approaching.

Across the ice, she spotted what looked like a Sno-Cat. The tracked vehicle slowly chewed its way through the snow and ice. A flashing red light atop the cab helped mark its position while the bright red paint made it stand out in contrast to its surroundings.

Annja hefted her duffel bag and stood on the leeward side of the plane, trying to shield herself from the wind as much as possible. At last, the Sno-Cat trundled to a halt almost right in front of her and the cab door opened.

"Annja Creed?"

"That's me."

"Climb on in—weather's getting worse. I want to get you back to town before it gets any nastier out here."

Annja hustled over to the Sno-Cat and heaved her duffel bag into the open door before climbing up on part of the tracks and sliding into the passenger compartment herself.

As soon as she did, she felt a bellows of heat pumping up between her legs. The interior windows were coated with condensation. The driver next to her held out his hand.

"Dave Rasmudsen. Geology."

Annja shook his hand. "Annja Creed. I have no idea why I'm here."

He laughed. "I'm sure you'll find out soon enough." He pointed at the vents. "Too warm in here? Myself, I like to keep it toasty in the cat. But some folks like it a bit more temperate."

"As long as I don't show up all sweaty, I think I'll be fine for the trip back. How long does it take?"

"About a half hour," Dave said.

"That long?" Annja asked.

Dave patted the dashboard. "This thing doesn't do sixty, so we have to settle for a snail's crawl. But she does the job she was designed to do, which is to say she gets us where we need to go and does it without complaining. So, that said, I can't complain if she takes a little bit of time to do so."

"Fair enough."

"Where you hailing from?"

"New York," Annja said.

Dave nodded. "I'm outside Anchorage, myself."

Annja smiled. "So this kind of weather doesn't really bother you, huh?"

He grinned. "Well, that depends. Now, it's true Alaska has herself some of the nastiest weather around, especially out on the Bering Sea, but Antarctica can give her a run for her money if she wants. I've been here before in storms that would make you get down and hide under your bed. Winds howling and screaming outside—you wonder if the station is going to hold or if you'll be buried in snow."

"Sounds delightful," Annja said.

He laughed. "It's not bad. I gotta be honest with you, I love her. I mean, where else can you get access to the kind of rocks and soil I can study here? We've got projects going on right now that can tell us mounds of info about what happened millions of years ago. It's tremendous stuff."

"Or you could be a truck driver."

Dave grinned. "Exactly. You know what I'm talking about. We only get one shot—we have to live her the best way we know how."

"You married, Dave?" Annja asked.

He looked surprised. "Me? No, no chance of that. I'm afraid I place my career ahead of everything else. Too much to study and not enough time to devote to a family. I dunno. Maybe that'll change one day, but not anytime soon. I've just got too much to do."

And too much to say, Annja thought.

"Why do you ask, anyway?" Dave said.

"Just that I noticed you use 'her' a lot when you're describing things. I thought there might be a logical explanation for it."

Dave nodded. "Oh, there is, there is. My father used to use that all the time. I guess after he died, I kind of took it to heart and started using it as a way of maybe remembering him better on a daily basis."

Annja smiled. "That's awfully insightful of you."

"I just miss him is all," Dave said. He took a breath and flicked the wipers as snow started coming down outside.

Annja glanced back over her seat. In the darkness, she could barely make out the LC-130 sitting in the snow as it was refueled.

"Will they be able to get out of here?" she asked.

Dave nodded. "Those guys? They're amazing. You know you landed on skis, right?"

"Yes."

"Well, invariably, what ends up happening is the skis stop the plane through friction. Yep, the pilot doesn't even use the throttle or brakes to control her when she comes in."

"How nice to know that after I'm already here," Annja said.

Dave laughed. "Yep, they don't tell you that ahead of time, no siree."

Annja smiled. "Go on."

"So the friction melts the snow, you know? Then once the plane stops, the melted ice refreezes pretty darned quick and keeps the plane in place. You might have noticed they weren't tying her down."

"I thought that was because they were going to be leaving very quickly."

"Nope, just no need to do so. The ice keeps her in place."

"And what—they have to dig the plane out when they're ready to leave?" Annja asked.

Dave shrugged. "You know, sometimes that does happen. But most times, the pilot will put the wheels down to break up the ice and then retract them back into the plane. Then the skis can move again and the plane can take off."

Annja sighed. "It's fascinating."

"Dangerous, too. Those aircrews, they're amazing people. Some of the folks down here owe them their lives," Dave said.

"The woman with breast cancer, right?" Annja asked, recalling the news story a few years earlier.

"Yep, and another doctor down near the pole. Both of them had to be evacuated out of here when the weather wasn't too spectacular." He glanced at Annja. "You know, kind of like how you were just flown in."

Annja looked at him. "I guess that's a bit unusual, huh?"

"You could say that. This time of year, things get mighty ferocious down here. Lots of folks are still down at the various outposts and stations, and by and large, we're cut off from the outside world."

"You're trapped here?" Annja asked.

Dave sniffed. "If we're being honest?"

"Always."

"Yep. We're trapped here. Unless one of us is important

enough to warrant sending in another plane. But that doesn't happen all that often. For the most part, what you see when we get to McMurdo is what you get."

"The pilot said there was a place to get a drink," Annja said.

"Three places, actually," Dave said. "Depends on what your pleasure is, I guess."

"Meaning?"

Dave eyed her. "You smoke?"

"No."

"Okay, so I'm guessing you wouldn't want to hang out at Southern Exposure. It's a bit small anyway, and with the smokers, you'll have the hazy funk infecting your clothes if you go in. Still, it can be a fun place."

"What else have you got?"

Dave tapped his fingers along the steering wheel. "If you're into wine and cheese, you can check out the coffeehouse. It's pretty mellow. A lot of folks head on over there to relax after a day at work."

Annja frowned. The thought of spending too much time at a coffeehouse didn't excite her much, either. "Anything else?"

"Yep. We have a place called Gallagher's."

"Gallagher's?"

"Named after a guy who died out on the ice of a heart attack. Our way of remembering him, I guess."

"It's a good place?" Annja asked.

"Oh, yeah. Nonsmoking so there's no funk. Bigger than any of the other places and the dance floor is usually packed." He eyed her. "You a dancer?"

"Depends on my mood," she said with a grin.

"Fair one. Anyway, we've got some pretty old beer for fifty cents a can. I never touch it. But they're getting some pretty good stuff down here these days, too. Bottles of Sam Adams, which are damned good brews. Plus, you've got the wine and the mixed drinks, too. And if you're up for it, we've got a pretty kick-butt group of folks who love to do karaoke. Swing night just got started, as well."

"All that?" Annja asked, amazed.

Dave smiled. "Even though there aren't that many of us, we have to make it as much like home as we can. It gets tough sometimes, but that's how we do it."

Annja peered out of the windshield. The snow seemed to be falling harder now than it was before. "You weren't kidding about the weather."

Dave frowned. "You'll find that's about the one thing no one kids about down here. When we say it's getting bad outside, take us at our word. It's not going to be nice."

"Noted."

Dave pointed at lights in the distance. "That's McMurdo. What we call Mac Town."

Annja tried to pick out details through the dark and the snow, which seemed to be coming in horizontally. She could see the dim outlines of shapes that she took to be buildings. She could just make out a few vehicles, parked up in a ragged line with snow already draping over them like a heavy woolen blanket.

"Is anyone still awake?" she asked.

Dave laughed. "I know what you mean. You see the dark and think it's the middle of the night, right?"

"I guess." Annja realized she had no idea what time it was.

"Well, it's six in the evening. If I guess right, most folks are enjoying a nice warm supper right now."

"Guess I'd better get squared away and do the same," Annja said.

Dave nodded. "I'm taking you right to your quarters. Not sure how long you're staying there, though."

"Oh?"

"I hear tell you're headed out of town pretty fast. Seems like you've got some folks down here who are keenly interested in getting your eyes on something."

"What kind of thing?"

Dave shook his head. "Annja, I'm just a guy who digs rocks. Literally. Anything else going on down here? I don't want to know about it."

"That sounds ominous," Annja said.

He glanced at her. "In case you forgot, you're at the bottom of the world. Something goes on down here, there aren't a lot of eyes looking at it, you know what I'm talking about?"

"I suppose."

Dave pointed again. "Here we are. Welcome to Mac Town."

Annja peered out of her window and wondered what exactly was going on with Zach.

3

McMurdo Station housed about one hundred buildings of every size. Most were the kind of box shape Annja imagined was the prerequisite for design under the harsh Antarctic conditions. Many had smaller doors and few windows, along with a thick cylindrical tube containing power lines and communication gear.

As they drove down the main street, Dave pointed out various things. "There's aboveground water and sewage systems in place. We've got a good electrical system with some redundancy to it in case of outages."

"You get a lot of those?" Annja asked.

"Depends, like everything else, on the weather." He pointed at a larger building. "A lot of the research for the station goes on there. Of course, we just came from the direction of Williams Field, and then maybe if there's time, we can take a run down toward the harbor if you like."

"Sure, a nice balmy breeze would feel great. Maybe after that we can go for a swim."

He laughed. "You know, they've been trying to organize

a polar bear dip around these parts for a while now. Not too many people are keen on the idea, though."

"Wimps," Annja said.

"That's them." Dave laughed.

Annja continued to look out of the windows at the buildings. Here and there, someone could be seen rushing through the snow and going into a building. But really, Annja thought, the place looked like a ghost town.

"You weren't kidding about it being quiet down here," she said.

"You think this is bad, you should visit some of the other stations across the place. Some of them, there are maybe a dozen people. That's if you're lucky. There are a few other isolated joints scattered about, as well. Temporary fixtures that we've set up for one reason or another. As soon as the research is done, they get dismantled. Places like that might have four people."

"Lonely life you guys lead down here."

"Well, we find ways to amuse ourselves." He slowed the Sno-Cat. "I'm going to drop you off here and wait while you stow your gear inside. When you're done, I'll take you down to Gallagher's."

"That's mighty nice of you."

He shrugged. "I can use a drink anyway."

"Fair enough." Annja zipped up her hood and grabbed her duffel bag. As soon as she turned the door handle to leap outside, a blast of wind slammed it back in her face.

Dave laughed. "First one's always a killer."

Annja tried again and this time managed to get out of the Sno-Cat without getting the door kicked back at her. The wind howled in her ears and she could feel the pores on her face freezing.

Inside, she thought. Just push through the wind and get inside.

She groped for the door handle and pushed into the building.

A wall of heat greeted her, and she slammed the door shut behind her. "Wow, that's some wind."

"You must be a virgin," a voice said.

Annja removed her hood and goggles and stared at the main room she'd entered. There was a long wall separating the entrance from the rest of the bottom floor, but she could see a wide-screen TV set playing what looked like a fairly recent release from Hollywood. A few people lounged on sofas and chairs. Some of them were eating.

The man who addressed her looked quite young. And his dark skin stood out in contrast to the mostly white environment. Annja grinned. "That obvious, huh?"

"Yep. Everyone says that the first time they come down here. Like they expected this place to be all warm and sunshiny."

"Well, I knew it was snowy, but I didn't think it was quite like this."

He grinned. "I know it. Your name Annja?"

"Yes—"

"Don't ask me how I knew. You're the only one coming down this time of year. Folks with good common sense wait until later in the summer. Our summer, that is."

Annja unzipped her jacket. "I guess I'm staying here?"

"Temporarily. Least that's what I heard." He handed her a key. "Your room's upstairs. Number five. You need me to show you where it is?"

"I think I can handle it."

"Okay."

Annja looked at him. "You got a name?"

"Trevor. Trevor Howard."

"You don't look like much of a cruise director, Trevor. No offense."

He smirked. "I'm not. But you're in my building, so I like to know everyone when they come in for the first time. But don't think of me as your local tour guide or anything."

Annja pointed outside. "Already got one of those. What do you do here?"

"Try to stay warm," Trevor said. "What most of us are doing here. Enjoy the room." He turned and went back to watching the movie.

Annja grabbed her duffel bag and headed up the stairs to the second floor. She found number five easily enough and immediately heaved her duffel bag on top of the bed. She could always unpack later.

Her room was Spartan, but she hadn't expected much. A double bed with a drawer underneath it occupied most of the room. She had a desk and chair near one wall and a small television on the table by the door. There was an overhead light and a red lamp on the nightstand.

I feel like I'm back in college, she thought.

She resisted the urge to grab a shower and instead headed back downstairs. She glanced quickly at Trevor's back, but he made no attempt to talk to her again, so she slipped back outside and into the Sno-Cat.

Dave sat there whistling a tune. "All set?"

"Guess so."

He slid the Sno-Cat into drive. "What'd you think of the place?"

"Like a college dorm."

Dave nodded. "Sure is. And sometimes, the Air National Guard guys have a keg-tossing contest down at the bars."

"Wonderful."

"You meet Trevor?"

"I guess you could call it that."

"Yeah, he's like that with everyone. But honestly, he's a good guy. You need anything, he'll be there to help you out.

Just don't take it personally that he comes off as a royal pain in the ass."

"Okay," Annja said.

They drove back down the main street and then turned left. Through the snow, Annja could see bright lights. "Neon?"

Dave shrugged. "Like I said, gotta make it look like home."

He slid the Sno-Cat in next to another vehicle and then killed the engine. "We'd better get inside. In this weather, even the cab freezes after about five minutes."

Annja clambered down again and Dave waited as she walked around. Then he held the door open for her and she ducked inside.

Annja could hear the steady throb of a bass line drum beat. It sounded like they'd just walked into a nightclub. Dave unzipped and showed Annja where she could hang up her parka. "Drink?" he asked.

She nodded. "Definitely."

They headed for the bar. Annja could make out about twenty people throughout the club, most of them in smaller groups. Some of them ate dinner and others seemed to be laughing over a round of drinks. A few tipsy folks hammed it up on the small parquet wooden floor.

"It's imitation," Dave said. "But it looks the part and that's all that matters sometimes."

Dave ordered a beer for himself. "What can I get you?"

"Gin and tonic," Annja said.

The man behind the bar had a white beard longer than the ones worn by the guys in ZZ Top. "We're out of limes," he said.

Annja nodded. "That's fine."

He slid her the drink and Dave passed some money across. "First round's on me."

Annja held up her glass. "Thanks for the warm welcome."

He clinked his beer bottle and then drank long and deep.

Annja sipped her drink and found it packed a wallop. She turned back to the bartender. "You put any tonic water in this?"

He grinned. "You just got here, right? I figured you could use the extra kick. That flight rattles a lot of people's nerves."

Annja smiled and hoisted her glass. "Much appreciated."

"My pleasure."

Dave nodded at an empty booth. "Want to sit down?"

Annja shrugged. "Sure. I'm not sure how the heck I'm supposed to find my friend."

"Zach'll find you, I'd expect," Dave said.

"I guess."

"No, seriously. I'm sure he will. He asked me to bring you here, so he knows you're in town."

"Oh, all right." Annja frowned into her drink. It was a little weird, the entire situation. Being here in this isolated outpost away from the rest of the world. The people here seemed nice enough, but she wondered what kind of person could work in an environment like this and not go crazy.

Dave leaned back and sighed. "So what is it exactly that you do?"

"Me?" Annja grinned. "Mostly I file reports for a show called *Chasing History's Monsters*. But occasionally I end up in remote parts of the world in small bars with guys who buy me drinks."

"Interesting life," Dave said.

"It has its moments."

"Well, I'm sure Zach will be able to shed some light on why you're here just as soon as he gets here."

No sooner had he spoken than the bar's door opened. Annja felt a gust of cold air blow into the bar before the door closed again. She saw a huddled figure stooped over wrestling with his parka zipper before finally freeing himself.

He turned and headed right for their booth.

Zach Guilfoyle hadn't changed much since the last time

Annja had seen him. He wore his sandy-brown hair cropped close to his skull, and his Romanesque nose protruded like a hawk ahead of him. But his toothy smile made her grin even as he approached.

She climbed out of the booth and hugged him. "It's great to see you."

He hugged her back. "Glad you made it down intact. I'm sorry for not being able to speak with you first about all of this, but then, some things are better left unsaid until you're face-to-face."

"Okay, well, I'm here. So what's going on?" Annja asked.

He pointed at her drink. "You need a refill?"

"Not yet."

Dave spoke up. "I could use another."

Zach eyed him and smiled. "Sure thing. And thanks for picking her up."

"My pleasure."

Annja watched Zach walk to the bar. He seemed thinner, as if the weight of all the extreme-weather gear he had to wear had stripped him of some of his flesh and bones. But he seemed cheerful enough, if slightly preoccupied.

She noticed two men at the bar seemed interested in him. And judging from the grim expressions they wore, they weren't fans.

Zach came back with two bottles of beer and sat down across from Annja. "Well, here's to you getting down here safe and sound."

"Cheers."

They clinked bottles and glasses and drank. Zach wiped his mouth on a napkin and then glanced at the bar.

Annja could feel his apprehension. "You okay?"

"Yeah. It's nothing."

Annja looked at the bar. The two men continued to stare at Zach with frowns etched on their faces.

"They don't look all that nice," she said.

"They're not," Zach replied.

Annja took another sip of her gin and tonic. She felt uneasy. She closed her eyes. Not already, she thought.

But when she opened them, she knew it was coming. Zach's eyes had widened.

Annja turned.

The grim men were headed over to their booth.

4

Annja felt a twinge of apprehension at their approach. Neither of the men looked drunk and both seemed in excellent physical condition. She blinked and kept her eyes closed long enough to determine that her sword was ready, if need be. It hung in space, glimmering faintly.

But the last thing she wanted was to explain to anyone how she'd suddenly manifested a large two-handed sword.

The larger of the two men stopped about four feet from their booth and pointed a finger at Zach. "You Guilfoyle?"

Zach smiled. "Yes. Can I help you with something?"

Annja watched the man's eyes. They never shifted. They just stayed fixed on Zach. But she was aware of how relaxed he seemed, as well. And that wasn't a good sign. It meant these guys were so used to intimidating people, it had become second nature to them.

The second man hung back a bit, looking around to make sure people weren't taking too much notice of the conversation, one-sided though it was. His eyes roved the rest of the bar, never settling too long on anyone. He looked like he was maybe five feet ten inches and weighed around a hundred and sixty pounds. He was solid and lithe and he had a casual manner about him that told Annja a lot.

The first guy looked Zach up and down. As he studied Zach, Annja sized him up. He stood about six feet and weighed maybe two hundred pounds. It was a little more difficult to tell since he wore a thick turtleneck sweater that bulked him up some.

But the most telling thing about him were the calluses on his hands. Specifically, on the edge of his hands.

Annja pointed at them. "You study karate?"

He barely moved. *"Uechi-ryu."*

Annja whistled. "Hard style. How long?"

"I've got a black belt."

Annja shook her head. "Didn't ask what your rank was. I asked how long you've been studying."

"Isn't that the same thing?"

She smiled. "Not really. See, any two-bit jerk can go to a seminar these days and find a sham of a teacher willing to hand them a black belt. But only the people who have been around for years and years are worth a damn."

He looked at her now, eyeing her carefully. "Fifteen years," he said.

She nodded. "That would account for the calluses. Lots of *makiwara* training, huh?"

"Yes."

"I'll bet you've got one in your house, too, wherever that might be."

"I train constantly."

Annja glanced around. "Anything good to hit here in Mac Town? I only just got in, so I'm asking."

His eyes betrayed the disdain. "You study?"

"Sure do. Not any specific style—I'm too busy to devote a lot of time to any one form—but a lot of varied ones."

"Like?"

Annja took a breath. "Oh, wow, let's see. *Shotokan,* tae kwon do, some judo, boxing, a little Krav Maga, old-style jujitsu, and even some ninjitsu on occasion."

"Ninjitsu?" He smirked. "You must be joking."

Annja narrowed her eyes. "Not at all."

"Yeah, well, I've known plenty of supposed ninja guys and they all sucked."

"What about ninja girls? You ever known any of them?"

He frowned. "No."

"Well, then, there you go. Everyone knows ninja guys are horrible fighters. It's the women who are the deadliest of the species. But no one ever talks about it, so we just let them carry on. It's good for their ego and all."

"Who exactly are you?" the man asked.

Annja smiled and took a sip of her drink. "I'm the woman who asked you what was good to hit around here."

The man pointed at Zach. "I'm thinking he might be a good place to start. Looks like he could use a good beating."

"Why?"

"Because I don't like him. I don't like how he looks and I don't much like what he stands for."

Annja laughed. "You're kidding, right? What's not to love about Zach? He's the life of the party. I'll just bet if you and your friend there had a shindig, old Zach here would bring the house down."

"He's not invited."

"So you're going to just beat him up, is that it?"

The first guy cracked his knuckles. "Yep."

Annja shook her head. "No. That's not what you're going to do. You're not going to touch a hair on that guy. Not one single strand."

He eyed her again. "I don't like the manner you're taking with me, little lady."

"Lady?" Annja shook her head. "And I'm supposed to believe you're some kind of gentleman, is that it?"

He shook his head. "I don't really care what you think."

"Good, because it's not pretty. Really. Now, why don't you and your pal go on back to the bar and you can continue giving us the evil eye or whatever it was you were doing over there before you so rudely interrupted our conversation. I just had a long flight and I'm really in no mood for this kind of silliness."

"You just flew in?" the man asked.

"That's right," Annja said. "And, boy, are my arms tired." She smirked. "Or did you hear that one before?"

"If you just flew in, that means you're with him, right?"

"He hasn't proposed yet, if that's what you're asking."

Zach cracked a smile. "Yeah, she's with me. What about it?" he asked.

The first guy leaned on their table. "I don't like either one of you people. So you'd better just watch yourselves. Or there might be trouble."

Annja cleared her throat. "Well, how come Dave here gets a pass? I mean, after all, he's sitting with us. Aren't you mad at him, too?"

"I got no problem with him," the man said.

Annja sighed. "See, that's just like the world, isn't it? I have to be friends with the trouble magnet. And Dave here gets off free."

Dave shrugged. "Maybe I'm just more lovable."

Annja looked back at the first man. "Well, thanks for coming by. I know I certainly appreciate it. And I think Zach does, too, in his own peculiar way. It's always nice to know who the assholes are in any town you travel through."

He leaned closer to Annja. "You keep your tongue wagging and I just might forget about my previous hard-line stance against beating the crap out of women."

"Something tells me you might have already broken that position," Annja said. "You look like just the type of jerk who would beat up a woman for kicks."

He smirked. "Maybe you're right."

"Oh, I know I am," she said. "And that's fine. Because there's nothing I like better than taking an idiot like you to task. It will be my tremendous pleasure to redefine the meaning of the words *smack down* in your precious little stegosaurian noodle."

Annja could see his fists clench. The vein in his forehead seemed to jut out a little farther now that she'd riled him up. She glanced around. The music had gone quiet and people were paying close attention.

"Whoopsie, looks like you've got yourself that audience you didn't want. Might be a good time to pack up this snake oil and peddle it elsewhere," she said fiercely.

The first man glanced around and then nodded to his friend. He looked back at Annja. "We'll be seeing you again. Real soon."

"Great. I appreciate the welcoming committee making me feel so comfortable," she said loudly.

Both men wandered back to the bar, downed their drinks and then stalked off into the cold night. Once the door closed behind them, the music came back up and people returned to their tables and friends. Annja could feel more eyes giving her a once-over.

"So much for keeping a relatively low profile," she said.

Dave smiled and polished off his second beer. "Anyone for a refill?"

Zach nodded. "I'll take one."

"Annja?"

"May as well."

Dave got up from the booth and headed for the bar. Annja leaned closer to Zach. "Okay, pal, just what in the hell have you got me mixed up in here?"

"What do you mean?"

"What do I mean? I mean, why the hell are you getting hassled by two professional thugs?"

Zach shrugged. "I don't know."

Annja leaned back. "You don't know. Of all the places in this town, they just happened to wander in here and didn't like you much. Yeah, that makes sense. Especially when it's the height of tourist season."

Zach smiled. "I never could put one over on you, huh?"

"Never could. Never will."

Zach looked at her, his eyes gleaming in the dim light. "I'm glad you're here, Annja. Seriously. Not just because you always know how to handle guys like that, but just because I'm genuinely glad to see you. It's been too long. Too much time has passed between us."

"I won't argue that," Annja said. "But the next time you get all sentimental about seeing me, how about not sending the men-in-black goon squad to my house?"

"Sorry about that. It wasn't my idea. When you didn't respond to the letter, the people in charge decided a more aggressive approach was needed."

"I feel like I'm being worked over for a mob debt here." She looked up as Dave came back and set a fresh drink in front of her. "Thanks, Dave."

"You bet." He slid into the booth. "What'd I miss?"

"Zach here telling me how he likes sending government agents to my home to strong-arm me into coming down to the bottom of the world."

Dave looked at Zach. "You did that?"

"Not me. Them."

"Oh," Dave said knowingly.

Annja sighed. "If I don't get some answers soon, I'm hopping the next plane out of this ice cube."

"You're better off swimming," Dave said with a slight belch.

"Why?"

He examined his beer bottle. "No more flights are expected here for weeks."

Annja frowned. "They told me I'd be back within ten days. I've got work to do back home, you know."

"Yeah, well, they lied," Dave said. "Unless it's a vital emergency, no one is going anywhere."

Annja slumped back in her seat. Great, she was trapped down on the coldest continent on Earth, with no clue as to why she was there and no real chance of getting home for quite some time. "This day just keeps getting better."

Zach looked at her. "Annja, listen, I'm really sorry about this. I didn't know who else to turn to, though, and you're the best person I know for this kind of job."

"Now it's a job?" Annja frowned. "I've already got a job."

"Yeah, I've seen the show. I think it's a waste of your talents."

Annja smirked. "Yeah, well, thanks."

Dave took a long drag on his beer. "It's not so bad once you get used to the place. There's bowling. You like to bowl?"

"Not particularly," Annja said. "But I guess I could be persuaded, you know, if it's between that and say, freezing to death."

"Darts league, too," Dave said. "We compete against the other stations. But we have to call in the results by radio. I think the other teams cheat."

Annja smiled. "All right, whatever. I guess I can make the most out of this. After all, isn't this the last great unexplored region on Earth?"

"Land-wise, yeah," Dave said.

"So what gives, Zach?" Annja said.

He smiled. "I've found something amazing."

"That's not exactly illuminating. I want details and I want information. And I don't want to think that you're holding anything back."

Zach shifted in his seat. "There's kind of a lot to tell."

"Great. Well, I've apparently got a lot of time to spare. So if there's any way to rustle up some food in this joint, then let's do it and then sit back and hear you tell me what was so damned important I had to get kidnapped from my nice Brooklyn loft, herded around the world and dropped into the freezer here."

Dave slid a menu in front of her. "The wings are good."

Annja glanced at him, cracked a smile and then looked at Zach. "Spill it, pal. And don't stop until you've told me everything."

5

Zach took a long pull on his beer bottle and then slapped it back down on the table. "As I said, I've found something."

Annja sipped her drink. No one was paying attention to them anymore, which made her feel at least somewhat protected from prying eyes. "All right. What did you find?"

Zach put his hands to his neck and reached inside his turtleneck. With a great deal of maneuvering, he managed to slide a necklace over his head. He rested it on the tabletop in front of Annja. "This," he said simply.

Annja looked at it. It was a simple design of three snakes lying parallel to each other, the curves in their backs suggesting motion. She could see the elaborate work done to denote scales, eyes and parts of forked tongues. She reached for it, but looked at Zach first. "May I?"

"Of course."

Annja hefted the piece and found it surprisingly heavy. "I thought it looked like a piece of aluminum almost, but it's far too heavy."

Zach nodded. "Exactly. And you see how thin it is?"

Annja turned it over. It had the thickness of a soda can. "Incredible. Is it lead or pewter or something?"

"No. We ran it through a battery of tests. We can't figure out what it is. The metal doesn't register."

Annja eyed him. "You're telling me this has no basis in science?"

"Yes."

She turned it over in her hands. The metal seemed to catch any available light and change colors as she moved it in her hands. The illusion made her think that the scales on the snakes could actually ripple. "This is incredible," she whispered.

"I thought you'd say that."

Dave looked over her shoulder as she studied it. Annja passed it to him. He was as shocked as she had been at its weight. "Wow."

Annja looked at Zach. "How old is it?"

"That's the other curious thing."

Annja leaned forward. "Well?"

"According to the carbon dating we did, it's over forty thousand years old."

No one spoke for a moment. Annja was acutely aware of the silence hanging between them all. She heard the clinks of glasses and the low murmurs of conversation at other tables. Even the music that had resumed playing seemed hushed now.

"Forty thousand?"

Zach held up his hand. "I know. It seems crazy."

"It seems impossible. There's no way humans could have made this forty thousand years ago. I mean, I'm not a metallurgist, but this is pretty complicated stuff. It would take some seriously skilled people to pull this off given what conditions were like on Earth back then," Annja said.

Zach didn't say anything but kept staring at her as if he

wanted her to take the next leap on her own. Annja took another sip of her gin and tonic and felt the liquor slide down her throat.

After a moment she set the glass back down. "You're not, no, there's absolutely no way…"

Zach's eyebrows waggled. "Why not?"

Dave handed the necklace back. "Why not what?"

Annja sighed. "Extraterrestrial? You can't be serious."

"It's possible, though, you have to admit," Zach said, sounding excited.

Annja shook her head. "I'm not admitting anything. You've got something curious here, sure, but to think little green men from Mars planted this here is a bit far-fetched, don't you think?"

Zach frowned. "If you've got any better theories, I'd be more than willing to entertain them."

"I don't have any theories. I just got off a plane. I can use some good sleep. Maybe a few pleasant dreams. And in the morning, maybe we'll be able to look at this in a more logical light."

Dave pointed at the necklace as Zach slid it back on. "Where in the world did you ever find that?"

"I'm on a dig at the base of Horlick Mountain."

Dave whistled. "You're out on that one, huh? I heard some whispers that some sort of secret dig site was going on somewhere in the Transantarctic Range, but no one had any idea where it was."

Zach nodded. "Well, do me a favor and don't tell anyone now that you know. We don't need the publicity."

They took a moment to get their order of wings from the bar. Annja tore into one of them and her mouth watered as the hot sauce hit. She wiped her mouth on a napkin and then glanced around. "Why no publicity? Have there been problems?"

Zach shrugged. "Sort of. Down here, you'll find a lot of different camps on the whole idea of how Antarctica should be used. The scientists want to study it because it's a fascinating look back at our own history. We can learn a whole lot from this place. Antarctica used to be warm and lush, connected to Africa, India and Australia through the Gondwana supercontinent. When the continents broke apart, the land started to cool, which is why we don't have fossil records dating later than twenty-five million years ago."

"Too cold," Annja said.

"Exactly. Earlier than that, we've got reptiles, plants, all sorts of connections to those continents I just mentioned."

Dave frowned. "Which is why I'd guess your discovery of this necklace has made such an impact on you, huh? It's from a time when there was supposed to be nothing much here."

"Right. Meanwhile, the business folks come down here and see the natural resources this place has—all the coal, copper, chromium—and start seeing dollar signs. If it was up to them, they'd rape this place and leave it for dead."

Annja sighed. "Wonderful."

"And then you've got the various political machinations at work. No one is supposed to lay claim to any part of this great land, but they do so subtly anyway. Specifically, the U.S. and Russia. They've reserved the right to stake claims here. It's ludicrous."

"What else?" Annja asked.

Zach sighed. "Then you've got the people who have forgotten there's another world outside this place. They've been here far too long. They get snow crazy. Think of themselves as protectors of this frozen paradise. They can be real nuts."

"Did we just meet a few of them?" she asked.

Zach grinned. "I think they work for another faction."

"Oh, great."

"In the meantime," Dave said, "you'd obviously like to figure out where your necklace came from."

"You got it, pal. We've got a mystery here."

Annja smiled. "So you called me."

"I don't know very many other archaeologists who can drop what they're doing and fly down here at the last minute."

"Well, technically, I'm not one of them, either, but your friends in the black suits had a very persuasive way about them."

"Which brings me to the other part of this whole thing," Zach said.

"That being?"

Zach leaned closer to her. "The government wants this investigated and kept strictly hush-hush."

"Why?" Annja asked.

Dave smirked. "Every other country on the planet has basically come out and confirmed that they've been buzzed by flying saucers, and our government still tries to con the public with stories about weather balloons."

Annja frowned. "Well, in some ways, you can't blame them."

"Why not?" Zach asked.

"Look at the timing of when we started hearing reports about extraterrestrials—right around the end of World War II. Right after we exploded the first nuclear weapons."

"You're saying there's a connection?"

"I don't know," Annja said. "But we'd just finished demolishing Japan and ended the war. Then the Soviet Union entered the Cold War arms race with us, each nation trying to protect itself. And all of a sudden, oh, by the way, there are aliens, too?"

Zach smiled. "I've always loved the way you're able to break everything down to the simplest terms possible."

"Well, look at it from their perspective. Acknowledging the existence of space invaders would have sent the general public into absolute hysteria. As if it wasn't bad enough we had to deal with the Soviets, we've got flying saucers prowling the skies? And we didn't have anything technology-wise that could compete with them. The government had to make sure that the public felt we could protect ourselves," Annja said.

Zach finished the last drops of his beer. "I suppose that makes sense, but I still don't like the way they've continuously lied to us all these years."

"Agreed, but you can at least appreciate their need to do so," Annja said.

"I can appreciate it during the 1950s. I can't understand it now when the Cold War is a thing of the past," Zach said.

"Old habits die hard," Dave said. "And some of those guys in the power circles of Washington look older than dinosaurs. Maybe we've been infiltrated."

Annja laughed. "Next time say it without that smile and you might be more convincing."

Zach patted his chest. "So with all that said, we've got ourselves a real interesting conundrum here."

Annja leaned back. "So you found the necklace and told the government about it?"

"Not quite. I was on a small team at the dig site, and one of the people on the team was a government plant."

"A plant? Why would they have a plant on a dig site in Antarctica? Last I heard, there were no weapons of mass destruction here," Annja said.

Zach grinned. "Yeah, well, that was my fault for trusting people I thought were scientists when in fact they were scummy agents with the intelligence community. No sooner had I unearthed the necklace than I had a visit from some people who called themselves concerned representatives."

"These the same folks who drafted me?" she asked.

"Probably."

Annja glanced at Dave. "Lovely folks. Truly. Real warmhearted souls."

Dave smirked. "I'll bet."

"So they told you what?" Annja asked.

"That I had to figure it out. That I had to go back on the dig and see if I could unearth anything else. They sent me down some gear for the job and told me I could have a crew of whoever I wanted."

"Guess that's where I come in."

"Yeah." Zach sighed. "In the meantime, the dig site has been declared an environmental emergency."

"What?"

"It's how they're containing it. They've claimed we spilled some sort of chemical compound there that they're cleaning up. No one buys it, of course, but it gives the U.S. the right to put security people in place so they can control access."

"Good grief, this is starting to sound like something out of a science fiction movie." Annja craned her neck, trying to relieve some of the tension she felt starting to creep in.

"It's getting out of hand," Zach said. "I figured the least I could do was bring in some people I actually trust, so I don't have to work exclusively with professional liars."

Annja nudged Dave. "I take it you're on the team?"

"Yep. Just the rocks, ma'am."

Zach looked at Annja. "So what do you say? Are you in?"

"Could I ever get out?" Annja smiled. "I'm basically stranded here now, anyway. I guess my choices are pretty limited. Besides, I'm more than a little intrigued by what you've told me so far. I'd like to check it out."

Zach clapped his hands. "Awesome. Thanks, Annja. I really owe you for this."

"Oh, I'll collect. And I'm sure you'll regret it later, but what the hell. When do we leave for the dig site?"

"Tomorrow morning. First thing," Zach said.

"Dawn?"

Zach shrugged. "You can call it dawn, but it won't be very light out when we leave. We're entering the dark times around these parts. Sunlight won't be a frequent visitor for a number of months."

"Okay, so I'll see you at what time?"

Zach checked his watch. "We leave at four o'clock."

"Ouch." Annja finished her drink and stood up. "That barely leaves enough time for a decent sleep." She smirked. "But that's cool. I'm going back to my luxurious digs now and taking a nice hot shower."

"You mean a lukewarm bath," Dave said. "Uses less hot water, which, as you might have guessed, is a bit of a premium in these parts."

"Bath, then." Annja smiled. "I'll see you gents in the morning."

"Wait," Dave said. "Don't you want a lift?"

Annja shrugged. "Back that way two blocks and up one on Main Street, right?"

"Yeah, but it's probably twenty below out there," he said.

"I can use the fresh air," Annja said. "But thanks anyway."

"Annja, your skin can freeze inside of two minutes if it's exposed to the frigid air," Zach said.

"Well, I guess I'll have to make sure I don't expose myself on the way back to my room. Good night." She walked back to the front door of the bar, slid into her parka and zipped up. In another moment, she eased out into the dark cold.

6

Dave was right. It was absolutely frigid outside, and the cold slammed into Annja like a five-ton truck zooming along at eighty miles per hour. She took a breath and felt her throat freeze. Her sinuses instantly shriveled, and she tucked herself down into the wind and started walking back up the road.

The gale-force winds howled around her, screeching through the nooks and crannies of the buildings that clustered in this part of McMurdo. The fallen snow was deep, as well, making her footing unstable. Twice she slipped and had to right herself before continuing. Every once in a while, she would look up to make sure she was still headed in the direction she needed to travel.

But it was slow going.

Maybe I should have opted for that ride, she thought.

But the truth was, she needed some time to think as she walked. Zach's proposition that the necklace was alien in origin didn't sit well with her. Sure, she'd seen plenty of things that regularly defied logical explanation. Her own situation as the inheritor of Joan of Arc's mystical sword was just one of the many instances that had caused her to reevaluate her philosophies.

But extraterrestrials?

Annja couldn't believe that. She knew a little about Antarctica's history and how it had once been linked to other continents. She also knew that its mountain ranges were something of a peculiarity, with scientists believing that neither earthquakes nor tectonic smashes had formed them.

And the continent had plenty of volcanoes—eleven of them at last count. Some were active and continued to shed lava into the sea. The whole region was a fascinating trip into the primeval past.

But aliens?

The necklace was peculiar; there was no doubt of that. The weight of such thin material had caused Annja to wonder if it might have even been radioactive. But she dismissed that immediately, knowing the government would have already run tests on it. And there'd be no way Zach would wear it unless it was safe.

She frowned. Why was Zach wearing it? Didn't he trust the people around here enough to leave it in a safe or something? Or had the government people ordered him to have it with him at all times?

But that was dangerous, too. Zach was a good guy and Annja knew he could hold his own in a fight if need be, but the two hitters she'd met earlier would have been able to take him without breaking a sweat.

She reached the top of the street and turned left. Main Street stood before her. Some of the buildings had lights on them that helped illuminate Annja's path. She felt a bit foolish trudging through the frozen town, but then again, she did enjoy being independent.

She kept walking, knowing that her building lay up the

street a few hundred feet. Once she got there, she could take that bath and then settle in for a nice sleep.

Sleeping on the flight down had been difficult at best. The interior of the LC-130 was Spartan, barely recognizable as a place where passengers sat. It also had no lavatory on board, just a drum filled with chemicals at the back of the plane. Annja had used it a few times and each time, the stench got grimmer and grimmer.

The noise had been oppressive, as well. Jet engines were noisy, but the turboprops were even louder. By the time she got to New Zealand, Annja had needed some serious migraine medicine.

Her boots got stuck in a bit of snow and she paused, yanking at the drift until she felt it give.

Annja glanced around. Somewhere in the distance, she thought she could hear an engine starting up. Maybe Dave was coming to look for her to see that she'd gotten home safe and sound.

Or maybe someone else was still up. After all, it couldn't be much later than nine o'clock at night. Still, she didn't know what passed for daily schedules around these parts.

She could see her building ahead. Annja huddled in against a harsh blast of wind and started to cross the street.

As she hustled, a Sno-Cat turned the corner and crawled toward her. Annja paused, trying to see into the cab beyond the bright headlights. She could see one person inside but only in shadow.

She waved.

The Sno-Cat kept coming at her.

Annja frowned. Maybe they didn't see her. She turned and kept moving across the street.

Someone flew into her, tackling her from the side. Annja felt the wind rush out of her lungs and she and her attacker shot into the hard-packed snow together with a crash.

She could hear him huffing as he kept driving his elbow right into her midsection, slamming it repeatedly into her.

Annja grunted and tried to roll.

She heard a crack and felt her ribs explode in pain. "Dammit!"

The immense weight on top of her shifted and then vanished. Annja lay on her back in the middle of the street. Her breath came in spurts, and the needles of agony lancing through her came with every breath.

The headlights of the Sno-Cat continued to bear down on her.

So that was the plan—tackle her and try to immobilize her while the slow-moving snow vehicle stalked her. If she couldn't move, she'd get run over.

She stared at the headlights. The Sno-Cat was only forty feet from her now. She tried to get up, but the weight of her clothing made movement tough, combined with the incredible pain shooting through her. She felt as if she were a beetle trapped on its back.

She had to move!

Her fingers fumbled for her zipper and found it. She tore it down and then took a deep breath. Clenching her teeth, she squirmed out of the jacket. Finally free of it, she rolled and screamed as the pain almost became too much.

Then she was up and across the street as the Sno-Cat crawled past, crushing her parka in the snow.

A few more seconds and that would have been me, Annja thought.

She staggered toward her building, aware now that she was terribly exposed to the harsh cold. She reached the door and fell inside, collapsing on the floor.

"Annja?"

She looked up and saw Trevor's face. "Someone tried to kill me," she gasped.

His face hardened. "What? Here? When?"

"Just now. Outside." Annja took a breath. "My ribs. Someone tackled me. I think they're broken."

She felt Trevor's hands under her armpits. "Okay, okay, let's get you upstairs where you can lie down. I'll send for a medical team. They can check you out and make sure you're okay."

He lifted her and Annja cried out. The pain felt like a hot poker being pushed into her lungs.

"Easy," Trevor said. "I've got you. Just rest all your weight on me. I think I can handle it."

They took the stairs slowly and made their way to Annja's room. Trevor sat her on her bed and then removed her boots, got a wool blanket and covered her.

"Don't want you going into shock. I need to elevate your feet, too," he said.

Annja took a breath and nodded when she was ready. Trevor was mercifully quick, getting her settled and sliding another folded blanket under her heels.

Annja closed her eyes. She could hear Trevor using the telephone. "I need a medic over at Building 5. Possible broken ribs. Okay. Thanks."

He hung up and then leaned in close to her. "Who did this to you?"

Annja shook her head. "I don't know. I was walking—"

"Walking? What the hell were you out walking for? You know how cold it is out there?"

Annja smiled. "Needed some fresh air."

"That's not fresh air, Annja. That's death air. That stuff'll kill you dead before you know what hit you. Don't mess around down here. You can get disoriented way too easily. And you might not even be found before it's too late."

Annja opened her eyes and looked up at him. "Someone tackled me."

"You said."

"They wanted me dead. They got me on my back and then they were going to run me over with the Sno-Cat."

Trevor frowned. "Who the hell would do that?"

Annja had a few thoughts. The two thugs in the bar earlier hadn't seemed very warm. But who were they? Annja didn't even know their names. "I don't know. There were some threatening guys at the bar."

"Which bar?"

"Gallagher's."

Trevor shook his head. "Most of the bad characters hang out in the smokers' bar. Gallagher's is usually okay. We don't normally have any trouble. Especially this time of year."

Annja looked at him. "You have police down here?"

Trevor frowned. "Didn't you get the in-briefing?"

"The what?"

"You were supposed to be met by the special deputy U.S. marshal. He greets everyone who comes in here, especially Americans. He gives the in-briefing about the fact that if you commit a serious crime down here, you can be extradited back to the U.S. for prosecution. It's boring and stuff, but we all have to go through it. Some kind of legal thing."

"Never saw him," Annja said.

"Huh." Trevor got off her bed and walked toward the door. "I'll go see where the medics are. And then, maybe you'd better have that talk with the marshal. His name's Dunning."

Annja closed her eyes. "Okay."

Trevor closed the door behind him and Annja sighed. How many times was she going to fly into some place new and within hours get someone pissed off at her? She really had to work on how she interacted with the percentage of permanent losers that seemed to inhabit the planet.

She laughed. "Yeah, right."

Her voice seemed quiet in the thickly insulated bedroom. She couldn't even hear the wind howling outside. She pulled the blanket up under her chin and felt the first waves of drowsiness starting to wash over her.

At least she'd made it back alive.

Someone knocked on her door. "Come in."

Trevor entered first, followed by a man and woman wearing red parkas that they quickly stripped off. They both carried big bags of gear.

The woman took the lead. "Annja? I'm Martha, the head medic on duty right now. You want to tell me what happened?"

"Tackled and driven to the ground. I felt an elbow go into my ribs, heard a crack. I think it might be broken."

"What makes you so sure of that?" Martha asked.

Annja smiled. "It's not the first time it's happened to me."

"Do you get into a lot of fights?" the medic asked.

"Trouble seems to have fun hanging out with me. But it's not something I go in search of, if that's what you're getting at."

Martha grinned. "Ah." She felt for Annja's pulse and checked her pupils. "Well, you seem in okay shape. You mind if I take a look?"

"It's going to hurt like hell, isn't it?" Annja asked.

"Probably."

Annja grinned. "At least you're honest." She tried to maneuver on the bed and Martha helped her. Annja lifted her shirt and Martha ran her hand over Annja's rib cage.

Annja felt her gently prod the area and then her fingers went a little farther and Annja grunted loudly. "Yow."

Martha nodded. "Yeah, well, that's the area. There's some nice bruising, but it's not as bad as you think. I don't think the break went all the way through. Someone heavier, yeah, then maybe. But whoever did this was lighter than necessary to get the break clean."

Annja nodded. "So now what?"

"You know the drill. Taped up and some painkillers. A few weeks from now, you should be good to go. Sleeping will be a pain in the ass for some time, though."

"Great," Annja muttered.

Martha and her teammate wrapped the thick, stiff tape around Annja's midsection until it felt as if she were wearing a girdle. Annja took some breaths and everything seemed as well as could be expected.

Martha handed her a small bottle. "These are powerful. Don't overdo it with them, okay? Just one when you need it, no more."

"Got it."

She stood and packed her gear. "I'd say welcome to McMurdo, but it seems someone has already done so. So I'll just wish you a better stay than what you've had thus far."

"Thanks."

The medics left and Trevor stood there smiling at Annja. "You okay?"

Annja dry-swallowed one of the pills. "As soon as this bad boy hits, I should be fine."

Trevor nodded. "Yeah, well, try to stay awake a little while longer."

"Why?"

"I called the marshal. Dunning. He's here now. And he wants to see you."

7

When Dunning walked into the room, Annja could tell right away he was a cop. He had the hard-edged look to him, and his eyes betrayed the cumulative experience that all cops acquire after years on the job. The crap he'd seen, the faces and the pictures of tragedies, they clung to him and he carried them everywhere. Combined with the bristling short hair that was gray at the temples and the strong jawline just starting to soften, Annja knew he was a career law-enforcement type.

He held out his hand and Annja shook it. It was hard as stone. "Thanks for coming," she said.

"You missed my engrossing briefing."

Annja tried to shrug but was rewarded with a stab of pain. "No one told me there was any such thing."

"I had slides and everything planned. Got my new laser pointer just for the occasion."

Annja smiled. "Sorry about that. Someone grabbed me at the plane before I could figure out my bearings."

Dunning frowned under the bushy mustache he wore. "Yeah, I'm working on making it mandatory, but this area presents its own unique problems in that regard."

"Like what?"

"Well, there are over a dozen nations down here doing this and that, and not one of them wants to have anything to do with a little law and order. Antarctica, they say, represents the last real frontier in terms of land on Earth. And, of course, they don't much like the idea of Americans telling them what to do."

"That's understandable," Annja said.

Dunning smiled. "I agree. But even on a frontier like this, where everyone is ostensibly your next-best friend, people get into spats. And if that happens, there's got to be someone around who can protect the population."

"And that would be you."

"At least for this year, yeah. We rotate down for a year-long stint. I've got a partner with me, so we can back each other up. Plus, if things get really hairy we can always call the New Zealanders in from Christchurch. Their department is top-notch, and we have a good working relationship with them."

"You ever have to call them in?"

"Not for anything too horrible. Most of the people down here are reasonably stable folks. The snow gets to you, but if anyone starts showing signs of becoming a problem, they get rotated out pretty darned quick."

Annja winced as another stab of pain sliced through her breathing. The pain medication wasn't yet working. "I think there are two guys down here who might be good candidates for being shipped home."

"Yeah? Tell me about it?" Dunning said.

Annja filled him in on what had happened at Gallagher's. Dunning listened and stroked his mustache thoughtfully as she supplied the details. "And you didn't get their names, huh?"

Annja shook her head. "I doubt they would have obliged me, anyway. They seemed fixated on my friend Zach."

"Why so? What do you think made him so interesting to them?"

"I don't know," Annja said. Zach had asked her to keep the necklace confidential and she wanted to respect that.

Dunning looked into her eyes. "You sure about that?"

"Of course. Why would I lie about that?"

"I have no idea. I just find it tough to fathom why two guys would walk over and look to start trouble with your friend. Unless there was some underlying reason for their interest."

"None I can think of, that's for sure."

Dunning patted her bed. "All right. Well, I'll head down to Gallagher's and see if anyone there can give me some more information. Unfortunately, you know how this is going to play out."

"How?"

"Your word against theirs. That's if we even find them. It's not like our streets are crowded around here at this time of year especially. If you guys were tussling out there, no one saw it. People get into bed early during the winter. And without another witness, I can't really do all that much except warn them to be on better behavior, that I'll be keeping an eye on them, that sort of thing."

Annja nodded. "Well, maybe that will be enough."

"Yeah. Maybe it will." Dunning stood. "Well, try to get some sleep. At least you're safe now."

"Until tomorrow," Annja said.

"What's tomorrow?"

"I'm going off-site."

Dunning frowned. "Whereabouts?"

Annja thought hard. "I've been asked to take a look at the environmental situation out at Horlick Mountain."

"Ugh, I don't envy you. It's a long trek to get there and from what I've heard, the place is a real mess."

"Wonderful."

"Well, best of luck to you, then. Mind those ribs and if you can think of anything else you haven't mentioned yet, give me a call."

Annja watched him shut the door and then she slumped back on her pillow. She felt drowsy and exhausted from everything that had happened so far.

She glanced at her clock. Ten o'clock. She'd need to be up by three to get herself squared away and then meet Zach and Dave for a four-o'clock departure time. That left five hours to get some rest.

Not much time. But she'd survived on less.

Trevor poked his head in again. "You need anything else for the night, Annja? Or are you all set?"

Annja smiled. "Just need some rest now, Trevor. But thanks."

"My pleasure."

"And thanks for all your help just now. I really appreciate it."

He nodded. "I'm going to fix the lock on your door so it locks as I shut it. That way you don't have to get out of bed, okay?"

"Okay."

"Rest well."

Annja closed her eyes and listened as the door clicked shut. Trevor tested the doorknob outside and couldn't open the door. Annja turned and set the alarm, then reached for the light switch closest to her bed and managed to find it without putting herself into too much pain.

She slumped back on the bed.

She lay there in the dark thinking. What would make two guys want to kill her so soon after meeting her? Annja smirked. Yes, she thought, my personality can be abrasive when I want it to be. But was that all there was? Or was there another reason why she'd been marked for death so quickly? Why would someone want her out of the way this fast? She'd only just arrived in town and someone was measuring her for a coffin.

It didn't make sense.

Unless Zach's necklace was more of a threat than they thought.

But to whom? And why?

I need to rest, Annja told herself. And I need my ribs to heal fast or else I won't be much good on the site.

She took a deep breath and sank into herself. In her mind's eye, Annja could see the sword hovering in space, waiting to be used. Annja reached for it and touched the handle. A jolt of energy seemed to surge through her body as it always did when she prepared to unsheathe the blade.

The dull glow extended from the sword blade up her hands and wrists now. Annja watched it spread farther. Can I will this to cover my body? she wondered. On cue, the glow spread farther up her arms until she could feel the prickliness of its energy encompassing her entire upper torso. Annja willed it farther down toward her cracked rib. The energy seemed to vibrate and then pulse.

Annja continued to breathe deeply, feeling the sword's energy flow through her entire body now like the pulsing effect she'd heard mentioned in relation to *ki* energy in Japan.

The sword glowed brighter and the energy seemed to increase.

Annja could feel a more powerful flow rushing through her body. She started to sweat and then shiver as alternating currents flowed through her.

And then the glow of the sword started to diminish.

She opened her eyes in the darkness of her room. Her side didn't ache nearly as much as it had only moments before. Perhaps her pain medicine was finally kicking in.

Or perhaps the sword had helped heal her.

It wouldn't be the first time she'd been aided by the

mystical blade. Or by the strange plane of existence where it resided.

Thank God I have that, Annja thought. Otherwise, there was no telling how much of a liability she'd be to Zach and Dave on the mountain.

She yawned and took a deep breath.

It was time to sleep.

And time was already ticking toward her three-o'clock wake-up call. The last thing she wanted was to be sleepy tomorrow when they set out.

She had a lot of questions for Zach.

And she intended to get some answers.

"JUST A CRACKED RIB."

"That's what I heard."

"For all that trouble and you only managed to bust her rib up? What's the point of doing something if you can't even manage to carry it out all the way through?"

"We tried."

"You didn't try hard enough. And now you've got the marshal's attention, haven't you?"

The man from the bar listened to the voice on the other end of the phone. "Yeah, well, he'll get a bunch of descriptions. We could be any two guys down here."

"In the summer, that would be fine. But how many people are in town right now?"

"Maybe two hundred."

"Exactly my point, you idiot. Two hundred lowers the odds substantially, doesn't it? All the marshal needs is one good description and at the very least, he'll want to talk to you."

"He can't hold us on any charge, though. No one saw us try to take her out. No witnesses."

He heard a sigh on the telephone. "That doesn't matter.

You've drawn attention to yourselves. And the marshal will be keeping an eye out now for potential troublemakers."

"We can take her right now. Go to her place and break in. I know where she's staying."

"The idea, you louse, was to make it look like an accident, albeit a bizarre one. Now you want to go charging in and just kill her? That's not exactly the most intelligent thing to do, now, is it?"

"I guess not."

He heard another sigh. "You guess not. How wonderful."

"So what do you want us to do, then?"

"Nothing."

"Nothing? But I thought—"

"No," said the voice in his ear. "You didn't think. You didn't think at all. And that's why this simple little matter has suddenly become infinitely more complicated than it ever had to be. You and your partner there will do nothing more against her. Do I make myself clear?"

"Yes, sir."

"Tomorrow, when she and the two others leave, you will follow them. Covertly, mind you. I don't want them knowing you're tracking them."

"Then what?"

"Follow them out to the dig site. Make sure they get there intact and that nothing happens to them."

The man frowned. "You want us to make sure they're okay?"

"Yes."

"I don't understand."

"Obviously. You get them out there intact. Once they're on the site, their attention will be focused elsewhere."

"Okay."

"At which point," the voice on the phone said, "I will be able to ensure none of them ever returns to McMurdo Station."

8

When Annja's alarm clock erupted at three o'clock, she moaned and wanted nothing more than to slam the snooze bar down and sleep for another year. Her dreams had been mostly scattered images of her past adventures and how many injuries she'd sustained throughout them. It felt as if she'd been reliving the greatest hits of her past rather than enjoying the deep levels of sleep that would heal her.

Despite the reckless smorgasbord of dreams, Annja woke with her rib feeling much better than it had when she'd gone to sleep. She probed around the injury and decided that it must not have been as bad as she'd feared.

"That's something, anyway," she said to herself as she gingerly got out of bed. Her feet touched the warm carpet and she padded into the bathroom.

Once there, she carefully stripped off the tape around her midsection. The deep purple that had colored the bruised area last night was now a light yellow. Annja frowned. Was it really possible that the sword had healed her?

She started the water for her bath and watched the clouds

of steam fill up the bathroom. Annja added some soap and waited as the bubbles blossomed in the water, rapidly filling the entire tub.

She took a deep breath and finished stripping off the rest of her clothes. She felt as if she had thousands of miles of road grunge on her. She hadn't bathed in over a day and was certain that she must have a peculiar array of scents wafting about even now.

The bathroom was filled with steam when she finally turned off the spigot. She looked at the bubbly surface and then eased herself into the bath. The water greeted her like a warm blanket and she slid all the way into the tub, letting the water cover her.

The scent of the lavender soap filled the air as the bubbles began popping from her movements in the water. She lathered up and felt as if she were molting a layer of grimy skin.

When she was done she stepped from the tub and wrapped a towel around her head and a plush robe around herself. At the mirror, she wiped off the condensation and then checked herself over. She looked fatigued, but she was rapidly waking up. She ran a brush through her moist hair and noticed there was a hair dryer plugged into a wall-mounted unit.

Annja laughed. Probably not the smartest thing to do, go running outside with wet hair. She took the hair dryer and used it until she was satisfied that her hair was completely dry.

She put on some moisturizer that contained a bit of sunblock. She knew the harsh environment would be hard on her skin.

Back in her bedroom, Annja let the robe slide to the floor and stepped into a pair of thermal underwear. Not exactly glamorous, she thought, checking herself out in the mirror. Over the thermals, she added a turtleneck shirt and then a flannel shirt on top of that before pulling on her flannel-lined jeans. She slid two pairs of thick woolen socks over her feet and then stood again.

She felt a lot thicker now.

And hungry.

The wings she'd eaten last night hadn't done much to relieve her hunger. She poked her head out of the bedroom and wondered if the rooming house had a galley kitchen where she could find some food.

Annja wandered downstairs. A couple of people slept on couches. Beyond the sitting room, she could just make out the kitchen. The lights were on and someone moved around inside it.

Trevor.

"You're up early," she said.

He grinned. "Good morning to you, too. How you feeling today?"

"Actually, not all that bad."

Trevor looked shocked. "Really? A busted rib would set a lot of people on their heels for a few weeks. But you're okay, huh?"

"It's only cracked and I guess it wasn't as bad as we thought."

"That so?"

Annja shrugged.

He gestured at the stove. "You hungry?"

"Starving."

"There's oatmeal. I just made a batch. It's as fresh as we get it down here. Coffee's in the pot. Help yourself."

"Thanks." Annja got herself a bowl and a mug and scooped some oatmeal into the bowl. As she poured herself a cup of coffee, Trevor came back and handed her a bottle of maple syrup.

"Not sure if you like it—"

"I do."

He nodded. "Here you go, then."

Annja poured some on her oatmeal and then followed Trevor out to a small laminate table. She sat and started right in on the oatmeal.

Trevor watched her for a few minutes without saying

anything. Finally, he cleared his throat. "You're up awfully early."

Annja nodded. "I'm headed out this morning."

"When?"

Annja checked her watch. "In about a half hour."

"This early? Where's the fire?"

Annja smiled. "Horlick Mountain."

Trevor whistled. "Wow, that's some haul. Gonna be a long day for you, Annja. I hope your ribs are up to it. Those Sno-Cats aren't the most luxurious way to travel, if you get my meaning."

"It's far?"

"About five hundred kilometers. In good weather. With those Sno-Cats, you guys are going to be looking at a full day, maybe a day and a half of travel. Be better if you just flew."

"Why aren't we?"

Trevor smiled. "Weather. It rules the roost around here. This time of year, it's not safe for a routine flight. We only put planes up if there's no other alternative."

"I see." She sipped her coffee and moaned. "Wow, that's good stuff."

Trevor nodded. "I import some nice blends down here. It's my guilty pleasure, I guess."

"How long have you been here?" she asked.

"Nine months."

Annja ate another spoonful of her oatmeal. "Quite a haul."

"Money's good. You come down here and you can earn more in a year than you do in five back in the real world. It's a hefty cost, though, being alone and cut off from the rest of the world. Especially this time of year. The darkness can get to you. But there are benefits, too."

"Such as?"

Trevor swallowed some coffee. "The landscape is utterly amazing. In a lot of ways, it's like being on another planet.

When you're out there and away from any signs of civilization, you can almost imagine what it's like to be out in space."

Annja nodded. "You miss home?"

"All the time."

"What about your family?"

Trevor shook his head. "Grew up in orphanages. And I don't have any emotional attachments. I guess that's why I'm something of a poster boy for Antarctic employees. No strings back home aside from a few friends who think I'm nuts for coming down here."

"But you do it anyway," Annja said.

Trevor nodded. "Maybe the real world just isn't my cup of tea. I think I like it down here better than I ever would back there."

Annja finished her oatmeal. Trevor stood. "You want some more?"

Annja held up her hand. "I don't think I have time. Still have to brush my teeth and then climb into my gear. Oh—"

Trevor smiled. "I got your parka from Dunning. I'll see you off when you come back down, if you don't mind."

Annja nodded. "Sure. Thanks."

She went back upstairs and used the toilet and then brushed her teeth. Trevor seemed like a nice guy and he'd certainly been a big help to her last night. But what would make a guy like that want to run away from the real world? What had driven him down here in the first place? she wondered.

She slid a thick hat onto her head and then climbed into her snow pants and boots. She'd left the parka downstairs. She could put it on when she was headed out the door.

She took a final glimpse at her room. Comfortable, she thought. And it had certainly been a nice place to crash last night. She wondered where she'd be sleeping from here on out.

Trevor was as good as his word and met her at the bottom of the stairs by the front door. "Got everything you need?"

Annja nodded. "I think so. But honestly there's not much to bring. Just my laptop in my bag and a few articles of clothing and toiletries. Beyond that, what's the use?"

"You left the bathing suit at home, in other words."

"Exactly."

Trevor smiled and held up a small resealable bag. "Here, take this with you."

"What's this?"

"Some of my coffee. You seemed to like it an awful lot, and I can't imagine where you're going there's anything nearly as good as this. So, please, take the bag of it. I insist."

"Thanks, Trevor, that's awfully nice of you."

"Just remember me when that coffee's the only thing keeping you from freezing your ass off out in the woolly cold."

Annja smiled. "I will."

From outside, she thought she could hear an engine somewhere off in the distance.

Trevor seemed to hear it, too. "Sounds like your ride," he said.

"Guess so."

"You be careful out there, Annja. Okay?"

She looked at him. "Why so concerned?"

Trevor shook his head. "You seem like a smart woman. I don't like seeing good people get into things over their heads, you know?"

"Okay."

"All I'm saying is be careful. I've heard what happened out there—the environmental spill and all. I just hope it's not all that bad. Spoiling the natural beauty of this place would be a great shame. And I'd hate for you to get mixed up in any of that crap."

Annja squeezed his shoulder. "I'll be careful. I promise."

"All right, then."

The engine noise grew louder. Annja turned for her parka.

"Let me help you with that," Trevor said.

"Thanks." Annja slid into the parka and then zipped up the front. Trevor eyed her. "Ribs still feeling okay?"

"Pretty good, actually, yeah."

"Okay then, Miss Creed, I hereby pronounce you ready for Antarctic exploration. Godspeed to you."

Annja smiled and pulled her hood up. The engine noise had diminished to an idle right outside the door.

Annja stepped outside and felt the Antarctic morning greet her with a solid one-two punch in the blast of frigid air. She hustled over to the Sno-Cat and heaved her bag up into the cab.

She climbed up on the track and slid inside, pulling the door shut tight behind her.

"Good morning," Dave said. "How are you feeling?"

Annja smiled. "Oh, let me tell you about that."

Dave slid the Sno-Cat into gear. Annja looked out the window at Trevor, who still stood silhouetted in the doorway.

Just as she was about to wave goodbye, he closed the door.

9

"Someone attacked you?"

Annja nodded. "That's right. It happened right after I left the bar. As soon as I turned onto Main Street."

Dave shook his head. "Sometimes, I tell you, this place seems less and less like the Antarctica I fell in love with and more like Dodge City."

Annja shrugged. "Well, whoever it was, they definitely wanted me out of the way. And they did it in such a way that it would have looked like an accident. A strange one, but an accident nonetheless."

Dave steered the Sno-Cat farther out of McMurdo. "You talk to anyone about it?"

"Uh, yeah. I needed medical attention for my ribs and then the marshal came to see me. And he was a bit peeved that I hadn't had my in-briefing with him as of yet. Apparently, someone neglected to tell me it was standard procedure for all new arrivals."

Dave cleared his throat. "Yeah, sorry about that. Zach told me he wanted you brought into McMurdo as quickly as possible. Plus, it was suppertime. I didn't see much point in bothering Dunning about it."

Annja watched the dark sky lighten just a little. "Any other procedures or protocols I need to know about?"

"Nope. I think that's it."

Annja nodded. "Good."

"So who do you think it was? I mean, you weren't exactly in town all that long. Certainly not long enough to make any enemies—unless, of course, you count those two guys at the bar."

"I'm counting them," Annja said.

"Yeah, but you really think they'd do something like that? I mean, it just seems a bit extreme for a couple of lug nuts like them. I can't see them wanting to kill you just because you had some words."

Annja took a breath and didn't feel much pain in her side. "Dave, if there's one thing I've learned in my various travels, it's that you can never overestimate how low someone might be willing to sink."

"I suppose," Dave said. "Just makes me kind of sad, that's all. I don't want to think about crime infecting my home here." He flipped on the wipers to whisk away the snowflakes that had started falling. "Guess it just bums me out."

"Well, I was bummed out, too, but for obvious reasons— I was lying in the middle of the street with a Sno-Cat bearing down on me."

"Death by Sno-Cat," Dave said. "That's a new one. Especially considering how slow these things trundle along. Not exactly a high-speed rundown."

Annja looked out of the window. "We really have a long way to go, huh?"

"It's a good stretch, yeah. But we'll be all right. We've got plenty of provisions and equipment with us."

"But we won't get there tonight?" she asked.

"It's impossible to say. It all depends on the weather. As long as we arrive by late tomorrow Zach will be happy."

"Where is he, by the way?"

Dave pointed over his shoulder. "In the cat behind us. He joined us as we left Mac Town. He's got the equipment so we deemed it best that we take two cats instead of just trying to burden one of them. This way, if we run into trouble— one of them breaks down or something—we can hitch a ride on the other."

"Makes sense," Annja agreed.

"Plus, we can always radio for help. It might not be quick in getting to us, but at least they'll know what's going on."

Ahead of them, through the window, Annja could see very little in the darkness. The sky seemed to melt into the landscape, leading her to wonder how Dave would know how to reach their objective.

"I don't suppose there are any gas stations out here, huh?" she said.

Dave laughed. "Not quite. If you have to take a pit stop, I'd suggest you get used to using the jerrican behind your seat. It's a lot more comfortable than taking a powder outside. The conditions aren't exactly merciful to those who obey nature's call."

"How do you know when we get there?" Annja asked.

Dave patted the dashboard. "Global positioning system. We had them installed in all the cats a few years back. The things are a definite lifesaver. For years we had to go out with maps and take our chances. But now we know where everyone is right down to a yard or so."

"Anyone ever been lost since you got GPS?"

"Nope."

Annja nodded. The landscape looked incredibly foreboding. She could see small hills and peaks and long, irregular lines of ice sheets that jutted out of the ground. Snow seemed to fly at them from all sorts of odd angles.

"I can't imagine getting lost in this stuff," she said.

"Yeah, your chances of survival aren't great if you do. But people have done it before. And then when you think back to those early explorers, well, they didn't have much in terms of fancy gear with them. Just a willingness to go the extra mile and stake a claim for humanity in this frozen wasteland."

Annja smiled. "That was almost poetic."

Dave looked at her. "Don't let that get out. It'll ruin my reputation as a complete loon for staying down here as long as I have."

"And how long is that?"

"Ten years."

Annja looked at him. "You've been here for a decade?"

"Yep."

Annja shook her head. "You weren't kidding. You are a loon."

"Considering I came from Alaska, it's not too much of a stretch. And besides, in the summer, we get an almost balmy forty degrees outside. That's practically warm enough to go for a dip in the harbor."

"Well, sure." Annja rolled her eyes. "How long has Zach been here?"

"Oh, not long. A few months. He's green by comparison to a lot of folks. The research stations work primarily on rotations of crews who come down. There's overlap so everyone has good continuity on the various projects."

"And you were assigned to help Zach?"

"Something like that, yeah."

"By who?"

"Pardon?"

Annja looked at him. "Who assigned you to help Zach?"

Dave smiled. "My uncle. And yours."

"Ah. You're one of those guys, huh?"

Dave shook his head. "Nope. Not a spy or a soldier or anything like that. I'm just one of the few who have been down here long enough to know his way around and be able to safeguard the interests of the country. I'm not a zealot or ultranationalist. In fact, I'm much more liable to vote my conscience about keeping this place beautiful than for some political agenda. But I have my uses anyway."

"Such as looking after Zach."

Dave took a turn and brought the Sno-Cat onto a new ice sheet. The engine groaned, then the tracks gained purchase and they jerked forward again. "I get him to where he needs to be. This dig is an important one, as you can see from what he showed you last night. It's my job to make sure he does what he's being paid to do."

"Which is?"

"Figure out exactly what that necklace represents."

Annja nodded. "And do you believe that it could be from another planet? That aliens made it?"

"I don't know. This continent has a lot of history to it. Who knows, maybe some early tribe of humans made their way down here at some point. They could have dropped it and then we find it thousands of years later."

"So you're not into aliens."

Dave smiled. "If I see something conclusive, then sure, I might change my mind. Until that happens, though, I'll be a bit skeptical about its origins."

"Is that a view shared by your uncle?" Annja leaned back, trying to stretch. Her ribs felt tender but pretty good.

"I don't know, Annja. I'm not privy to a lot of what they talk about. I get my orders, and do what I'm asked to do. They deposit money into my bank account. That's how our relationship works."

"But Zach seems to trust you."

"Yeah, well, he's got no reason not to trust me. I wouldn't do anything that would hurt the guy. He's a good apple."

Annja let the conversation stall for the moment. She yawned and fought to keep her eyes open. The sleep last night hadn't revived her as much as she'd hoped it would. Plus, the injury had given her body more work to do, even if it had been helped by the power of the sword.

A nap would really be great.

"How long until I spell you at the wheel?"

Dave smiled. "You know how to drive one of these things?"

"Nope. But I'm a fast learner."

"Is that so?"

"Ask Zach."

Dave smirked. "All right." He reached forward for the radio handset and keyed it. "Zach, you back there?"

There was a pause and then Annja heard Zach's voice. "Yeah. What's up?"

"Annja here says that she's a quick study on vehicles. Is that true?"

"Why, is she asking to take a turn at the wheel?"

"Something like that, yeah."

Zach's laughter floated through the speaker. "I wouldn't if I were you. There was this one time, in Paris, where she tried to work the controls of this giant wrecking ball and ended up—"

Annja grabbed the handset. "We don't need to go into details about that just now, Zach. Why don't you just be a good guy and tell Dave that I am perfectly capable of working the Sno-Cat so he can get some rest when he feels tired?"

Zach paused. "Well, I guess she could relieve you if you explain how those controls work."

Dave smirked. "That's quite a vote of confidence you got yourself there."

"Zach's always been like that. He's convinced I can't drive, either. And that Paris thing was just a big misunderstanding. Really. I'm much more accomplished now on heavy machinery."

"Really?"

"You bet."

Dave nodded. "Well, I'm fine right now and we only just started out. I'd like to get us a good hundred miles out before I give much thought to releasing the controls. I'm well used to long hauls like this anyway, so it's no real big deal."

Annja sighed. "Fine."

Zach's voice came back through the speaker. "Dave?"

Dave took the handset. "Go ahead."

"You tell anyone else that we were coming out here today?"

"Me? Nope. No need."

"Annja? How about you?"

Annja frowned. "Just that guy Trevor at my dorm. He seemed to know already, though. He mentioned something about being careful out here and that he's heard it was a big old environmental disaster area. He told me I should be really careful. He seemed genuine enough."

Dave keyed the microphone. "Why do you ask? Something wrong back there?"

Zach paused. Then Annja heard his voice again. "I don't know."

"Zach?"

"It's probably nothing," he said. "I just thought I saw something behind us, that's all."

"Behind us? As in what? Another vehicle?" Dave asked.

"Yeah."

Dave shook his head. "Not very likely. It's tough going out here, and unless whoever's driving is experienced, they can easily get lost, even with the GPS system."

"How so?"

"They have to be able to navigate with it. And the GPS isn't quite as easy as what you'd find on a car. It's a bit trickier."

Annja frowned. "But what if there is someone back there? What would they be doing?"

"I don't know. Tracking us?" Zach said.

"But why?" Annja turned in her seat and felt a slight twinge in her side. "Ouch."

"Take it easy," Dave said. "Don't damage yourself any more than you already have."

"Okay." But Annja turned anyway and peered through the back windshield. She could see the lights from Zach's Sno-Cat. But nothing behind that.

If there was someone else out there, the snow and ice seemed to have swallowed him completely.

10

By midday, they'd traveled a little more than half the distance to the dig site. True to his word, Dave had stayed at the wheel, only taking small breaks to use the jerrican situated in the back of the Sno-Cat. During those times, Annja had kept the tracked snow vehicle trudging over the ice sheets and on course with the GPS system, which was actually very easy to follow.

"I don't know why you said this was tricky," she said as Dave zipped back up. "Any idiot could use this thing."

"Yeah, I know. I tend to exaggerate a little bit."

"I can take the wheel a while longer if you want to sleep."

Dave slid into the passenger seat. "Let's see how Zach's doing. He might be looking for a break."

He keyed the microphone. "How you doing back there, pal?"

"Tired. You guys?"

Annja yawned. Dave laughed. "I think Annja could use a break."

Zach's voice came back. "Let's take a break, then. We haven't eaten since before we left and I could use some grub. Not to mention a fresh cup of coffee."

"All right." Dave replaced the handset and studied the GPS screen. "There ought to be a place we can rest about a mile farther on." He jabbed at the screen. "There. Steer for that and once we get there, we'll get some food going."

Annja followed the course he'd plotted on the screen. As the snow vehicle traveled on, the line on the screen showed her position exactly. After another two minutes, she could see the flashing icon indicating they were just about at the rest point.

Dave peered through the window. "Pull it in over there behind that hill."

"Is that safe?"

He nodded. "Yep, and we should be on the leeward side, so we'll be out of the wind. We can actually get out and stretch our legs. You know, keep the blood flowing so we avoid having a stroke."

"Funny." Annja turned the Sno-Cat in and then turned it around.

"Keep the engine on. Otherwise she'll freeze up and we'll never get it started again," Dave said.

"Okay."

Zach maneuvered his Sno-Cat into position right next to their vehicle. A moment later, Dave opened the door and hopped out, sinking up to his knees in snow.

Annja followed and was amazed at how good she'd been feeling throughout the trip thus far. Her ribs had ceased aching and now, only a dull throb every once in a while remained. She still wasn't sure if the sword had helped her heal.

The fresh air felt marvelous on her face, despite being drastically cold. Zach waved at her. "How you doing?"

Dave spoke up. "Did you know she was attacked last night after she left us at the bar?"

Zach's face showed concern. "Are you all right?"

Annja nodded. "I had a bruised rib, but frankly, it's feeling fine right now."

"When we stop for the night, you'll have to tell me all about it. For right now, let's get the cats tanked up with gas and then get some food on. I'm starving."

Dave was already getting five-gallon gas cans out of the back of Zach's Sno-Cat. They took turns tipping them into the gas tanks, eventually topping them off.

"I can't believe how much gear these things can haul," Annja said.

Dave nodded. "They're built for this kind of thing. And luckily, they can tolerate the conditions, provided we treat them right."

"I'd hate to get stranded out here," Annja said.

Zach walked over. "We've got beef stew for lunch. And it's piping hot."

Annja looked at him. "How'd you manage that?"

"Space-age technology," Zach said. "You'd be amazed at what you can fire up even down here."

Dave threw the empty gas cans back into the Sno-Cat and they all got back into Dave and Annja's Sno-Cat for lunch. The cab was filled with the sweet smell of the bubbling beef stew.

Annja leaned over her bowl and sniffed. It smelled incredibly good. "Wow, that smells great. Almost fresh."

"It almost is," Zach said. "One of the cooks I know back at McMurdo makes a great recipe of this stuff and she gets the freshest vegetables she can when the supplies come in. She owed me a favor and here's the result."

Annja spooned up some of the beef stew and tasted it. Her mouth swam in the juices and broth and she moaned. "Even the beef is pretty good."

"As fresh as we can get it," Zach said. "Which, honestly, isn't all that fresh. But it's still good."

Annja smiled. "I've only had wings since I got here, so this is a feast by comparison."

Dave handed her some coffee. "Here you go."

"Actually, is there any water? I'm feeling a little dehydrated."

Dave nodded. "Good point." He rummaged around in the back of the cat and came back with three large bottles of water. "With the almost zero percent humidity down here, it's good to keep drinking water. People don't even realize they can dehydrate so quickly."

"Well, I've been dehydrated before, so I'm familiar with the warning signs." She drank deep of the water bottle and then replaced the cap. "That's good stuff, too."

They ate in relative silence, with everyone going back for seconds. Annja's stomach seemed to appreciate the sudden infusion of food and energy. And the water was a godsend. She wondered why she hadn't thought of asking for some before and then remembered what Dave had just said. People wouldn't even recognize they were thirsty simply because the humidity was so low.

"You sure you're okay?" Zach asked. "I mean, after being attacked and all last night."

"It was a weird run-in," Annja said. "They clearly hoped I'd be dead by now. The first guy tackled me and left me squirming on my back, unable to flip over so I could get out of the way of the oncoming Sno-Cat."

"How'd you get out?" Zach asked.

"I unzipped my parka and wriggled out that way. Hurt like hell, though, after having my ribs cracked."

Zach shook his head. "Had to be those guys from last night at the bar. You weren't in town long enough for anyone else to be pissed off at you."

"Yeah, but why would they just opt to kill me?" Annja asked. "Doesn't make any sense. We were just having words. Are things so serious down here that you can't get into a disagreement without folks resorting to lethal force right away?"

Zach shrugged. "So what did the marshal say?"

Annja spooned more stew into her mouth. "Not much he could say. He promised to keep an eye out for the two guys. Said he'd head down to Gallagher's and have a word with folks, that kind of thing. But honestly, I'm not all that hopeful about getting any results."

"I wouldn't be, either," Zach said. "Even though it's the dead of winter here and the places are by and large isolated with lots less people, there are still ways to vanish around here if you know where to go."

Dave nodded. "He's right. Some of the buildings in the settlements are virtually abandoned. Someone who knows what they're doing could make themselves scarce, hide out and emerge only a few times. It would be like they were ghosts."

"Speaking of which," Annja said. "You said earlier that you thought you saw something behind us. What was that all about? You think we've been followed?"

Zach shrugged. "Damned if I know. I caught a glimpse of some red flash in my rearview mirror. I looked back but the snow had obscured my view. I couldn't be sure, but I thought a few times during the trip I spotted something."

Annja frowned. "I'm not that crazy about the idea that we're being followed."

"Nor am I," Dave said. "You think it's trouble?"

"Annja's friends from last night, you mean?" Zach asked. Dave nodded.

Zach sighed. "I don't know. Truth is, the dig is probably what's causing the problem. It's almost impossible to keep anything a secret down here. People talk all the time. And the settlements are in constant communication with each other. Hell, if need be, the folks back at Mac Town can punch a couple of keys and see exactly where this Sno-Cat is right now."

Dave eyed Annja. "Privacy is almost nonexistent down here. Everyone knows each other's business."

"Which is why this dig site has remained so covert," Zach said. "And amazingly so given the scope of the project."

"What do you mean?" Annja asked.

He grinned. "What I mean is we aren't going to some base camp with just a few pitched tents. The government folks have come in and set up a pretty elaborate camp. They don't do things half-assed. Well, at least not anything like this."

"Will we get there by nightfall?" Annja asked.

Zach looked at Dave. "We're doing pretty well so far. What's your take on that?"

Dave nodded. "Theoretically, if the weather doesn't get any worse, I think we can continue and make it in time for dinner."

"Excellent. I'd rather get a bunk than have to sleep in the cat."

Annja nodded. "My ribs could use a flat surface to rest upon. I'm feeling okay, but I think as the day wears on, I might be in more pain again."

"Did the docs give you anything to take for it?" Zach asked.

Annja nodded. "Yeah, but I'm one of those people who doesn't like to keep tipping pills into my system every few hours if I can possibly avoid it. I'd rather let nature handle things and just try to coax the healing process along where I can."

Dave smiled. "I like good strong pills myself."

Annja patted his arm. "If I don't need mine, you can have the unused portion of my prescription, okay?"

"Great."

Zach smirked. "You'd think you just offered him the chance to lick the icing off the bowl."

"Hey, I sell them to the penguins. Guy's gotta make an extra buck where he can, you know?" Dave said.

Annja shook her head. "Hopped-up penguins. Excellent."

Dave checked his watch. "We should get going. Idling too long puts too much pressure on the cats. And the last thing we want is to break down out here."

"Has that ever happened to anyone?" Annja asked.

"More often than you'd think," Zach said. "In the short time I've been here, there were already two fatalities."

Dave shook his head. "That's only because they were damned fools and didn't stay with the cats." He glanced at Annja. "Survival protocol is to stay with the vehicles. Since they can track them with GPS, the rescue teams know exactly where to go. But the two who died insisted on leaving the shelter of the cats."

"Their last transmission claimed that the engines had died entirely," Zach said.

Dave frowned. "They were still out of the wind, and that's the killer down here. A blasting gale will strip body heat even faster than temperature alone. They should have stayed put."

"Maybe something else was bothering them about their predicament," Annja said.

Dave shook his head. "Nope, they were just a bunch of damned fools. They'd only been here a week and then that happened. Just another reminder that you can't fool around with Mother Nature. If you don't respect her, she'll kill you."

A blast of wind rocked the cat and snow pelted the windows. Dave put his spoon into his bowl. "I'll clean up the dishes." He collected Annja's and Zach's and then hopped out of the cat.

Annja watched him washing the dishes in the snow. "He seemed a bit upset by that story."

Zach leaned closer to the windshield. "Yeah. The two people who died were friends of his."

"They were?"

"Yeah. They were close. And they came down because he

recommended they come down. But he was sick that day and I think he blames himself for their deaths. He hides it by being angry with them, but deep down, I know he blames himself."

Annja shook her head. "Couldn't be helped, though. How long is he going to carry that guilt with him?"

"Dave's a complex guy despite seeming simple. I haven't known him all that long, but I'd trust him with my life."

"That's good, considering my little run-in last night."

Zach nodded. "Yeah, well, if there is trouble at the dig site, Dave is the one guy you'll want at your back."

Annja looked at Zach. "You expect trouble?"

"I don't know what I expect. But given how things are going, anything is possible."

"And the necklace? What about that?"

Zach sighed. "Probably the catalyst for anything bad that's going to happen."

11

As the afternoon dragged into the evening hours, Annja could clearly make out the peaks of the Transantarctic Range stretching in front of her. What surprised her the most was how small they seemed. She mentioned this to Dave, who only smiled.

"That's because the majority of their mass is buried under the snow and ice. What you're seeing are the very tops of them."

"How tall are they?"

"In total? I think about forty-four hundred meters is the tallest we have down here. Certainly not the size of the Himalayas, but sizable nonetheless. They can be impressive in their own right."

Annja nodded. "So when we say we're actually going on a dig, we really are digging down, huh?"

"Yep. No real need to climb up. All of the history of this continent is buried down deep. Makes things a little easier in that regard, rather than having to trek lots of equipment up a steep slope."

"Incredible." Even through the windshield, the peaks of the mountains looked as if they could easily be on the set of a science fiction movie. The bleak sky, barely light, looming over the jagged teeth of the mountaintops. And the ever-present horizontal snow gave the environment a true sense of foreboding.

Inside the cab, the heat continued to pump out of the vents, making a marked contrast to the exterior conditions. Annja sucked down some more water and then replaced the cap. Since she'd started drinking the water, she'd had to use the jerrican a bit more frequently, but she knew that was a good sign that she was ingesting enough water.

She turned in her seat and her ribs felt almost back to normal.

Dave eyed her. "You seem to be handling that broken rib easily enough. And you haven't touched your meds."

Annja nodded. "Yep, I guess I'm a pretty fast healer."

"Never seen someone bounce back from busted ribs quite like you."

"I imagine there are plenty of things I could probably do that you haven't seen before."

Dave laughed. "I'd bet on that."

Through the back windshield, Annja could make out Zach's vehicle following in their wake. His caterpillar tracks chewed up the snow being churned out by Annja's Sno-Cat and seemed to spit it sideways into a nice blazed trail.

Anyone following them would have no problems doing so. The trail would be easy to follow, even from a distance. It would take at least a day of heavy snows to erase their presence from the landscape.

If anyone was following them.

Annja glanced at Dave. "What do you think about the possibility of someone being on our tail?"

He shrugged. "Honestly, maybe there is someone back there. I don't know. With this dig, the folks upstairs could have easily called a few more into the fray and if we don't have a need-to-know, then we wouldn't know, would we?"

"Guess not."

"On the other hand, if it turned out that our guests weren't the friendly type, then, yeah—I might be a bit concerned about that."

"This is a mighty isolated stretch of journey we're undertaking," Annja said.

"At this point, if we get into trouble, we're screwed. The station at the very South Pole might just be a hair closer than McMurdo. But either way, without a flyover, any rescue would take the better part of a full day to get to us. And it looks like the weather's getting worse."

Annja looked out of the front of the Sno-Cat. Dave was right. The amount of snow flying at them seemed to have increased exponentially. The flakes were tiny, reflecting how utterly cold it was outside. And at times, it looked like a wall of white was headed right for them.

But Dave continued to steer the cat according to the GPS. He nodded at the dash. "Now, if that thing kicked out, then we'd be in a world of hurt. My map-reading skills are about on par with my skills at golf. Which is to say, completely nonexistent."

Annja cocked an eyebrow. "You can't map-read?"

"Nope."

"I find that hard to believe."

He glanced at her. "Why so?"

"You seem much more capable than that."

Dave smirked. "You flatter me. But the truth is, I'm mostly self-taught about a lot of stuff. Just how I've always been. Never had much use for school and the like, so I escaped as soon as I could and came down here once I found I had a certain skill set that translated well to this environment."

"What skill set is that?"

Dave shook his head. "Nothing special."

"Okay, I know enough not to pry too much." Annja went back to studying the landscape.

The radio crackled. "Guys?"

Annja grabbed the handset. "Hey, Zach, what's up?"

"I've got a bit of a problem back here."

Dave glanced in the rearview mirror. Annja turned in her seat.

"Where are you?"

The radio sounded staticky. "You see that huge pile of snow in the middle of the path?"

"Yes."

"That would be me. I caught a snowslide. It buried the cat. I'm dead in the water here."

"Jesus." Dave wheeled the Sno-Cat around and started back.

"We're coming back for you Zach," Annja said. "Hang on!"

Dave leaned close to the windshield, trying to judge his distance to Zach's cat. "I don't want to stray too far away. We need to get him out of there as fast as possible."

Annja keyed the microphone. "Is your engine dead?"

"Yeah. The snow clogged the intakes and it shut down."

"Carbon monoxide," Dave said, zipping himself up. "We have to get him out of there. You feel well enough to help out?" he asked Annja.

"Absolutely." She zipped up her coat, as well.

Dave nodded. "Follow me."

Annja jumped out of the idling vehicle and followed Dave around to the rear of the cat. He handed her a shovel and then leaned close to her head. "We need to dig the cab out first and extricate Zach. If we don't get to him, he'll be dead if there are any trapped fumes. Understand?"

Annja nodded. "Got it."

The wind howled. Dave pointed at the mound of snow. "Let's go!"

The wall of snow blew into them hard, whipping past

Annja's head as they walked through the deep snow toward the mound of snow that had buried Zach.

Annja marveled at how calm he'd sounded on the radio. Being buried alive wasn't something she ever wanted to experience.

Dave jumped up and into the mound. He landed awkwardly and Annja watched him topple back down. He got up, brushed himself off and pointed at the side he'd tried to climb. "There's a track here. Climb up with me."

He held out his hand and Annja took it. Together, they scaled the side of the cat.

Dave got his shovel and started leaning in and scooping off the snow. Annja got her own shovel in and tried to shove some of the powdery snow off. Her ribs protested and she felt her side strain somewhat. She moaned with the sudden pain.

Dave glanced at her. "You say something?"

Annja grinned. "When it hurts, I know I'm alive."

Dave grinned and nodded before going back to work.

Gradually, they cleared part of the windshield. Inside the cab, they could see Zach. He'd zipped up and looked quite calm sitting there. Annja waved but she got no response from him.

"Is he okay?"

Dave pressed his face against the glass and peered in. He shook his head. "Keep digging!"

Annja drove her shovel down into the snow and kept clearing. They worked at the side door to the cab and finally got the handle exposed.

"Stand back!" Dave got in front of Annja and grabbed the handle. He gave a grunt and yanked on it.

Annja heard the door pop open and then the wind took it, slapping it open. Dave was already inside getting his hands on Zach's coat. "Give me a hand, Annja!"

Annja got next to him and saw Zach. He was completely

limp. Dave heaved him out and they all slid down together into the snow. Annja grabbed a handful of snow and wiped it all over Zach's face.

Dave slapped him. "Wake up, you lazy bastard."

But Zach didn't stir.

"He couldn't have been in there long enough, could he?" Annja asked.

Dave shrugged. "Don't know." He bent down low and blew three breaths into Zach's mouth. Dave came up, and then checked Zach's pulse.

"There's a pulse."

Zach coughed and sputtered. Annja grabbed him. "You okay?"

Zach turned and threw up in the snow. The pile of vomit steamed in the frozen air. Annja blanched.

"Yuck."

Dave slapped him again. "Next time don't wait so long to call in the cavalry, okay?"

Annja rushed to their cat and got Zach some water. When she walked back, he was already on his feet. He took the bottle and took several swigs, which he then spit out. Finally, he took a long drag and swallowed.

"Thanks."

"You're welcome."

Dave came walking back from the cat. "I don't think it's going to be salvageable. The engine seems pretty well shot. I'd guess the snow and ice did a number on it." He glanced at Zach. "What the hell happened?"

Zach shrugged. "I was following you guys and then all of a sudden I heard this weird sound, like a rumble, and the next thing I know, this wall of snow just engulfs me. In a split second I was buried."

Annja frowned. "You get a lot of avalanches around here?"

Dave smiled. "Considering where we are, yeah."

Zach took a breath. "Just glad you guys weren't that much farther down the trail. Any longer and I would have been a goner."

Dave nodded at their cat. "Let's get you warmed up. Annja and I will try to salvage what we can from your cat and pack it into ours."

"Okay."

Dave led him over to their cat, and Annja watched as Zach climbed inside the cab. Dave came trudging back through the show, leaning into the wind as he approached her. "You okay?"

"Yeah, just concerned about Zach."

"He'll be okay now. The fresh air did him good." He nodded at the disabled cat. "We need some of the fuel and the equipment. As much as we can get into our cat."

Annja helped him with the fuel cans first. They topped off their cat, then Dave pulled out a number of heavy-duty boxes that were taped up with all sorts of strange-looking tape.

"What are those?"

"Zach's stuff. I don't ask about it."

They dragged them through the snow to the back of their cat. Dave got them situated inside and then headed back to the buried cat one final time.

Annja watched him move through the snow. He seemed at ease in this bizarre landscape, as if he'd been born to the snow in some weird way.

She shook her head and then looked up at Zach. He seemed to be focused on something far away.

Annja tapped on the glass. He glanced down at her and smiled.

Dave came walking back. "Okay, I think we've got as much of the stuff as we're going to be able to haul with us. As it is, we're going to be a lot heavier now than we were."

"Is that bad?" Annja asked.

"It slows us down and burns more fuel."

"Will we make it?"

Dave nodded. "If we don't, we'll be close enough to radio for help."

"I thought you said that the South Pole station was the closest."

"It is. They're the closest known station. But there are plenty of folks at the dig site we can call on to help if we need it."

"That's a relief," she said.

"C'mon. Let's get going. We've been out too long as it is."

Annja climbed back in the cab and got herself situated behind Zach, who now sat in the shotgun seat. Dave climbed in and gunned the engine. With a jerk, the Sno-Cat spun on its tracks and headed off again, following the path laid out on the GPS.

Annja glanced out the back windshield. She could just make out part of the cab jutting out of the mound of snow. But then the flakes flew in and obscured her view.

The cab would be buried in minutes anyway.

12

"An avalanche?"

"Not quite, sir. More like a snowslide. But their second Sno-Cat was completely buried."

"Was anyone hurt?"

"No. They turned back and extricated the driver before he died."

There was a pause on the phone. "Did you have anything to do with that?"

"The avalanche?"

"You called it a snowslide a moment ago."

He frowned. "No, sir, we didn't have anything to do with it. We were following your orders and hanging back. We only observed what happened to them."

"I told you to make sure no danger befell them en route to the dig site."

"There was nothing we could do about it. It was just a freak occurrence."

Static crackled over the phone and then the voice came back again. "For your sakes, you'd better hope nothing else happens to them on their journey. It's imperative they reach the dig site safely."

He frowned. "You mind me asking why? I mean, it sounds like you're going to kill them anyway once they're there. So why not just do it right now?"

"You have no appreciation for how things should unfold. You will take no action against them—do I make myself clear?"

"Yes, sir."

"Good, continue to observe and report anything out of the ordinary."

"Fine." He hung up the phone and turned to the man sitting next to him in the Sno-Cat. "Let's go."

"He wasn't happy?"

"Is he ever?"

DAVE HADN'T BEEN JOKING about the increased weight slowing them down. Their speed seemed to dip from a solid twenty-five miles per hour down to just under eighteen. The tracks continued to grind up snow and ice as they crawled along in the shadows of the mountain range to their right side.

The fuel gauge took a hit, as well. They'd had to stop once more to top off the tanks.

Zach seemed to have recovered himself and napped intermittently. Annja watched him. Through his shirt, she could make out the links of chain that attached to the necklace he wore.

Dave eyed him, as well. "He seems fine now, if that's what you're thinking."

"Yeah."

"Carbon monoxide is tough stuff. Can't see it or smell it. An invisible killer. That's why they passed all those laws about people getting detectors. Just too many folks losing their lives to it."

Annja nodded. "Guess you really never know how quick it can go wrong until it starts to go wrong, huh?"

"Something like that."

Annja sighed and stretched. She was tucked behind Zach with all of the equipment. She didn't have a lot of room to maneuver or make herself comfortable, and it felt as if she'd spent the past several hours bunched up. She desperately wanted to stretch her legs.

"How much longer?" she asked.

"About an hour, maybe less."

"We're that close?"

"Yep."

She took another breath. "Well, that's good news at least."

Dave nodded. "The getting there is always the toughest part. But I'm sure it will all be worth it once you get a look at the place."

"It's that amazing?"

He shrugged. "Far be it for me to comment adequately on it, but considering what Zach found, who knows what other kinds of marvelous things might be there. In some ways, this is a lot like unearthing some Egyptian pharaoh. Personally, I can't recall when I've had this much fun."

Annja eyed him. "Last night you made it sound like you'd never even seen the place. Or that you hadn't known Zach was involved in it."

Dave nodded. "Yeah, well, that was before I got a chance to know you. I don't like putting all my cards on the table until I know who holds the deck. That way, I keep the surprises in my life to a minimum."

Zach stirred. "Talking about the dig?"

Annja nodded. "Dave was just prepping me for the first views of it."

"Have you ever seen a big hole in the ground?" Zach asked.

"Of course."

He smiled. "There you go."

Dave chuckled. "So much for romance, huh? Zach's much more the pragmatist in the equation."

Zach patted his chest. "This thing weighs heavy on my heart. I want to figure out where it came from and who it might have belonged to."

"Can I see it again?" Annja asked.

Zach turned to her and took off the necklace. He handed it to her and Annja was again surprised at its weight.

"Where did you find it at the dig site?"

Zach leaned back against the seat and took a deep breath. "I was hired to come down and check things out, as I told you."

"Who hired you?" Annja asked.

"A company out of Milwaukee. Navstar. Supposedly they do a lot of work for the oil conglomerates, but I felt pretty sure they were a front for some government operations. Sometimes you just get a feeling about these things."

"So what happened?"

"They approached me about coming down to look a site over for possible paleontological finds. As far as I knew at that point, there wasn't much down here worth examining in any great detail. I mean, sure, I'd heard about the fossils and plants that had been found down here, but beyond that? It seemed like a dumb assignment. Just a way for the oil companies to cover their asses."

"What changed your mind?"

"The paycheck."

Annja looked at him. "You're motivated by money now?"

"Trish and I got divorced. She took the kids. I didn't have a chance at custody, being away throughout the year like I was. The judge granted her sole custody. I get visits when I'm home, but—" he took a breath "—it's been tough making ends meet with the alimony and child support."

"And the job came along at just the right moment."

"Yep."

Annja glanced at Dave. "This is sounding more and more like a government conspiracy all the time."

Dave nodded. "Oh, it most definitely is. We know that now. They control every aspect of the dig site. The oil companies aren't even involved, believe it or not."

"So who's running the show? CIA?"

Zach shrugged. "I heard something about a DARPA project. They'd be the ones looking to scoop up anything extraterrestrial and reverse engineer it so it becomes the next iPod or something."

Annja smirked. "I'm surprised they let you have the necklace."

"Oh, it's not mine. I'm returning it to them. They let me take it out so I could use it to secure your interest."

"Ah."

"Anyway, they flew me down here and we trekked out to the site. By the time I got there, they already had a series of tents and hardened prefab shells in place. There's a hole that literally goes right into the base of the mountain. You can descend the better part of a half mile right into the mountain itself."

"Incredible."

Zach nodded. "That's what I said, too. On that first day, they got me outfitted and showed me a map of tunnels they'd made. It had a number of branches on it, and I wanted to go off exploring. They said no, that they weren't sure how structurally sound it was yet. But I sneaked off anyway, and down a long winding passage in the dark, my headlamp caught something amid the ice."

"The necklace," Annja said.

"Yeah. When I pulled it out, it felt like I was trying to jerk an anchor out of the water. But then when I held it up, it was almost a magical experience."

Dave smiled. "Maybe there is a little romance in that heart somewhere."

Annja shifted in her seat. "And what happened when you showed it to them?"

"They ran the tests we spoke about last night. When things started coming back…odd, they got really interested. Of course, it's all very compartmentalized. I'm positive there are people on the site who know how this is all supposed to fit together, but damned if anyone's talking. So, in the meantime, they've been bringing in more scientists and I requested the only person I knew I could trust—you."

"I'm flattered."

"I need someone watching my back. Someone who knows how to think and can maybe make sense of all of this stuff."

"Well, I can't wait to get there."

Dave pointed at the dashboard. The clock read just past 5:00 p.m. "I'm betting we'll be there inside of twenty minutes now."

"Good," Zach said. "They're probably freaking out that the necklace has been gone this long. They're not exactly the most trusting people on the planet. But they do recognize the power of persuasion."

"I would have come anyway," Annja said. "Not like I have much else to do while I wait for my return flight."

"Good point," Dave said. "And she doesn't look like she's very good at darts, either. That rules her out for team competition."

"Funny," Annja said. "I'll have you know I'm quite adept at throwing pointy things into small targets."

"I'll bet." Dave chuckled.

Annja turned back to Zach. "Sorry to hear things didn't work out with you and Trish. Was it a long time coming?"

"Yeah, I guess so." Zach sighed. "I tried to make adjustments. I changed my work schedule. Stopped going off on long hauls away from home. But even when I made the changes, it just didn't seem like she was into the marriage anymore. I got the feeling she'd rather be off doing her own thing without the likes of me around."

Annja took a deep breath. "Maybe it's for the best."

"Honestly, I'm not so much broken up over her. But I miss the hell out of my kids. I can't stand thinking of them living with another guy and calling him 'Dad.'" He shook his head. "Pretty juvenile, huh?"

"No," Annja said. "It's not. It's completely natural to think that way. After all, you helped bring them into the world in the first place."

Zach grinned. "I figure with this paycheck I'm getting, at least I can secure their futures for them. Even if their mother thinks I'm a bum, I can rest easy knowing they've got money for college and maybe a head start on life. It's more than what I had growing up."

"Me, too," Dave said. He glanced at Zach. "You're a good man, dude. Maybe she didn't realize that, but it's true. You care about your kids and it shows. You're willing to do whatever it takes so they have a better life. That's the definition of a hero in my book."

Annja patted Zach on his shoulder. "It'll work out, Zach. It'll work out in the end."

"I hope so. This job could be a good stepping stone for me."

"I'm sure they'll be pleased with your work. And I'll do my best to make sure you get the credit necessary. Okay?"

"Thanks, Annja. I really appreciate that."

Their radio came to life. "Attention, unmarked vehicle, you are approaching a United States government secured area. This area has been officially recognized as an environmental disaster area. You must proceed no farther. Please turn around and head back the way you came."

Zach smirked. "Like they don't know it's us."

Dave shrugged. "They have to be sure, I guess."

"Better give them what they want."

Dave nodded and picked up the handset. "This is Romeo-One-Five-Whiskey. Requesting permission to proceed."

There was a pause. "Authentication code?"

"One-One-Zulu-Delta."

"Confirmed. You're cleared to proceed. Report directly to in-processing upon arrival."

"Roger that." Dave switched off the handset and glanced back at Annja. "You ready for this?"

Annja smiled. "Always."

"Then here we go."

13

As they rounded the bend, immense lights that had been set up to illuminate the entire area blinded Annja. She blinked several times before finally being able to focus again.

"Slow it down," Zach said. "They'll want to check us out."

Sure enough, Annja heard a bang on the side door. Dave opened it and a soldier dressed all in white stood there with his rifle.

"Identification?"

Dave removed an ID card from his wallet and passed it over. The guard studied it and then handed it back. "All right. Make sure you park this and head over to in-processing."

Dave closed the door again and drove the Sno-Cat into a parking area that looked well sheltered from the elements. Other Sno-Cats sat there along with smaller snowmobiles.

"This is quite the setup," Annja said.

Zach laughed. "You haven't seen anything yet, Annja. Just wait."

Dave parked the vehicle. "All right, let's get out and get the in-processing done. Then I need to find a toilet."

"Thanks for the image," Annja said.

Dave led them toward a hard-shell prefabricated unit with lights strung up. Inside, warm air greeted them, and they all unzipped their parkas. Dave approached a desk and the soldier sitting behind it. A sidearm was clearly visible.

"Evening."

The soldier nodded. "I'll need IDs from everyone."

Zach handed his over while Annja struggled to get her passport out. Finally she managed to extract it from her bag and handed it to the soldier, who looked her over.

"Do I know you from somewhere?"

"TV," Annja said. *"Chasing History's Monsters."* She hoped that's all it was.

He nodded. "Yeah, that's it. Hey, I really love that show. Especially when what's-her-name is on."

"Kristie Chatham. Yeah, she's a doll." Annja tried to smile, but it came out like a zigzag line across her face.

The soldier handed back her passport. "Enjoy your stay."

"Thanks."

They started to leave when the soldier stopped them. "Wait, don't forget these. You have to wear them at all times. Just in case."

Annja took a small credit card–size box from him. "What's this thing?"

"Radiation detector," the soldier said.

"Radiation?" Annja turned to Zach. "Just what the hell is going on here anyhow?"

He shook his head. "I don't know. This is all new to me."

"Just a precaution, most likely," Dave said. "Come on, let's get the gear."

They walked back into the biting cold. The wind was screaming now, and anything not tied down was flapping about in the wind. Annja spotted an American flag stuck into the ground and noticed that the cold air had frozen the fibers.

"So where's this big environmental accident?" she asked.

"Later," Zach said. "Let's get the gear and get settled. We can check it out later, like tomorrow morning."

"I thought we were under the gun here," Annja said.

He shrugged. "Right now, I want to rest and get some food into my belly. I also want to find out what's been going on since I left."

"All right."

They got back to the Sno-Cat and opened the rear compartment. Zach handed Annja one of the boxes and she was pleased to find it wasn't heavy at all. Dave heaved out another long box, and Zach grabbed the final bit of stuff. They walked over to another series of prefab shelters.

Zach ducked into one of them and then waved them on in.

Inside, Annja could see four beds set up with space heaters blasting out warm air. The lighting was great and although sparse in creature comforts, Annja did notice a closed-off toilet stall at the back.

Dave headed right for it.

Annja glanced at Zach. "So what's with all the gear?"

"Just some standard boring stuff. I wanted to see if I can get down farther into the earth with it and possibly see if there are any other items that might help describe the necklace."

"You think there might be?"

He shrugged. "I don't know. At this point, even being away for a couple of days, things can change on a dime. Who knows what's been happening since I left."

Someone knocked on their shelter. "Yeah?" Zach said.

Annja saw a head poke in. "Okay to come in and talk?"

"Sure."

The hooded figure entered and removed his parka. Annja saw an older man of about fifty standing before them. He removed his gloves and headed right for Annja.

"So you're our newest addition here."

"I guess so."

"Welcome. My name is Colonel Thomson. I'm in charge of the operation here at Horlick."

"Nice to meet you. But what is this operation exactly? I was under the impression it was just a dig site," Annja said.

"Oh, it is, it is. But when Zach here found that necklace, the scope of things changed a bit. Now it's more of a recovery operation than anything else."

"Recovery? What are you talking about?" Zach said.

Colonel Thomson sat down on one of the beds. "Since you left us, Zach, the crews kept digging. We've found some more items."

Zach looked startled. "More? Like what exactly?"

"Evidence of a race of people living here long before most scientists would agree it was possible to fashion items like we've found. From what we've discovered, they were extremely advanced. And we still can't fathom what the metal is. We've even sent some back to the States for analysis, and they can't determine its origin."

"Incredible." Zach sat down again.

Colonel Thomson nodded. "So what we're hoping is that you and Miss Creed here—"

"Please, call me Annja," she interrupted.

He smiled. "Very well…Annja." He glanced at Zach. "We're hoping that you will be able to go down into the dig site tomorrow morning first thing and help us try to figure out who these people were."

"Do you have any ideas?" Annja asked.

Colonel Thomson shook his head. "None whatsoever. The ideogram of three snakes keeps popping up, however. We feel certain that they somehow associated themselves with a serpent of sorts. Three perhaps. Maybe it figured into their mythology in some way."

"The other items you've found have had this ideogram on them, as well?" Annja asked.

He nodded. "We've got a pot of sorts and some kind of kettle, it looks like. All made from the same type of metal. And both of them are emblazoned with that trio of snakes. It's quite unusual."

"And what about the possibility of these items being extraterrestrial in origin?" she asked.

Colonel Thomson smiled. "Well, now, I suppose that's an idea that Zach had put forth." He pointed a finger at Zach. "You're far too obsessed about this alien thing. I just can't see it. At least not yet."

"So you admit there's a possibility," Zach said.

"Oh, sure, there's always a chance. I mean, it's certainly got all the makings of a good theory—unidentifiable metal, strange ideogram, evidence of a race existing here long before it should. Sure. It could be aliens. Why not?"

Annja looked at him. "You seem awfully open to the idea."

"Annja, when you've been in the military as long as I have, you see things. Sometimes you ask questions—only if it's permissible. But you still see things. And I've seen a lot. Certainly enough to know that nothing is as impossible as it might at first seem."

"I understand."

Thomson stood up. "All right, then. Glad we had a chance to meet up and discuss things. I look forward to seeing you both down on the dig bright and early tomorrow. Did you have any troubles getting out here?"

"Snowslide," Zach said. "It took out my Sno-Cat. We had to double up in the second one."

Thomson nodded. "All right. I'll send a recovery team as soon as the weather breaks. I can't do it until then—don't want them exposed to the elements unless they can get it back. How far away was that?"

"A couple of hours back," Zach said.

"Good enough." He put his parka on. "Have a good night." He ducked back through the door and out into the cold night.

"Nice guy," Zach said. "He likes to rib me on my obsession with aliens."

"I can tell. You've known him long?"

Zach shrugged. "Just since I got here. He was in charge. I didn't even know it was a military operation until I arrived. Up to that point, I was still thinking the oil companies were behind it."

"Not a chance, huh?"

Zach smiled. "Not a chance."

Annja heard a flush and then the stall door opened and shut quickly. Dave emerged, looking much more relieved. "I really hope you guys don't have to use the can anytime soon."

Zach sighed. "Great. I hope you left the fan on."

"Oh, yeah, definitely."

"Thanks."

"No sweat." Dave lay down on his bed. "So what did the bird have to say?"

"Bird?"

"Full bird. A colonel. Thomson."

"Oh," Zach said. "He was just filling us in on the discovery of some more items. A pot and a kettle."

Dave nodded. "So what's the plan, then?"

"First thing tomorrow," Annja said, "we head down into the dig site."

"Cool."

"In the meantime," Zach said, "we need to get some food and then some sleep. It's going to be another long day tomorrow. There's a lot of stuff to check out. And I want to be ready for anything."

"Is there a galley or a mess hall here?" Annja asked.

Dave nodded. "Got a mean cook here, too. I hear tell that

Colonel Thomson's a real foodie, so any place he goes, he makes sure he brings along a good cook in his unit. And this guy is top-notch."

"You've got all the gossip, huh?" Annja asked.

Dave shrugged. "Well, not all of it, but a fair chunk. Anything food-related, that's a given. I love to eat."

"I'm getting hungry," she said. "What say we head on over and see how good the cook really is?"

Zach yawned. "Can I get one of you to bring me back a doggie bag? I'm kind of wiped out here."

Dave frowned. "You feeling okay, pal?"

"Yeah, why?"

"Just checking. I don't want you having any lingering effects from the carbon-monoxide inhalations earlier. You think you want to get yourself checked out? Just to be sure?"

"I'm fine. I just need some good rest. Sitting up in a Sno-Cat all day long can wear you out."

"Don't I know it."

Annja looked at Zach. "You sure you're all right?"

"I'm fine. Get going. Just bring me back some dinner and some cookies if you don't mind."

"Fair enough." Annja looked at Dave. "Looks like it's just you and me."

He bowed low. "After you, then."

Annja glanced back at Zach. "We'll see you in a little while, okay?"

"Yeah."

She glanced at Dave, who just shrugged. "He'll be all right. Let's go."

And they ducked back out into the Antarctic night.

14

Annja bit into the sliced honey ham and leaned back in her chair. "Wow, that is good."

Across from her, Dave nodded and chewed his food slowly, as if savoring each morsel of the meal. "Told you," he said around bites. "The man is gifted."

They sat in an elongated cylindrical hut with kitchen facilities at the back and several long folding tables set out in the front. It was a sizable setup, and judging from the number of staff and people eating, the dig site numbered at least one hundred people. Not exactly the small outpost she'd expected.

Dave raised his glass of orange juice. "This is a rarity, as well, and it sure tastes good." He drank it down and then rose to get himself a second glass while Annja continued to survey the scene.

She spotted a lot of soldiers, all men and all looking very tanned and heavily armed. Their conversations were hushed, as if they trusted no one but the close brotherhood they had with each other. Their weapons were always close by, leaning against the table or in between their knees while they ate. It looked as if they were expecting trouble.

Dave sat back down. "You okay?"

"Just curious about the guns. It's like they think they're going to be attacked at any second."

"Maybe they know something we don't," Dave said. But when he caught Annja glaring at him, he grinned. "It was just a joke."

"Not so funny," she said.

"Sorry. But these guys, they're professional soldiers. People like us, we dig into the ground. We'd probably feel the same way about our shovel or pick, right?"

"Maybe."

"So they like their guns. No big deal."

Annja noticed another group seated away from the soldiers. "And what about them? What's their story?"

Dave glanced over at the three men and two women sitting about twenty feet away and shrugged. "Bookworms. Scientists. We'll probably meet them on the dig tomorrow. Right now, they look pretty worn-out."

It was true. Annja could see the streaks of dirt on their faces. Their coveralls were caked in dark mud, and their boots seemed to have tracked in part of the mountain. They spoke very little, and ate in relative silence.

Dave finished off his ham and macaroni and cheese and went back looking for more. Annja spooned some macaroni and cheese into her mouth and marveled at the taste. The cook was damned good at his job.

Dave came back instead with a slice of chocolate cake. "Can you believe what this guy can do back there? He's like a genius or something."

"And what about you?" Annja asked.

"Me?"

"I thought you dug rocks."

Dave shrugged. "I've been known to."

Annja leaned forward. "Just what is it you really do, Dave? You told me you were a geologist when we first met."

"Did I?"

"Yes."

Dave chewed another bite of his cake. "And you think I was lying about that?"

"Well, then you told me you do things for the government, and I'm left wondering what kind of geologist does favors for Uncle Sam, looks after my good friend Zach and generally safeguards things. I'm coming up blank."

"Is it that important that you know?" Dave asked.

"Would you trust your life to someone who wasn't a hundred percent up-front with you?"

Dave shrugged. "Fair point, but sometimes we can't reveal all we want to reveal. It's just the way things go."

"I understand that," Annja said. She took a drink from her glass and set it back down on the table. "The problem is, I've been attacked once already and then we had that snowslide earlier. I'm not paranoid, but I am cautious. And when strange things start happening, I start looking around at the variables in my life."

"And I'm a variable."

"Definitely."

Dave leaned back. "Well, you've got nothing to fear from me," he said plainly.

"If only you knew how many times I've heard that before."

"Annja, you're starting to strain our friendship. I don't really enjoy being called out like this."

"So just tell me—are you a spook or what?"

Dave wiped his mouth. "You're convinced I am, apparently."

"I'm not convinced of anything except this entire dig site seems weird. And it's filled with some odd characters, and this whole continent might just be ripe for the loony bin for all I know. I'd like some answers. Preferably honest ones."

Dave pointed at her plate. "You finished with that?"

"I was going to get some cake."

"Get it to go," Dave said. "We need to bring something back for old Zach anyway."

"Fair enough." Annja headed up to the counter and asked for some food to go. She watched the assistants put some together for her, thanked them and then turned and saw Dave standing by the door, ready to head back out.

Outside, the wind blew across the open area. Dave leaned forward into the wind. "I was trained as a geologist," he said.

"Was?" Annja asked.

He nodded. "Yeah, but rocks never did much for me. I worked for the oil companies. I did some conservation work. I was bored."

"So what happened?"

"I met someone."

Annja glanced at him. "Who?"

"His name's not important. He recruited me to come and work with him on a project he guaranteed would excite me like nothing else."

Annja bent into the wind, struggling to hear what Dave said. "Go on."

"Turns out it was a project examining rocks taken from one of the Moon missions back in the 1970s."

"Moon rocks? What was the big deal about that?"

"The rocks were *found* on the Moon," Dave said. "But they didn't come from the Moon. Originally."

"Yeah, but aren't there meteorites slamming into it all the time? They could have come from clear across the galaxy for all you know. I'm still not seeing the connection."

Dave shrugged. "We're back. Let's continue this conversation tomorrow. Okay?"

Annja frowned. "All right. Whatever." She knew there was

no point pressing the issue. She headed inside and found Zach just starting to wake up.

"Hey, how was dinner?" Zach asked.

"Fantastic," Dave said. "Ham and mac and cheese. Delicious. We scored you some chocolate cake, as well. The cook delivered tonight. He really did."

Annja handed Zach the food and sat down on her bed. She leaned back and ran a hand over her ribs. They felt fine and she could even prod them without any pain.

Dave noticed. "How are they?"

"They seem fine."

"Cool."

Annja removed her boots. As each one came off, she wriggled her toes and rotated her ankles, relishing the release. "Oh, that's nice."

Dave slid his boots off, as well. "You aren't kidding. I think I forgot how my toes feel."

Zach tore into his meal with a lot of moaning and groaning. "Damn, this is good stuff."

"Told you," Dave said. He leaned back on his bunk. "Anyone up for some cards?"

Annja shook her head. "I don't think so. I'm actually pretty exhausted from the day. I think it's lights-out for me."

Zach nodded. "I'm with Annja. I think I'm still feeling a little light-headed from earlier. This food is fantastic, though. But seriously, we should grab some sleep. Get ready for the morning. I expect we'll be quite busy tomorrow."

"Fair enough," Dave said.

"Did you see any of the rest of the team at dinner?" Zach asked, yawning.

"A couple of them were seated close by," Annja said. "But Dave suggested we hold off on the intros until tomorrow. They looked pretty tired anyway."

"Yeah, it's no picnic down there. But it will be fascinating."

Annja leaned back and took her snow pants off. She'd sleep in her thermal underwear. The blankets on the bed felt extremely lightweight but warm. She got up, pulled them back and slid under the covers.

"Don't forget your hat," Dave said.

Annja looked at him. "Really?"

"If the heat goes out, you'll lose a lot through your head and be well on your way to hypothermia before you even realize what's going on."

"Good advice." Annja grabbed her hat and slid it back onto her head. "I'm going to have an outrageous do tomorrow," she said with a laugh.

"Comes with the territory," Zach said. He crumpled up the aluminum foil and tossed it into a waste can near the door. "Thanks for dinner, guys. That hit the spot."

Dave was already under his covers. Annja heard a light snore start coming from his mouth. "Is he loud?" she asked.

"Depends on how much beer he's had to drink," Zach replied.

"He didn't have any that I saw."

"Then we should be okay."

"Good." Annja settled back down into her bed. "Good night."

Zach flipped off the lights. "Sleep well."

Silence seemed to settle over the camp. Annja could hear muffled bits of noise from outside, but by and large the sound of the howling wind seemed distant. The outside lights stayed on, silhouetting various shapes against the exterior of their shell.

Annja closed her eyes and thought about the long trip she'd undertaken. The monotonous crawl of the Sno-Cats seemed long ago, and it wasn't something Annja would look forward to repeating anytime soon.

She dreamed about digging into the mountain. Rocks and

soil surrounded her and then in the center of a spot, she saw something gleaming in the dark soil. Her hands reached for it, withdrawing it from its earthly tomb.

Three metallic snakes looked up at her, their skin covered in scales that gleamed different colors as the light from Annja's headlamp hit them.

And in an instant, they came to life, wriggling and wrapping themselves around her hands as their tongues flicked out, tasting the air.

They headed right for Annja.

Annja woke up gasping for air.

Across the shelter, Dave's snores flittered about the air in some discordant rhythm. Zach's deep inhalations continued uninterrupted.

She realized it was just a dream.

Annja lay down, taking a moment to calm herself by breathing deeply. She hadn't even been down to the dig yet and she was already having nightmares about it. She wondered if Antarctica was getting to her already.

She turned onto her side and was surprised at how little pain she felt. She was healing well and quickly. She thought about her sword for a moment. Could it have helped the process?

Outside, the lights shifted every once in a while as the wind blew them little by little. She thought she could hear them creaking, but knew the walls of the shelter would inhibit that noise from reaching her ears.

She saw movement, though. A vague shape started near the bottom edge of the shelter.

And grew.

The shadow approached, silhouetted by the outside lights. Annja recognized the shape of a man. He stood right outside their shelter and seemed unsure of whether he was going to knock or go away.

Was he there to greet them?

Or was this something else?

Annja felt uneasy. She rolled herself out of bed. She closed her eyes and saw the sword hanging in the opaque mist, ready if she needed it.

Annja stole over to the door, careful not to make any noise. There was no time to put on her coat or boots. If this was trouble, she wanted to handle it immediately. She wanted to know who was stalking her shelter.

The shadow showed no signs of moving.

Annja reached for the door handle, took several deep breaths and steeled herself for the waiting wind outside.

She jerked the door open and ran outside.

As soon as the wind touched her exposed skin, she gasped. But she looked around the shelter, searching for the shadow.

It was gone.

15

Dave was out of the shelter before Zach. The pistol he held in his hand stood out in the light. The look on his face was harder than anything she'd seen before. He saw Annja and came right over.

"What the hell happened?"

"I saw someone standing out here."

"So you came to investigate without putting on any boots or even your coat?" Dave shook his head. "Get inside, for crying out loud, before the whole camp wakes up."

Annja walked back inside and instantly the heat of the shelter started warming her. She stood by one of the space heaters and felt the waves rolling over her. Dave shook his head.

"You should be okay, but that really isn't something I'd recommend doing again. You can get frostbite very quickly. And I'm sure losing fingers or toes isn't on your list of things you want to do."

"Not really," Annja said.

Zach wiped the sleep from his eyes. "What happened?"

"Annja saw someone outside," Dave said.

"So?"

Dave smiled. "Good point."

Annja shook her head. "You don't understand. He was outside. Just standing there. It wasn't like he was on his way to someplace else. He just stood there. It was weird."

"And apparently, common sense got sacrificed in the name of finding out who it was," Dave said to Zach. "She ran outside without her gear on."

Zach sat up. "You nuts or what?"

Annja frowned. "I thought it was weird. And I wanted to know who it was. It's my fault I ran out without the gear. I just figured there was no time."

Dave led her back to her bed and then wrapped her in the blankets. "I'll get some dry socks."

"Better make it two pairs," Zach said. "She'll be lucky if she doesn't lose a toe or something."

"Thanks for that cheerful prognosis," Annja said.

"Hey, I wasn't the one running around in the freezing snow."

"Touché."

Dave got a couple of pairs of socks, and Annja slid them onto her feet. Her feet tingled from the freezing conditions outside, but she didn't think there'd be any lasting damage.

"I'll be okay," she said stubbornly.

Dave looked at her. "The way you gasped, I thought someone had taken you."

"Thanks for coming to my rescue." She eyed the pistol lying on the blanket. "Interesting bedmate you've got yourself there."

He nodded. "Yeah, well, you weren't actually supposed to see that. But then again…"

"It's all right," Annja said. "I understand that you've got some secrets you may not want to share with the rest of us."

Zach flopped back down on his pillow. "Can we get back to sleep now? I'm really wasted."

Dave eyed Annja carefully. "You sure you'll be okay?"

"Yeah," she said.

"Okay, then. Good night." He patted her leg and then walked back to his bed with the pistol.

Annja watched him go. Does he sleep with that thing under his pillow? she wondered. She tucked herself back under the blankets and closed her eyes.

Who had been standing outside her shelter? And why were they just standing there? Was it the same person who'd tried to kill her back in McMurdo? Or was she now in danger from an entirely different person here in this camp?

Annja was troubled by the prospect of not knowing who was after her and why. She didn't like not knowing who her enemies were. She always got along best when she was able to determine who meant her harm and who was a friend.

Maybe in the morning she'd be able to figure it out better.

"You awake?"

Annja cracked open one of her eyes. The lighting hadn't changed all that much. It was still dark in her shelter and bright outside from the electrical light system. Annja groaned and rolled over. "Wake me in another five hours, please."

"It's 0600. Time to rise and shine."

She turned back. Dave stood there smiling at her. "C'mon, sleepyhead. Up and at 'em."

Annja frowned and glanced at her watch. "How is it possible for so much time to go by? I feel like I just closed my eyes and now I'm getting up again."

"Brings back memories of high school, doesn't it?"

Annja frowned again. "I hated high school. Those are memories better left relegated to the past, thank you very much."

Zach slid out of his bed, oozing to the floor. Dave glanced at him. "You okay?"

"I feel like I've been drinking heavily. I'm still worn-out."

Annja pointed at the necklace. "Maybe you ought to try taking that thing off. It's probably weighing you down anyway," she said with a grin.

"Funny," Zach said. But he lifted the necklace over his head and let it rest on his bed. "Still, it's not a bad idea. I'll hand this back in as soon as we're ready to get some breakfast."

Zach went to use the bathroom. Dave looked at Annja. "You feel okay today? All your limbs intact after your field trip last night?"

"They seem to be fine, yes. Thanks."

"Good."

Zach came out of the bathroom, and Annja used it to freshen up as best she could. When she emerged, Zach and Dave were already zipping themselves into their gear.

"Jeez, guys, I was just in there for two minutes. How about waiting for me before you go running off to explore the mountain?"

"It's breakfast time," Dave said. "Rumor is the cook's making pancakes this morning."

"How'd you know that?" Annja asked.

Dave pointed at his nose. "The schnoz has a gift."

Zach laughed. "Guy's like a shark and blood. Food doesn't stand a chance around this man."

Annja stepped into her snow pants and then her jacket. She zipped up and followed them out of the prefab shelter. Outside, the area was still dark. Sunlight was an endangered species in the Antarctic this time of year, and Annja found it tough getting used to the idea that it would stay dark.

"How do you deal with it, the lack of sunlight?" she asked.

Dave shrugged. "Believe it or not, you get used to it. You should be here in the summer when it's sunny all the time. You wouldn't believe how fast you can get tired of that extreme, as well."

"It really is like being on another planet," Zach said. "And of course, I don't mean to influence you guys into thinking about the whole alien thing."

"Oh, no," Annja said. "You'd never do that."

AFTER THEIR BREAKFAST of pancakes and eggs, Zach led them over to one of the command shelters. They found Colonel Thomson sitting inside at a bank of computers. Annja saw bundles of cables running out of the tent.

"How do you guys power this station, anyway?" she asked.

"Generators," the colonel said. "We keep them running twenty-four hours a day. That gives us the juice we need."

"But all that gas…how do you have enough of it?"

Thomson looked at her. "Gas? Who said anything about gas?"

Annja frowned. "But if it's not gas, then…?"

"Nuclear power," Thomson said. "DARPA perfected a smaller generator model some years back for use in remote outposts like this. We can generate enough kilowatts to keep everything we need going indefinitely. It's an easy setup and teardown operation."

"Provided there are no accidents," Zach said.

Thomson smiled. "Well, that's always a risk, but then again, no nuclear sub has ever had an accident in all the years they've been at sea."

"A setup like this must have a host of its own unique challenges," Annja said.

Thomson smiled. "I'd rather not get into the specifics of nuclear power right now. Suffice it to say, we believe things here are perfectly safe."

"They'd better be," Zach said. "Otherwise that cover story about the environmental disaster just might come true."

"Indeed." Thomson looked at him. "You have something for me? A necklace, I presume?"

Zach nodded. "Here you go. Back safe and sound."

The colonel accepted it from him and gestured for another soldier to take it. "Place in the containment area. No one handles it unless I authorize it."

Zach frowned. "That's new."

"We started picking up readings," Thomson said. "The day after you left. Down in the dig site, the Geiger counters started going off the scales. We couldn't pinpoint the source. It seemed to fluctuate wildly from time to time and then it would simply disappear."

"You couldn't determine the source?" Annja asked.

"No. So we took the step of giving everyone portable rad detectors. What you've got on your parkas now."

Annja had almost forgotten about hers. She looked down and saw the strip of red across her chest.

Thomson pointed. "If that turns blue, get the hell out of wherever you are—otherwise you'll start to glow in the dark."

Zach nodded. "Understood."

"Good. Now, what else?"

"We'd like to head down if that's okay with you."

The colonel nodded. "Fine, fine. Just be sure to take the necessary survival gear. They've gone deeper than when you were last here."

"I've only been gone two days," Zach said.

"Yes, well, things have been stepped up. Our new orders are to thoroughly penetrate the mountain and determine whether or not the artifacts we're uncovering are of an earthly origin or not. In the event they are not, then we are to try to determine where they come from."

"Well," Annja said. "That ought to be easy enough. We'll just search them on the Internet and see what planet pops up."

Thomson frowned. "That'll be enough. This is a serious matter and the people upstairs aren't taking any chances."

"Hence the armed militia," Zach said.

"Hence prudence," Thomson replied. "We're not here to turn this into a military operation. It is still primarily a scientific exploration of a possible alien environment. But we also like to be prepared."

"How so?" Annja asked.

"Washington has sent down another adviser."

"Another scientist?"

Thomson shook his head. "No, he's something of a specialist on security issues. He's to take command in the event we uncover something we can't control."

"What—like Godzilla?" Zach asked.

"No, like something otherworldly," Thomson said. "Something that might be slumbering right now beneath our very feet."

"You're kidding," Annja said. "It's just a mountain."

The colonel shook his head. "We don't know that yet. And until we do for certain, we will take whatever precautions we deem necessary to secure the safety of the people in this camp."

Behind them the door to the shelter opened and a hooded figure strode in. The colonel rose with a smile. "Allow me to introduce you to Major Braden."

The figure paused and slipped his hood off.

Annja caught her breath at the sight of the man standing before her with a broad smile splayed out across his face.

16

The first thing Annja wanted to do was shout, "Garin!" but something deep inside her stopped that from occurring. Instead, she merely smiled and extended her hand. "Annja Creed. Nice to meet you."

Garin shook her hand and bowed slightly. "Likewise."

Annja couldn't help but grin. Garin's normal continental manner seemed to have been replaced—almost painfully so—by the brusquely polite personality of an American military officer. It wasn't a mantle he looked comfortable assuming, and Annja could only wonder why in the world he'd shown up at the bottom of it.

Dave and Zach introduced themselves and then Thomson came around and clapped Garin on the back. The gesture seemed to shock Garin, who looked as if he wanted to punch the colonel for doing so. But as quickly as that expression rolled over him, it was gone. Garin slapped the disguise back into place and immediately smiled instead.

"Major Braden here is one of our most experienced professionals in the field of unorthodox security procedures. He's been trying his best to push through several new protocols that will help us deal with the possibility of alternative security threats."

"Alternative security threats?" Annja asked. "That sounds utterly engrossing and frightening at the same time."

"Oh, it is," Thomson said. "I was up late one night last week reading over his latest brief. Truly incredible suggestions. Of course, some of them will take time to win over the more temperate members of senior staff, but I think there's a good chance they'll eventually be implemented."

Garin tried to grin. "You flatter me, sir. But I appreciate your support and that of your staff."

"Not at all, not at all."

Annja smiled. "Maybe you could show me those briefs sometime, Major Braden. I'm always interested in reading up on military doctrine."

Garin eyed her. "Are you now? I wouldn't have believed a woman like you would be interested in such things."

Annja knew he wanted her to drop it, but somehow, she just couldn't. She really enjoyed seeing him squirm. "Oh, military strategy has become something of a hobby for me as of late. I'm working my way through a wonderful book detailing Frederick the Great's campaigns against the Austrians."

The colonel nodded. "You know, I think I read that book last year. It was a wonderful historical piece if I recall."

Annja smiled at him. "Now, don't you go and ruin the ending for me. I can't wait to see how it turns out."

The colonel laughed. "You're too much, Miss Creed. Really, you are."

"Isn't she, though," Garin said. He glanced at the colonel. "Sir, if you don't require any more of me for the moment, I believe I'd like to get a firsthand look at the dig site. It's probably as good a time as any to get down there and see what we might be dealing with."

"Yes, that's fine. But perhaps you can all go down together."

Garin coughed. "Together?"

Zach nodded. "We were just heading down there, as well. You're more than welcome to come along with us."

"Yes," Annja said, "the more the merrier."

Garin sniffed. "Yes, well, that sounds fantastic. Truly." He looked at the colonel. "I'll report back later, then."

"Excellent."

Garin turned and his eyes shot daggers at Annja. "After you," he said quietly.

Annja ducked back outside with Zach and Dave, neither of whom seemed all that interested in Garin. But Annja certainly was. His sudden appearance raised a whole bunch of new questions for her. Chief among them was why was he here? The last she'd heard of his whereabouts, he was somewhere deep in the jungles of Africa, off on a search for some valuable artifact.

And now he was here.

Annja frowned and stopped herself from turning, grabbing him by the parka and throwing him to the ground, demanding to know what the hell he was up to. Instead, she kept herself in check as they walked across the compound toward a part that she hadn't seen yet.

Zach and Dave carried the gear they'd brought with them in the Sno-Cat. Garin walked ahead of them, doing his best to stay clear of Annja. She followed in his wake, keeping herself just close enough to be a nuisance.

"Some weather, eh, Major?"

He nodded. "It's awful stuff."

Of course it was. Garin wasn't the biggest fan of the cold and snow. He much preferred a lazy summer day to negative fifty degrees Fahrenheit. Probably it was all he could do not to freak out and lose his cool.

"It's taking me a while to get used to it," Annja said. "But then again, I've only just recently arrived myself."

Garin grunted but said nothing more.

"How long have you been here, Major?"

He stopped and glared at her. "One week."

"Is that so? Sounds like you got down here pretty fast from…well, where were you before this?"

Garin glanced at Zach and Dave. "I'm afraid that's classified, Miss Creed. I'm sure you understand that I cannot reveal where I've been or what I've been doing. Security and all."

"Oh, sure." Annja kept on walking. "Just thought it would be a nice way to pass the time."

"Perhaps later," Garin said. "When we get to know each other a little better. A drink over dinner?"

Zach cleared his throat. "A drink over dinner? This isn't some five-star resort, Major."

Garin nodded. "Yes, of course, I was merely being facetious. Given our surroundings, a little levity is sometimes just the ticket for good conversation."

Dave shook his head but said nothing. Annja knew what he was thinking. Major Braden didn't act or talk much like any major he'd ever met. Garin would have to watch himself. His act might fool Zach and even the colonel, but Annja knew Dave was something else entirely.

They reached the entrance to a wide shelter. Zach paused. "This is it. We go inside and then take the path down into the mountain."

"The colonel," Dave said, "erected this sheltered entrance to try to cut down on the wind blowing into the dig site, stirring up all sorts of sediment and rocks. Plus, it helps keep the temperature much warmer than if we were exposed."

Annja nodded. "Makes good sense."

"Indeed," Garin said.

They ducked into the entrance and were met by two guards who gave them a once-over and then let them pass without incident. By the back of the shelter, Annja could see a hole roughly ten feet by ten feet going into the mountain itself.

A string of lights led the way and she could see the bulbs disappear into the darkness. She found herself wondering just what might be down there.

"Here." Zach handed her a headlamp. "Bring that hard hat with you. Just in case."

"In case of what?" Annja asked.

"Cave-in."

Annja shook her head. "You sure know how to make me feel nice and safe."

Dave chuckled. "I wouldn't worry about that. If something happens, I'm sure Major Braden here can support the entire cave. Isn't that right, Major?"

"Just like Atlas," Garin said. "I would knowingly sacrifice myself so that you all might live."

Annja laughed now. "Is that so?"

Garin frowned. "It's my duty."

Dave slapped a hat into his hands. "Here, Atlas, be sure you take a piece of cover for your noggin. We wouldn't want any of the rocks in there to smack into your brain."

Garin placed the helmet on his head and then shucked his parka. Annja removed hers, as well. The temperature inside the shelter was warm and Zach assured them it would get warmer as they headed into the dig site.

"Being out of the wind helps a tremendous amount," he said. "You can actually work up a sweat down there."

Dave checked their equipment. "We're good to go."

Zach nodded. "Shall we?"

He switched his headlamp on and Annja followed suit. Then they started at the entrance and began walking down the slowly sloping path that led them right into the mountain itself.

"It's been bored out pretty well," said Annja. "I wasn't expecting this much clearance."

Dave from behind her said, "They used one of those tunnel machines to break into this part. Basically, they came in here and churned up a whole bunch of the mountain. Not exactly the best way to go about preserving any possible finds."

"That's for sure," Zach said. "Once I came on scene I told them they had to remove the machine and let us work by hand. They grudgingly accepted that, but once the colonel came down, he was much more reasonable about it."

"I'd imagine," Garin said, "that's because the chance that there are more artifacts has convinced him of the necessity to proceed with caution."

"Definitely," Zach said. "And we have ever since."

"When did you say the colonel asked for you to come down here again?" Annja asked. "Last week?"

Garin shook his head. "The colonel didn't request me. I was assigned to come down here and offer my services."

So that explained part of it. Annja knew that Garin had a pile of money and acquiring proper paperwork, identity and security clearances were something he could pull together in no time. He'd apparently heard something about the dig site and come down to see what was going on. But did he know what this was all about? And if he did, why was he interested in it?

"Well, that was astute of your superiors to see you might be needed down here," Annja said.

"They're always looking out for the best interests of the country," Garin replied.

Annja smiled. The country, in this case, being the nation of Garin. "I'm sure they are."

They reached a fork in the tunnel. Zach pointed in one direction. "Workers are over there digging into a separate part of the mountain. One of the things they've found already is a huge deposit of copper. I'm not sure what their plans are, but I think it's a safe bet that if the mountain doesn't yield any more surprises, they may turn this over to a big mining company and get them to haul the copper out of here."

"That would turn this part of Antarctica into a huge eyesore," Annja said. "I thought mining was prohibited down here."

"It's a touchy subject," Dave said. "A lot of private companies have their eyes on this land. It's completely unspoiled and ripe for destroying. Some scientists in the employ of these companies have speculated that there might be untold reserves of petroleum, chromium and a bunch of other highly valuable things down here. You can imagine how many dollar signs that would represent."

Annja frowned. "I would hope they wouldn't cave in to the pressure from the companies."

"Of course they would," Garin snapped. "Since when has the government ever been able to withstand the influence exerted upon it by the private sector?"

Annja raised her eyebrows. Dave turned and looked at Garin. Zach had stopped, as well.

Garin recovered himself. "Which is to say, the government does exist for the needs of the people, so I'm sure that whatever they decide will be in its best interest."

Dave's eyebrows jumped once or twice and he glanced at Annja with a quick roll of the eyes. She smiled at him and they kept moving.

Zach pointed out veins running through the rock walls. "See that? It's all copper. This entire mountain seems to have an incredible amount of metal in it."

"Not the least of which is the unmined copper," Dave said.

"Is it possible," Annja said, "that there might be a new metal that has been previously undiscovered? Something stronger than what we know about now?"

Zach shrugged. "Anything's possible. Whether or not we'll find evidence of it is another thing entirely."

"But we do have evidence," Annja said. "The necklace is made of something we can't even recognize."

Zach nodded. "True enough. But whether that was mined here or indigenous to this place is what remains unknown." He stopped and Annja realized they were at a dead end in the tunnel.

"We're here," Zach said.

17

The hollowed-out part of the cave spread before them like the concave side of a saucer. Streaks of bright rock, veins of copper and tints of various colors all converged at a single point almost directly in front of them.

Annja ran her hand along the wall, feeling the jagged rocks bite into the palm of her hand. "It's warm to the touch."

Dave removed his bag of gear and set it down. "The mountain seems to conduct thermal energy up into the various caverns we've dug."

Garin leaned against one of the walls. "I thought I read one time about a large thermal flue of sorts that ran under this entire continent. Was that a mistake or is it true?"

Zach shrugged. "Given all the active volcanoes, it seems logical to imagine there's a pipeline of molten core and that the thermals work their way up to the surface. But I don't know that anyone's ever mapped such currents out to any degree."

"So we could be sitting right over one," Garin said.

"Sure. Anything's possible."

Garin nodded and busied himself with studying the walls of the tunnel. "Where will you dig?"

Zach pointed at the soil beneath them. "Right here."

"You didn't think we were going to bore into the rock, did you?" Annja asked.

"Of course not." Garin looked at the cave. "Although you did dig straight into the mountain. I was just curious."

Zach pointed at the wall. "If we went into the rock, we wouldn't get very far. What we're trying to do is get to the dirt. We've caused deliberate cave-ins where we know there's dirt above that can't be reached through the layers of snow and ice on top of it. So we come at it from below."

Dave smiled. "It's a lot of fun standing in a cave-in."

"You didn't," Annja said.

"I'm only kidding." Dave handed a shovel to Zach and then one to Annja. "Well, here's to getting filthy stinking dirty for the next few hours."

"And finding something worth our time," Zach added. "I'd really like to figure out whose artifacts we're in the process of digging up here."

Garin smiled. "I thought they were aliens."

Dave frowned. "We don't know anything right now. It could be some prehistoric race of humans who created that stuff."

"Using a metal alloy that is unidentifiable?" Garin smiled. "Something tells me that unless these people were the inhabitants of Atlantis, there's no way they could have forged the metal I've seen in that necklace. Heavy and lightweight at the same time? With such interesting properties? Even the simple serpent design defies what conventional scientists think possible for that time."

"We don't know everything about what happened back then," Zach said. "And we've been mistaken in the past."

"The carbon dating alone puts those pieces well out of the range of even the most advanced life-forms on the planet at that time," Garin said.

"That we know about," Dave replied. "You just said your-self they could have come from Atlantis. Or maybe even some other long-lost continent. Or hell, maybe this was Atlantis."

Annja could tell that in the close confines of the cave, per-sonalities were beginning to grate on each other. And Garin had never been one to be patient with the thought processes of mere mortals. He was getting disgusted with the limits of their logic, and she could sense it.

"Look, fellas, why don't we all just get digging. Get our minds on that and forget about where this might have come from. We can maybe figure that out later, okay?" she said.

Zach nodded. "Annja's right, we've got work to do."

"Fine," Garin said. "But just so you know, Atlantis is gen-erally believed to have been located off the coast of Spain. Not so far down as this."

Dave smirked. "Well, there are plenty of theories about that, I'm sure. You could probably dig up someone who will tell you the entire landmass was a big mobile alien ship, capable of moving through the oceans to wherever it wanted to go. How about that?"

Garin sighed and glanced at Zach. "Have you got another shovel?"

"Sure thing—here."

"Thank you." Garin settled himself into the far corner of the cavern and started digging.

For a time, the only sound was the rhythmic clangs of shovel blades sinking into the hard earth. Piles of loose gravel, dirt and small stones grew around them, like the walls of a great fortress.

Annja sweated now, aware that her snow pants restricted her movements terribly. She was feeling sore and hoped that she'd be able to have a long shower when this was over for the day.

Dave came by and tossed her a water bottle. "Make sure

you keep your fluid intake up. You'll dehydrate quickly down here without even knowing it."

"Thanks." She swallowed down most of the water and then paused. Dave made the rounds, handing bottles to Zach and Garin. Garin glanced at it as if it were dredged from the sewer.

Annja grinned. "Not your usual vintage?"

Garin swallowed some and blanched. "Not by the longest stretch of the imagination."

Dave frowned. "Yeah, well, it'll keep you from dehydrating and dying, so there's got to be something said for that."

Garin took another swig. "Indeed."

Annja finished her water and stowed the bottle in the loose pile of dirt nearby. She'd refill it later.

Dave was still hunched over by where Garin was digging. "Where were you assigned before you came down to these parts, anyway?" he asked.

Garin smiled. "I believe I told Annja earlier a little something about things being classified. Need-to-know, and all that good stuff. It's not really necessary information, anyway, is it?"

Dave shrugged. "Probably not. You just seem a little odd to me, that's all. You know, like when my gut keeps nudging me, it's almost like I've got to listen to it."

Garin frowned. "Does that happen often?"

Annja swallowed. "You should have seen him at dinner last night."

Dave glanced over and smiled. Then he got to his feet. "Well, whatever, Major. You just keep on digging and we'll see what we see."

Garin watched him walk away. For her part, Annja was amazed that Dave would have the courage to speak to Garin like that. Garin wasn't exactly the least intimidating guy on the planet. He was huge by comparison to Dave, but Dave showed absolutely no signs that it made any difference in the world to him.

It presented a problem. If Garin thought that Dave was too much of a bother, there was every chance he would simply kill him and be done with it. Of course, it would have to look like an accident to allay suspicion.

Annja didn't want anyone killing anyone. All she wanted to do was find more artifacts and try to piece together what had made them. The chances of that happening, however, seemed to be getting smaller and smaller with each passing minute.

Sooner or later, things were going to come to a head and Annja just hoped the damage wasn't too profound.

They dug for three more hours before taking a break for lunch. Dave had once again gone back up to get them the cardboard-boxed Meals Ready to Eat that soldiers ate in the field. He handed them out to everyone and then plopped himself down in the nearest pile of dirt and tore into it.

Annja glimpsed the ham stew and frowned. "This is going to be nothing like dinner last night, is it?"

Dave chuckled. "Not even close."

Garin held his up. "I abhor spaghetti and meatballs. Anyone willing to trade theirs?"

"Here," Annja said. She pitched her box to Garin, who threw his to her. Annja grabbed it and ate the spaghetti and meatballs in silence.

For a while, no one said anything. The ambiance of the cavern was relegated to the sounds of eating, drinking and the occasional belch.

Annja finished her pouch and then took out the peanut-butter package and a cracker. The protein tasted great and she knew it would help her get through the day. She took another swig of water and settled back against the dirt.

Zach looked at her. "How are you feeling, Annja?"

"Fine," she said with a shrug.

"Ribs?"

"A-okay."

Garin looked interested. "Ribs? What happened? Was there an accident of some sort?"

Annja leaned forward. "Yeah. There was. Back in Mc-Murdo, I was attacked walking back to my dorm room. Someone drove their pointy little elbow into my side and cracked a rib or two. Hurt like hell. Then they tried to run me over with a Sno-Cat."

Garin smirked. "They tried to run you over with a horribly slow vehicle? That makes no sense at all."

"I was trapped on my back and couldn't move."

"Ah. The proverbial beetle with its legs up."

"Exactly."

Garin shrugged. "Still, it was an awful lot of effort. Why not just put a bullet in your head if you'd pissed someone off that much?"

"I don't know. That's what has me wondering who it might have been. Obviously they wanted to make it look like an accident."

Garin shrugged. "An autopsy would have revealed the fractured rib. There would have been questions."

"I could have gotten the fractured rib slipping and falling on the ground."

"True. But they might determine the angle of impact as being inconsistent with a fall."

Dave held up his hand. "The important thing is she's okay. And she seems better every day. Hell, yesterday, I didn't think she was going to last twenty minutes in the Sno-Cat driving out here, but she weathered it like a trooper. I wouldn't have even guessed you had a busted bone in your body, Annja."

Garin's eyes gleamed. "Really? What did you do? Heal yourself overnight so that by morning you were perfectly fine?"

Annja smiled. "The power of positive thinking, I guess."

"Fascinating," Garin said. He tipped a small bottle of hot

sauce from his meal into his mouth and swallowed it with a grin. "Lovely."

Dave eyed him again. "Want some water with that?"

"Not at all," Garin said.

Zach bundled up his trash and placed it in a small pile by the entrance to the cavern. "Well, I'm all done. You guys ready to get back to work?"

Annja nodded. "Yeah." She handed out her trash, belched and then heaved her shovel back into the hole. Jumping down, her boots hit the loose dirt and she stood there for a moment, lost in thought.

Garin wandered by and looked into her hole. "You have healing powers now, Annja?"

She shrugged. "I don't think the injury was as bad as we first thought."

"Liar."

Annja laughed. "Pot, meet the kettle."

Garin wandered off and Annja hefted her shovel. She slid the blade into the soft earth and started digging again. It had been a while since she'd been on a dig like this. She'd forgotten how the close confines of working inside could have a claustrophobic effect on her. She shook her head and got back into a rhythm. With luck, they'd find something soon and then be able to get some fresh frigid air.

Around her, the steady clangs of more digging broke out. No one spoke; all were concentrating on their own hole and making sure they covered the ground allotted to them.

Annja felt an uneasy sensation deep in her stomach about twenty minutes later. At first, she thought the spaghetti and meatballs were making their presence known. But she quickly ruled that out.

This was something else.

Every time her shovel slid into the earth, she noticed it moved a little bit more to the right, as if on its own accord.

She slid her shovel into the earth.

Something stopped it.

"Guys? I think I've found something here."

18

Annja sensed a rush behind her as Zach, Dave and Garin all fell over themselves trying to be the first to see what she'd discovered. Annja smiled. "Relax, I haven't pulled it out of the dirt just yet."

Zach reached her first. "Where is it?"

"My shovel hit something."

"And you think—"

Annja nodded. "Yeah. I'm pretty sure."

Garin slid down toward the hole. "So let's see this grand discovery. I'm dying to see what you've managed to unearth."

Annja glanced at him. "Knock it off there, Major. I'm sure you wouldn't want me getting angry."

Garin frowned, but realized the meaning behind what Annja said. If he pushed too much, she could easily expose him as a fraud. "Fine. I apologize for my brash manner," he said.

Dave looked her over. "Okay, what have we got?"

Annja slid the shovel back into the dirt. A dull clang sounded.

Zach tensed. "Is that it?"

Annja nodded. "I think so." She handed Zach the shovel

and reached her hands into the soil. She was surprised at how warm it felt on her hands. It was almost like a mud bath she might have gotten at a spa.

Her fingers searched the soil, spreading out, until at last their tips brushed something. "I've got it."

Everyone leaned closer as she pulled the item free from the dirt. Clumps of soil fell away as she lifted it up.

"Wow," she said.

Holding it in front of herself, Annja studied the piece she'd found. It was comprised of three snakes again, each snake biting the other so they formed a triangle around a central circle that had a sparkling blue stone set right into the middle of it.

"Is that a sapphire?" Zach asked.

Annja shrugged. "Could be. I don't know."

Zach whistled. "You've certainly managed to find the most exciting piece so far. Is it heavy?"

Annja shook her head. "Seems to be made from the same metal as the necklace. And I'm assuming the kettle and the pot were made of the same."

"According to the colonel, they were," Dave said. "It's an incredible piece you've got there, Annja. May I see it?"

Annja handed it to him. Dave peered closer. "The cuts on this stone aren't something I would think could be accomplished with ordinary hand tools. Certainly not something that those living at that time would have been able to fashion."

Garin frowned. "So what are you saying? The stones were cut by a laser or something like that?"

"Some type of machinery I would expect," Dave said. "They're far too precise to be done by human hands and the tools they had. Of course, we're supposing that they didn't have elaborate machinery back then. It'd be hard to prove they did. There's just no evidence of it, in fact."

Dave handed it to Zach, who blew some more of the dirt off the piece. "This is fantastic." He smiled at Annja. "I knew

you'd be a source of good luck on this adventure. Look what you've found."

Annja smiled. She didn't feel particularly lucky, just fortunate that her senses seemed to be in tune with what was going on around her. She had somehow detected the piece, possibly because it wasn't a natural part of the landscape—the soil and rocks that made up the mountain.

Was the sword responsible for that awareness, as well?

She turned then, aware that Garin was staring at her. "Well done, Miss Creed," he said.

Annja frowned. "Thanks."

What was he doing there? His actions didn't make a whole lot of sense. But as much as she was suspicious of his presence, Annja did want to get him alone so she could ask his opinion on the sword and a variety of other questions that had recently come up.

But how could she do that without making everyone else suspicious?

Zach handed the piece to Garin, who took quite a few minutes to examine it. He turned it over and ran his fingertips over the surface as if expecting it to reveal something. When it didn't, he handed it back to Annja. "The stone is a phenomenal piece of workmanship. I should think it would fetch an astronomical sum if auctioned off."

Zach frowned. "It belongs in a museum. All of these pieces do. Just think of what this will do to the concept of human evolution on this planet. To think there were people living here who could work metal and precious stones this way. It's going to upset every theory of evolution to date."

"I imagine the warring parties between Biblical creationism and evolution will have lots to debate," Dave said. "I can see ammunition for both perspectives. Should make for some fun watching from the sidelines."

Annja sighed. "I thought we were trying to figure out if

these were made by people indigenous to this planet or not. I don't know if I see any way of presupposing who made these pieces. Where are the remnants of the rest of a civilization? We haven't found anything but a few scattered artifacts."

Zach nodded. "That's a good point. All we've done is find something new to gaze upon."

Garin cleared his throat. "I'd like to see if we can find any bits of wreckage to support the idea of extraterrestrial visitors."

Annja shrugged. "You really think this might be evidence of such a thing? You think they plopped down here and then just vanished?"

"You said yourself there aren't any other indications that a civilization even existed here. Suppose it was a craft from somewhere else that happened upon the planet during a period in its development. Suppose they experienced an accident that destroyed their means of leaving Earth. They would then be trapped here."

"But the same problems arise," Zach said. "Wouldn't they leave other traces of themselves than just these bits?"

"Perhaps," Garin said. "But depending on their biological makeup, they might have simply faded away—decomposed and become part of the very soil we're digging in."

"And their spaceship?" Dave asked. "Where would that be?"

Garin shook his head. "I've no idea. Perhaps it is buried even deeper in the earth just waiting for us to excavate it."

Dave sighed. "No offense, Major, but this is starting to get a little absurd for me to believe. I think what we've got here is proof of an earlier race of humans who were far more advanced than scientists would believe possible until this point. We've got artifacts that reflect an incredible history via the dating process."

Annja nodded. "I think people will be much more inclined to believe that explanation than the notion that they might have been created by aliens."

Garin stepped out of the hole. "Well, I'm going to get back to work and see if I can't find something of my own."

Zach chuckled. "None of this is ours, Major. It's all for the greater good."

Garin's smile looked forced again. "Oh, of course. Most definitely. I was only joking once again."

Dave frowned. "Yeah."

Garin eyed him. "Is there a problem between us, Dave?"

"Why?"

"Because I'm sensing hostility from you and I'm not sure exactly what to make of it. I can't recall doing anything offensive to you, but if I have, I wish you'd let me have the opportunity to apologize for my transgression."

Dave shook his head. "You haven't done anything…yet."

"Ah, so your animosity is simply a prediction of how you'll be feeling in the near future," Garin said.

"Something like that."

"How very enlightened of you."

The two men stood staring at each other for a full minute, and Annja could feel the tension building to an extremely uncomfortable point. She cleared her throat. "Yeah, well, okay, then. You guys can beat the crap out of each other later. For right now, I'm going to take this back up to the surface and get it logged in. I don't want to take responsibility for possibly losing this. I get the feeling it's pretty damned valuable."

Zach smiled. "Good idea. The colonel will be overjoyed to see it. I imagine he'll have some questions for you, as well."

Garin smiled at Annja. "Why don't I accompany you back? I think some fresh air might be a good thing."

Annja frowned. "Okay, let's go." She scrambled out of her

hole and she and Garin headed back up the path away from Zach and Dave. In seconds, Annja heard the rhythmic clang as their shovels resumed digging.

When she could no longer hear them, Annja turned to Garin. "What the hell are you doing here?"

Garin smiled. "Is that how you greet an old friend? I was hoping for something a bit more romantic."

"Keep dreaming," Annja said. "What gives?"

Garin shrugged. "I'm interested in artifacts. What can I say?"

"Right. Why the hell are you impersonating an army officer? Do you know how much trouble you could get into?"

Garin sniffed. "Please. There's nothing they can do to me that can't be thwarted. I'm perfectly safe."

"You think so? Dave back there has you in his sights. And he doesn't seem convinced that you are who you say you are."

Garin nodded. "Fair point. I might have to deal with him, although I'd rather remain low profile."

"No killing," Annja said. "I don't need that around me right now."

"Are you getting soft?" Garin smiled. "Old age starting to mellow you some? Slow you down a bit?"

Annja elbowed him in the side and he gasped at the blast. She nodded at him. "That feel like I'm getting soft?"

"Not even remotely."

"You'd do well to remember that," Annja said. "I'm not about to take any crap from you. Zach's a good friend of mine and I don't want anything bad happening to him."

"What about Dave?" Garin asked. "Is he a good friend, as well?"

"I just met him two days back."

"Ah, and you trust him?"

Annja shrugged. "How much trust can you build in two days?"

"Depends on whether you slept with him or not. Sex can be a fantastic bond between two people. Or three people. Sometimes, it's four."

"Enough," Annja said. "Spare me your lurid hedonistic philosophy. It grates on me."

"Only because you're such a prude."

"I am not a prude," Annja said. "I just don't see the need to have an orgy every night."

Garin took a deep breath. "You don't know what you're missing."

"A tangle of anonymous limbs? No, thanks. I'll pass." She kept walking. "Now, really, what the hell are you doing here? And don't feed me any lines. If I don't like what I hear, I'm liable to turn you in once we get up there."

"My background is without flaw," Garin said. "You could tell them anything and they wouldn't believe you. I've already been thoroughly vetted."

"How'd you manage that?"

Garin stopped her. "After all this time, do you really think I'd just show up without having the necessary backstopping to make certain I passed intense scrutiny? I'm a little insulted by that. You know I'm much more careful than to play amateur hour, especially with something like this."

"All right, so you've got the paperwork. How much did that cost you?" Annja asked.

Garin shrugged. "What is money but an excuse to have some more fun?"

"Too many questions," Annja said. "What I want are answers. And real answers, not more questions for questions."

Garin leaned closer to her. "You're extremely agitated about something. Is it your time of the month?"

Annja drove a right cross into his gut so fast he had no time to stop it. He doubled over and Annja kneed him as his head came down. Garin dropped to the ground, clutched his face

and stayed there trying to get his wind back. "That…wasn't… necessary…"

"Apparently, it was," Annja said. "Make any more cracks like that and your world is going to get a lot more painful."

Garin held up his hand. "All right. A truce."

"Fine."

He got back to his feet, rubbing his nose. "You really want to know why I'm here?"

"Yes."

He sighed. "Fine. I will tell you."

19

"So go ahead and tell me."

Garin looked around, as if convinced someone might be listening to their conversation. After a full minute of his not saying anything, Annja shook her head.

"There's no one there, Garin. Now spill your guts already or I'm going to get impatient."

He frowned but kept his voice low. "I heard there were strange artifacts being found down here."

"From where?"

"I'd rather not say," Garin said. "It's a very privileged source and if I reveal it, I'm quite certain it will dry up. I'd never have access to that information ever again. And I think it's in my best interests to protect it."

"Yeah?" Annja sighed. "All right, whatever. So you heard a rumor. And what—you just decided to come on down and see for yourself?"

"Something like that."

"But what made this dig such an interesting one to you? What piqued your interest in this rather than a dinosaur dig in Montana, for example?"

Garin sighed. "Annja, how long have we known each other?"

"Probably too long. You're like a bad set of luggage—I can't get rid of you. You and Roux. I'll be stuck with you guys forever at this rate."

A small smile played across Garin's face. "You know, it's quite likely you will at that."

"Lucky me," Annja said. "So what made you come down here?"

"The possibility that an otherworldly race created these artifacts. I need to be certain whether or not they were, in fact, created by extraterrestrials," Garin said.

"Well, join the club. But as we were discussing, I don't think we've got anything even remotely significant that might prove these are alien artifacts. In fact, I'm quite certain there's a more rational explanation for all of this," Annja said.

"Are you really?" Garin looked vaguely amused. "And just what makes you so certain?"

"It's nothing I can verbalize," Annja said. "Call it a gut reaction. Sometimes I have very strong intuition about this stuff, and right now, it's not saying these are from another world."

"And this intuition, is it a result of being with the sword that you possess?"

"Maybe."

"No *maybes* about it," Garin said. "I would suggest that your instincts and intuition have become far sharper since you've come into possession of the sword than in the time before you had it."

"Even still, it tells me these are not alien in nature."

Garin nodded. "Well, it just so happens that I agree with what your intuition is telling you."

"You do?"

Garin laughed. "You seem so shocked. Why is that?"

"I thought you had your own theories about this stuff. And

I guess I thought you were hoping that maybe they were alien in nature."

"Perhaps at another time I would have. But I'm far more excited about the prospects of what these artifacts truly represent than the wishes of people who like to dream about little men in spaceships."

"There's the condescending tone I was waiting for." Annja grinned. "At least you're being truthful. As near as I can tell."

Garin pointed at the triangular serpent item Annja held in her hands. "We'd better get this up to the surface and then get back or your little buddies are liable to think you've gone and had your way with me."

"Well, good heavens, we wouldn't want them thinking that now, would we? Those fantasies are never going to materialize anyway," Annja said.

Garin placed his hand over his heart. "Woe that you tease me so."

"Yeah, right." Annja walked away and along the trail toward the surface. Garin followed along behind her, his footsteps echoing throughout the caverns.

"When was the last time you spoke with Roux, anyway?" Annja asked.

"Why?"

"Call me curious."

Garin sighed. "The less time I spend communicating with the old man, the better. He has no appreciation or zest for life. All he wants to do is commune with the voices of the past. He lacks the ability to see his own future."

"What do you see for your future?" Annja asked.

Garin shook his head and was silent for a long time.

Annja waited, curious to see what Garin would say next.

He finally spoke. "I would like to see what else there is. What happens now. Clearly Roux and I have a part to play in

your development. Neither one of us aged before the sword was recovered and you assumed ownership. And thus far, neither of us has aged since then."

"You thought you might, though, didn't you?"

"Honestly? Yes. I think both of us did. Of course, I don't think Roux would ever admit that. He's much too much of an obstinate fellow to ever allow us entry into his grand vision for himself."

Annja smiled. "But you have no such troubles."

Garin spread his arms. "I am without guile, milady."

"Yeah. So where's that bridge you wanted to sell me, too?" Annja walked farther up the trail.

Garin caught up with her. "Annja, if I laid all my cards on the table, would you even recognize them as such? Face it, from the very first time we met, you've done nothing but suspect me of foul play at every opportunity."

"Uh, that's because you've been plotting foul play every time I've run into you." Annja shook her head. "Cripes, Garin, it's not like you're off fund-raising for orphans or something. You've tried to kill a lot of people I've known. Probably even me on occasion."

Garin leveled a finger at her. "You don't know nearly as much as you think you do. Let's get back to the reason we're here."

"Fine," Annja muttered, unwilling to let Garin know how much he unsettled her.

"Annja, if these artifacts aren't from an alien world, then they must be from Earth, right?" Garin asked.

"That would be the logical assumption, yeah."

"But then there's the problem of the history. Humans didn't start developing until long after the carbon date stamp of these items."

"Well, supposedly."

"Oh, please, you don't mean to tell me that you think there

could have been an early race of humans with the intelligence to design and manufacture these things, do you? Where's the proof? Wouldn't we have found skeletons by now that would corroborate such a theory? Wouldn't the scientists have been able to tell that they were older bones but more developed?" Garin asked.

"Yes."

"Well, where are they?"

Annja said nothing.

"They aren't there because there weren't any prehistoric races of humans out there living in some fantasy world," Garin continued.

"You don't think so, huh?"

"No. I don't. And I don't think you do, either."

Annja shook her head. "Don't tell me what I'm thinking, Garin. I don't like people who put their own thoughts into my head."

"Fine, fine. But I can see it in your eyes." Garin leaned in closer. "And you do have such beautiful eyes, Annja."

She looked up at him. Damn him for being so utterly charming when he wanted to be. The way he looked at her, it was as if he was trying to decide if he could eat her in one bite or if he would just slowly devour her.

As much as she hated to admit it, there were times when she loved being ogled like that. She knew enough about the vibe Garin threw to know that any time spent in bed with him would be utterly and completely earth-shattering.

She also knew that there was a strong chance she would never emerge from his lair alive.

Trust was a big issue between them.

Annja blinked and Garin withdrew. Had he been trying to hypnotize her? She wouldn't put it past him. He'd been around long enough to learn a whole array of tricks. He didn't need a crystal dangling from a pendulum to put her under.

Dangerous, she decided. Garin was simply far too dangerous.

"I wish you hadn't blinked, Annja. It could have been magical."

Annja ran a hand through her hair. "Oh, Garin. Here we are in the middle of a dirty, filthy dig in a mountain in Antarctica and you think that you can just charm me into your bed?"

"Why not?" he asked with a sly smile.

"For one thing, it rates about a zero on the romance meter. I tend to take things a bit slower."

"We can go slow. I've got all the time in the world."

Annja smiled. "Nice try, buddy. It ain't gonna happen, though, so let's say we cut the corny attempts at seduction and stick to the important thing here—figuring out who made these items."

"Fine," Garin said. "But I still say I could have had you in another couple of minutes."

Annja ignored his comment. "Your theory then is that these weren't made by aliens or by a race of prehistoric humans. Is that it?"

"Yes."

"Then who made them?"

Garin smiled. Ahead of them, the entrance to the shelter loomed. Annja could see people moving about inside the shelter. She turned to Garin. "Come on, tell me what you really believe."

Garin shook his head. "I'm afraid we're out of time. Please see the receptionist for a slot next week."

"Garin." Annja punched his arm. "I want to know what you think is so damned important about these artifacts."

"You've been asking the wrong questions, Annja," Garin said. "And for me to go ahead and just give you the answers without you doing the work involved wouldn't be any kind of fun, now, would it?"

"I could do without having to work for the answer every once in a while. I expect most people could," Annja said.

Garin nodded. "Sure, but there's no fun in it."

"So?"

"The goal is always to have fun, Annja. Always."

"Why is that?"

Garin sighed. "Because fun is the only thing I have left. Everything else has been stolen from me in this cruel world. I don't age. I don't get sick. I don't die. If I can't have fun, then truly, I am lost forever."

Annja looked at him for a moment. Garin caught her eye and she saw it coming. First the crow's-feet at the edges of his eyes started to crinkle inward. And then the lips parted. She saw his teeth. And then heard him laughing.

"Did I fool you?" he asked.

"Not even close. I know you too well."

Garin sighed again. "Ah, well, that's probably true. Well, here we are. Let's get this logged in and then you and I can take a nice shower together. How does that sound?"

"As appealing as a bout of food poisoning," Annja said. "I'll take a pass."

Garin smiled. "Well, just for that, I'm not going to tell you how I think these items were made by animals. So there."

20

Annja lay on her bed inside the shelter with her hands behind her head on the pillow. She was tired. And grumpy. Being alone seemed like the best thing to do.

She'd spent the better part of the afternoon digging in the cavern with Dave and Zach. Despite deep excavations, they'd found nothing else aside from the piece Annja had dug up earlier in the day.

Garin, meanwhile, had refused to make himself available for elaboration on his cryptic statement about animals creating the relics. He'd been busy with Colonel Thomson throughout the day, reassuring him of elaborate security measures that Annja was certain weren't even necessary.

Zach and Dave had gone for dinner, leaving Annja alone in the shelter. She had feigned a lack of appetite to get them to leave without her. She simply didn't want to be in the mess hall and forced to talk with people when she could be alone, relaxing and trying to wrap her mind around the situation and why she felt she was being played on many different fronts.

Her first source of frustration was with the attempt on her life.

Whom had she angered to the extent that they wanted her dead? Sure, there were plenty of people across the globe who would not shed a tear if she happened to get eaten by a great white shark or hit by a blimp, but would they bother to track her down to a remote research station in Antarctica to take her out?

She didn't think so. That meant that she'd run afoul of someone local and not back in the outside world. But the only two candidates for that were back at McMurdo in Gallagher's. She wondered if Dunning had had any luck tracking them down.

Had the two nitwits followed them to Horlick? Zach had insisted he might have seen another Sno-Cat back behind them. Was it possible someone was keeping tabs on her? And if so, who was it and why?

That brought her to Zach and Dave. Annja felt comfortable enough with Zach. She knew him and they'd worked together in the past. She trusted him implicitly. And besides, with his failed marriage looming over his head, Zach didn't really seem to be capable of planning some elaborate scheme. The dig was the one thing he could actually concentrate on to the exclusion of all the bad things happening in his life.

He needed this dig as a distraction from his personal life. She knew the feeling.

What about Dave? At times, he moved and acted like a bumpkin of sorts. Their first meeting in particular hadn't impressed Annja. He'd used his strange speech patterns to disarm her suspicion and put her at ease. If she thought he wasn't the sharpest knife in the drawer, she wouldn't figure out his true intentions.

But later on, Dave had let the disguise slip in spots. And when he did, he seemed a lot more formidable than he had before. While Annja wasn't necessarily convinced he was a full-on government agent, he sure had a way about him that made her think there was a lot more to him than he showed.

Garin's sudden appearance had surprised Annja far more

than anything else that had happened thus far. She hadn't seen him for months. And to see him striding about the camp in his military regalia made her want to break out laughing.

He was there for a reason. But she had no idea what it could be.

And the dig site itself confused her. She'd been on plenty. And she'd uncovered evidence before of ancient settlements. But this was completely unlike the others. Except for the discovery of the four pieces, there was no evidence that a race of people had lived here at all.

Of most concern to her was the fact that there weren't any skeletons. Nor were there cave paintings, or other tidbits that usually accompanied the dig sites she'd been on in the past.

It was as if someone had simply thrown four bizarre relics into the ground and then left.

But why would they do that? And where did they go after that? Were there other places elsewhere in the world with such relics buried in them? Or was this simply one strange incident that would have no real resolution to it at all?

As much as Annja hated to admit it, there were times when that was exactly what happened. For one reason or another, things wouldn't add up. There would be loose ends and an impossibility at ever uncovering the truth.

She hated that.

She closed her eyes and let her mind drift. The two killers in McMurdo were, as far as she was able to tell, still back there. She could do nothing about them at the moment. And concentrating on them would prove to be a distraction she didn't want right now.

She filed them away for later.

Dave was another matter entirely. He was on the site and a constant fixture in Annja's current situation. But fathoming what he was or what his motivations were would prove exhausting, as well. He didn't seem to be an enemy, at least

not yet. And he seemed genuinely concerned about Zach's welfare, which meant he had to be at least somewhat okay.

Annja filed him away, as well.

Garin's face swam into her mind's eye. What was his deal? she wondered. Why was he here and what was he after? Did he really want the artifacts? He'd seemed only mildly curious about the most recent discovery and certainly disliked digging at the site. If he was truly motivated to find the relics, Annja would have expected him to be right at the forefront of the work.

But he wasn't. And his actions called him into question. But Annja knew that he was a slippery character. If he told her one thing, he might have meant another and he might still have six other stories.

That concerned her.

Annja opened her eyes. Outside her shelter, she could see shapes passing back and forth as people walked in front of the lights. She smirked at the thought of all the generators running on nuclear power. Who would have thought, she wondered, that this entire installation was being powered that way?

She frowned. Wasn't it a violation of international law or some accord that there was nuclear power on the continent? She vaguely remembered reading somewhere that all the nations with an interest in Antarctica had signed something swearing they wouldn't bring nukes there.

Of course, she was sure the Americans would swear it was their right to do whatever was necessary if they thought they'd stumbled upon something that might threaten their national security. And the other countries would clam up because no one wanted to get on their bad side. Annja sighed. No wonder our reputation elsewhere in the world is the pits.

So what could she do about Garin?

She sat up. Lying on her bunk wasn't accomplishing a damned thing. She needed to get some answers. And soon.

Her mind didn't like a lot of unresolved questions about stuff she was so close to.

Annja checked the clock. It was just after 7:00 p.m. She knew a lot of people would still be at dinner.

She slid her legs over the bed and got into her snow pants and boots. She zipped up her jacket and then stood by the door, cracking it just enough to get a feel for the foot traffic outside.

A hundred feet away, she saw two armed guards on routine patrol. The military presence was very clear, but they seemed friendly enough and obviously had orders not to interfere in the scientific process.

Annja stepped outside the door into the frigid cold. The wind took her for a step to her left until she bent her knees and lowered her weight to get her balance. Then she righted herself and walked off toward Colonel Thomson's tent.

Rather than appear sneaky, Annja strode through the snow as if she had a clear mission in mind to see the colonel.

Once in his administrative tent, she could try to figure out where Garin was sleeping. And then she could have a sit-down with him. Or maybe she could just poke around in his tent and see if she could discover the real reason he was down here.

At the entrance to Thomson's tent, she paused. She heard nothing inside and so she stepped in.

A young soldier sat at the desk and looked up when Annja entered. "Can I help you, Miss Creed?"

Annja frowned. "You know who I am?"

He nodded. "We all do. Part of our orders are to know the names and faces of everyone in camp."

"I see." Annja glanced around. "Is Colonel Thomson around?"

"No, probably off at dinner, I'd expect. Something I can help you with?"

Annja smiled. "Actually, I was hoping to see Major Braden about something."

The soldier nodded. "He might be at dinner, as well."

Annja turned to leave. "Well, no bother. I'll stop by his tent in a little while and ask him then."

"Okay," the soldier said pleasantly.

Annja frowned. "His tent is over by the dig site entrance, isn't it?"

"No, Miss Creed, it's over by the generator station," he said.

Annja raised her eyebrows. "He's sleeping near the nuclear power core?"

The soldier grinned. "It's perfectly safe. And besides, he volunteered to pitch his shelter there. Said he was old enough that if he started to glow in the dark, it'd be better than any of us doing the same. Helluva guy, he is."

Annja smiled. "Isn't he, though?" She ducked back out of the shelter into the freezing air.

She turned and surveyed the camp. The nuclear power generator stood by itself, somewhat close to the dig site entrance, but far enough away that it seemed a little isolated. It might have been as safe as the young soldier had insisted, but psychologically, people didn't seem to want to be near it.

Except for one shelter.

Garin's.

Annja noticed the recent snowfall made it possible to see all the footprints in the area. She saw several sets, including what could only be Garin's large boots, leading to and from his tent. She walked carefully in one of the sets, mimicking the steps just because she didn't feel like advertising her presence.

She smirked. Garin would flip if he thought she was coming to his tent. His desire for her was ridiculous at times. And Annja wondered how much of it was an act designed to

simply flatter her to the point that she dropped her guard. She'd known plenty of women who were too easily disarmed by the flattery and supposed desire of a would-be conqueror.

Annja was determined not to let that happen to her.

Garin might make for an attractive mental stimulus every once in a great while, but she would never allow herself to bed down with him. Never.

The entrance to his shelter loomed ahead and Annja hurried to get closer. Garin had apparently set his shelter up so it was literally flush with the nuclear power generator.

Why would anyone—even Garin—do that?

She glanced around the shelter but saw nothing else out of the ordinary. Hoses ran from the generator out to all of the shelters, and Annja knew they carried the electricity that powered everything in camp.

The cold was becoming unbearable. She had to make a decision soon about whether she would stay outside or go in.

Annja paused by the door.

Here goes nothing, she thought.

She knocked on the door.

"Good evening, Annja."

But the voice didn't come from within the shelter. It came from behind her. She turned and saw Garin standing there.

"Is there something I can help you with?"

21

Garin looked imposing with his hood and goggles on, standing over her in the darkness. He smiled and clapped his hands together. "This is a very nice surprise. One I confess I never thought I'd see happening. But there you go. Just goes to show that we can't predict the future."

Annja sighed. "I wanted to talk to you."

Garin shook his head. "Well, I'm not going to talk to you out here. I'm cold and miserable. This weather is the absolute pits."

"We're in Antarctica, Garin."

"Regardless, I'm going inside." Garin opened the door. "Interested in coming in out of the cold?"

Annja stepped over the threshold. "Whether your sick little imagination wants to admit it or not, this does not mean I'm here to sleep with you," she stated.

Garin placed a hand on his chest. "Woman, thou doth slay me with your unkind words."

"Yeah, right," Annja said, laughing.

Garin removed his jacket and goggles, letting them fall over the small table near the entrance. "I didn't see you at dinner."

"No, you didn't."

He stopped. "Is this going to be one of those conversations?"

"What kind?"

"The ones where you simply confirm my statements and we do some silly dance around the topic you really want to resolve?"

Annja smiled. "You can tell we've been associates for too long. When you start predicting the flow of the talk, and all."

"Well," Garin said with a gleam in his eye, "you could always cozy up to me and take things in a direction neither of us ever expected. That might be a fun way to keep our relationship fresh."

"I'll give that some serious thought," Annja said.

"Please do." Garin removed his snow pants. Annja glanced away. He laughed. "I've got other pants on underneath, for crying out loud."

"What? I wasn't sure if you were naked under there or what. Knowing you, you might have planned it that way and all," Annja said, feeling a little embarrassed.

"Oh, might I?" Garin sat down on his bed. "There's a chair over there or you're welcome to sit here."

"Why did you pitch your shelter near the nuclear generator?" Annja asked.

Garin grinned. "Isn't it obvious?"

"Well, sure, but I like asking questions that have obvious answers because I'm a real fan of hearing myself speak," she said.

Garin frowned. "In case you didn't notice, I'm not exactly legitimate. And frankly, I like knowing that I have some separation, just in case I need to get out of here in a hurry."

"You're expecting to have to leave?"

"One never knows." Garin leaned back. "I've always found it's far better to be prepared for any eventuality. I had to live

that way for years while Roux and I tried to kill each other. After a while, that pattern gets ingrained in you. It's not something you can even choose to do or not do. It just happens."

"So you've got yourself an isolated bit of real estate here," Annja said.

"Yes."

"With the isotopes floating about."

Garin smiled. "The reactor is perfectly safe. It's a one-of-a-kind unit, I'm told. Straight off the DARPA assembly block. This is the first unit to use them in an actual field test. So far, I'm impressed."

Annja sat on the chair and stretched her legs.

Garin sat up. "So what's this all about, then? Why were you lurking around my shelter? Hoping to catch a glimpse of me in my skivvies?"

"Not even close." Annja frowned. "And I wasn't lurking. I asked where your shelter was and here I am."

"Who'd you ask?"

"The soldier in Thomson's tent."

Annja looked around the shelter. Garin had little in terms of personal effects. She spotted a backpack and that was it. "That's all your stuff?"

Garin glanced over. "That? Oh, yeah. Well, I travel light these days. I make better time than if I overpack."

"I haven't seen any weapons on you yet."

"Just because you can't see them doesn't mean they aren't there," Garin replied.

Annja looked at him closely. "Tell me why you said that thing back in the cavern."

Garin took a deep breath and leaned back onto the bed. "What thing was that?"

Annja sighed. "You said something about animals creating the artifacts we found."

"Did I?"

"You know you did."

"Well, I say a lot of things, Annja. And often, they make little to no sense at all. My mind, after all, is a bit addled. Fermented, you might even say."

"You're not going to tell me, are you?"

Garin smiled. "I could be persuaded to divulge my precious information. Perhaps."

Annja shook her head. "I'm not bartering sex for information."

"There are a lot worse ways to gain intelligence, Annja. You might give it some thought. I know I have."

"I'm sure." Anna stood.

"You're not leaving, are you?" Garin asked.

"I don't see any reason to stay. You've obviously got some sort of sexual fantasy you need to live out. And I'm not going to be a part of it."

Garin sighed. "But we were just getting going."

"No, we weren't. I was asking you a serious question and you were doing your best to derail us into hedonism."

"You say that like it's a bad thing."

Annja sat back down. "Look, Garin, I'm not going to judge you for being what you are—"

"Which is what?"

"A sex addict with questionable sociological tendencies."

Garin considered that and then shrugged. "Okay."

"But I do get frustrated with the constant parrying I have to do to try to get answers out of you. I don't have the time or inclination to spar ceaselessly with you. Really."

"All right, fine. So I said something about animals making the artifacts. What about it?"

Annja looked at him. "Do you really believe that?"

"I don't know. I threw it out there because I knew it would get under your skin. And obviously, I was right. Look at how

you've been obsessing about it. You're sitting here now because of one simple comment. That says a lot, I think."

"It says a lot because I'm a bit confused about my situation," Annja admitted.

"And you want to know where all the pieces fit together— is that it?"

"Yes."

Garin smiled. "You know what I envy about you, Annja? I mean, aside from your utterly delectable body."

"What?"

"Your inability to lie."

Annja frowned. "I can lie."

Garin shook his head. "My darling Annja, you cannot lie convincingly. There may have been times in your past when you told lies to save yourself, but in general, you simply don't possess the capacity for it."

Annja rubbed her shoulder. "So I need to be a liar all the time now? Be like you, in other words?"

"I don't lie all the time, Annja. But what I do is tell enough lies such that when I tell the truth, people can't tell the difference. It affords me greater opportunity to manipulate events to my liking."

"I'm not sure I follow," Annja said.

"Take this afternoon when I told you about the animals. You thought that was real. You then spent hours wondering about it prior to coming here and confronting me. But in truth, that was an offhand comment I made to distract you from other things."

"What other things?"

Garin held up his hand. "We were talking about the animals. Don't derail this conversation."

"So you don't believe animals created the artifacts?"

"I didn't say that."

"You just said that it was an offhand comment," Annja said.

"So?"

Annja frowned. "Forget it, I'm going."

Garin stretched out on his bed. "I once read the most amazing science fiction story about a mission to the Moon. The astronauts dug up bones on a site."

"What kind of bones?" Annja asked, wondering if she'd regret it.

"Dinosaur bones."

Annja frowned. "Dinosaurs? On the Moon? That is science fiction."

"Is it really?" Garin sat up. "We know now that dinosaurs were actually more intelligent than previously thought. So how is it far-fetched to assume that there might have been a race of animals intelligent enough to create metal and fashion it into artifacts like what were found in the dig site?"

"That belongs to the realm of writers," Annja said. "God bless them for their ability to tell stories, but that's pretty out there."

"Well, perhaps. But just because it doesn't make sense now doesn't mean it won't make perfect sense in the future."

Annja zipped up her jacket. "I'll think about it."

"Of course you will."

Annja put her hood up. "I wish I could say it's been fun."

Garin smiled. "Well, it won't ever be fun until you shuck those clothes and hop into bed with me."

"Good night, Garin."

Annja started for the door to the shelter.

"Annja?"

She paused and looked back. Garin lay on his bed with his eyes closed. His hands were folded across his chest as if he were a corpse resting in a coffin. Annja found the image vaguely unsettling and she wasn't quite sure why.

"What?" she asked.

Garin's eyes opened and he gave her a long look. "I think there's something you're forgetting."

"What's that?"

"With regard to the animals making the artifacts."

"Yes?"

Garin smiled. "Did Zach tell you anything about the various tests they conducted on the pieces?"

"Sure. He told me they ran a battery of tests trying to figure out exactly what their composition was, how old they were, that kind of thing."

"And?"

"And what?"

Garin sighed. "The metal used in the pieces. Remember? It wasn't from this planet. It's an unknown alloy. I believe that tends to discount the theory about the race of intelligent animals. Don't you?"

Annja stood there for another moment and then walked back out, unsure if she'd learned anything new or just gotten more frustration for her time.

22

"She's going to be a problem if she's around for much longer."

"We'll be there tomorrow. Can it wait until then?"

He gripped the satellite phone and his knuckles turned white. "I don't like delays. And yours have already forced me to push my timetable back considerably."

"Why not go ahead and complete your mission? If the woman gets in the way, you could always kill her."

The man sighed. He hated dealing with fools. Unfortunately, sometimes they were the only ones who could be used in certain situations. "If I kill her, it will raise too many questions. And I don't need the attention, not when I'm so close. It needs to be soon, though, or else she will discover what I've got planned."

"I think you put too much faith in her intelligence."

"Perhaps that's because I know her a bit better than you do. I know what she's capable of, and right now, what she's most capable of is being a nuisance to me. This was supposed to have been finished by now and it's not."

"It would have been if our Sno-Cat didn't break down. We couldn't do anything until we got rescued and brought back

to McMurdo. And once we got back, we had to dodge the marshal. He's been asking questions."

"If he becomes a problem, then you'll have to deal with him. Quietly."

"We will."

He glanced at the clock near his bed. "When will you be here?"

"At some point over the next day."

"The camp is very well guarded. You won't have an easy time getting in without paperwork."

"We don't need papers. You mentioned there wasn't much of a perimeter—is that still the case?"

"They haven't strengthened it, no. You could come in by coming down from the mountain face. It's a complicated route, but you and your partner should have no problems surmounting it, given your backgrounds."

"Good."

"Is everything arranged on your end?"

"Yes. The freighter will be in the harbor within thirty-six hours. It will stand by offshore, just shy of the ice packs. Once you're set to exfiltrate, they'll send in a Zodiac and get you out of there."

"It has to have a solid hull, not an inflatable one."

"It will."

He nodded. A few more days and this would all be behind him. "And you know what has to happen to everyone in this camp once I have what I've come here for?"

"They all die."

"And all traces of this dig must be obliterated."

"We understand."

"Good. Contact me when you're closer."

"Will do. Out."

The phone disconnected in his ear and he placed it back in his backpack. There was always a chance that the American

National Security Agency might have penetrated the secure communication system on the satellite, but he doubted they would be able to track it back to him. Ever since 9/11, the NSA—like its counterparts—had been far too focused on dealing with terrorist threats than with various other crimes.

He was sure he was safe.

But Annja Creed would have to be dealt with. If she wasn't killed, then sooner or later, they would come face-to-face and there would be no quarter.

The last thing he wanted was to kill her, but she was leaving him no choice. Her intelligence and capacity for discerning the truth were a danger to him. And he had no doubt that if she wasn't stopped, she would do everything in her power—including using all of her skills, skills she didn't even fully comprehend yet—to thwart his mission.

No, she had to die. And if his people could get it done properly this time, there would be no suspicion surrounding it. Her untimely death would simply be the result of a tragic accident. And the world would no longer have Annja Creed in it.

He lay back down and closed his eyes. Sleep would be a welcome respite for him tonight.

ANNJA SLEPT FITFULLY, tossing and turning every few minutes, aware of the rhythmic snores coming from Dave's side of the room. For a few moments, she'd hear nothing, and then he would spark up again, unleashing a cavalcade of snorts and whistles upon the room.

So much for sleeping tonight, she thought. And just when she needed every bit of herself rested. Her ribs no longer hurt, but in a lot of ways, her exhaustion was more mental than physical. There were so many loose ends, and seeing Garin hadn't helped much at all, except to dissuade her that a race of animals had created the relics—which she'd never believed in the first place.

What had Zach said about the metal? That they'd been sent out to a laboratory for analysis. And that the metal hadn't registered as being from Earth? How was that possible?

Annja rolled out of bed and nudged Zach awake. He started and then looked around. "Wha—"

"Shh, it's me. Keep your voice down or you'll wake Dave."

Zach rubbed his eyes. "Not likely. That guy can sleep through a herd of charging rhinos. What's the problem?"

"Tell me again about the necklace," Annja said.

"What about it? I've told you everything already. There's nothing left to tell."

"Back in McMurdo you mentioned that you had the necklace sent out for analysis, right?"

"Sure. Colonel Thomson handled it personally. Said he knew just where to send it."

"Do you know where that was?"

"What—the lab?"

"Yes."

Zach frowned. "No, I don't. What's this all about anyway? Why are you so curious about the lab work done on the necklace?"

Annja frowned. "I want to know about the laboratory and what tests they performed. Is there any way to find out?"

Zach shrugged. "Well, I don't know. I mean, they've probably got it logged in somewhere. Maybe in the admin tent on the computer. Maybe in Colonel Thomson's shelter. Hell, it could be anywhere."

"Yeah, that's what I was afraid of," Annja said.

"What's bothering you so much about it?"

Annja looked at him. "You said the metal didn't register, right?"

"Yeah."

"That the lab determined it wasn't from Earth?"

"Uh-huh."

Annja leaned closer to Zach. "Who told you the results?"

Zach frowned again. "Annja, you're not making any sense."

"Did you read a report or did someone tell you what the lab found out?"

"Well, Thomson called us all in and told us what the lab had reported. We were all cautioned not to tell anyone about it since it could get out and cause mayhem."

"So you never actually saw a report."

"No."

Annja walked back to her bed and sat down on the edge. "Interesting."

"What's interesting? I'm not following your train of thought here, Annja."

Annja leaned back on her bed. "If you never saw the report, then who's to say it's accurate?"

Zach sat up. "You think it was faked?"

"It's possible."

"But why? Who would fake a lab report?" Zach shook his head. "This is reaching, Annja. It really is."

"Sometimes we have to reach," Annja said. "And as for who would fake a lab report, I don't know yet. But obviously, it's someone who wanted to draw a lot of attention down here at the dig site."

"Yeah, but for what purpose?"

"I don't know."

Zach sighed. "And why would they tell us the metal isn't from Earth? You think they'd deliberately mislead us on that?"

"Very possibly. Especially if the relics are only part of the equation."

Zach took a deep breath. "Why do you always come up with this stuff in the middle of the night, anyhow?"

Annja smiled. "Dave's not letting me get my beauty sleep." She rolled over. "Tell me about how you got into this dig."

"Sure. If it'll help put this all to rest. It was just after I filed my final paperwork for the divorce. I was considering filing for bankruptcy because, between the alimony and the child support, I was going to be sunk. There was no way I could keep up with the payments. I was depressed. Lonely. I didn't even have my kids with me."

Annja shook her head. "I'm sorry."

"Me, too. I was sending out tons of résumés when I got this e-mail from someone who had seen my résumé on a networking Web site. Anyway, we exchanged a few e-mails. Turns out the guy was a recruiter and he told me they had something down in Antarctica and would I be interested in coming down. The pay was great, so I jumped at it. I think it was just what I needed to get my mind off my situation."

Annja nodded. "Nothing like a change of scenery, huh?"

"This is about as extreme as it gets, but, yeah."

"Go on."

Zach sighed. "I flew down, came out to the site, which was a lot less elaborate than it is now. We didn't have the generator for one thing, and that made life hellish."

"How'd you stay warm?"

"Lots of layers, kerosene and limited exposure to the elements. Plus, we didn't stay out here if we could avoid it."

"And what was your initial briefing like?"

"Just that they believed there was something peculiar about the mountain and that they had detected traces of something metallic inside the base of it. It was supposed to be for oil exploration under the guise of a scientific mission, but when they saw something unusual, they called me in."

"Of course they did," Annja said. "Having a real scientist gives the mission an air of authenticity and legitimacy."

"I found the necklace the first day. At that point, they wanted to know if I needed any more help. I thought of you

and how much you'd be interested in this stuff, and that's when they went for you."

Annja nodded. "Okay."

"That's it. You know the whole story."

"Did it ever strike you as strange that they contacted you right after you filed your divorce paperwork?"

"No. I just thought it was my good timing. I was a lucky bastard to get this assignment. They're paying me enough money to take all the stress out of my life."

Annja smiled in the darkness. "That's great. No one should have that much pressure."

"There something still bothering you about this, Annja?" Zach asked.

"Only everything."

Zach didn't say anything for a minute. "Well, tell me what you're thinking. Bounce your ideas off me."

"Not just yet, Zach. I need some more time to think this through. For now, I think we just need to keep on doing what we're doing."

"Digging?"

Annja nodded then realized Zach probably couldn't see her. "Yep."

"I get the distinct impression you aren't much into that part of the mission, though," Zach said.

"I'm not."

"You mind me asking why? It's really not like you."

Annja sighed. "It's nothing personal, Zach. And I'm flattered you thought of me when you were asked about help. But there's something else going on here, something bigger, and it's occupying most of my thoughts. I can't put my finger on it yet but I will soon enough. And when I do, I think that will be the time we need each other the most."

"Okay, well, whatever you need, Annja. You know that."

Annja smiled. "Thanks, Zach."

"So. What's your next step, then?"

"I think I need to see a copy of that lab report. I need to figure out for myself if those relics really are something special or just a bunch of trinkets thrown into the ground."

"Just a bunch of trinkets?" Zach sounded shocked.

"I know," Annja said. "It seems crazy, right?"

"Kinda."

"Just wait. If I find what I think I'm going to find, we'll have a lot more to deal with than just a bunch of crazy extra-terrestrials."

Zach flopped back down on his pillow. "Great."

Annja turned over and it was only then that she realized Dave had stopped snoring. Had he heard everything she'd said to Zach?

23

By the time Annja woke the next morning, she knew she had to get a copy of that laboratory analysis report and read it over. Both the metallurgic results and carbon dating seemed simply too bizarre to be fact, and she was surprised that none of the other scientists had requested to look it over.

This made her wonder exactly who the rest of the team was, and it was only then that she realized she'd been so obsessed with her own happenings that she hadn't properly met anyone else yet.

In the mess hall, Annja made a point of walking around and introducing herself to the other men and women. With each person she met, however, Annja found herself wondering exactly how they'd all been recruited for this particular mission.

"It doesn't make sense," she said to Zach and Dave over her eggs. "Who are these people? Have you ever heard of any of them before?"

Dave sighed. "Annja, are you saying it's necessary for you to personally know everyone in order for them to be valid researchers?"

"You know that's not what I'm saying, Dave." Annja frowned. "It's just that in our field, a lot of us know each other."

"But not everyone," he suggested.

"No. Not everyone," Annja admitted.

Dave shrugged. "Well, maybe these people have been hiding under rocks for the past couple of years. Or maybe they've been working on classified projects and haven't had a chance to broadcast their work in the usual journals."

"I suppose."

Zach sighed. "He's right, Annja. I think you're getting paranoid. And I'm honestly wondering if it's good for you to be here any longer."

"What?" Annja was horrified.

"I'm serious. I don't know what you were thinking last night, waking me up like that and broaching the questions that you did, but I sure as hell couldn't get back to sleep afterward."

"Well, sorry, but—"

"The idea that someone has gone through all of this to create some sort of subterfuge, which I believe is what you've been driving at, is really just out of the ballpark. I can't buy into it."

Annja ate a forkful of eggs. She was fairly certain Dave had heard the entire conversation so she didn't see any point in keeping it secret. "And what about the lab report?"

Zach shook his head. "Listen, go visit the colonel and see if he'll let you see a copy of it. If he does and you read it over, won't that allay your fears?"

"Possibly."

"Then do it. He should be at his office now, anyway. I'm sure he won't mind letting you have a peek at it."

"What if he does?"

Dave shrugged. "Maybe he's got a good reason. The report could have other details about stuff that we don't need to know. Once you start working with the government, this kind of thing comes with the territory. And as long as their checks

clear in my bank account, I can't say that I'm all that concerned about it."

"That's certainly taking the easy approach to the situation," Annja said.

"Maybe," Dave replied. "But at least I'm not losing sleep at night thanks to my crazy thoughts. Who says it's better to take the difficult approach to a situation anyway?"

Annja put her fork down. "And if it turns out there really is something strange going on here?"

"I'll apologize," Dave said.

"Me, too," Zach said. "And I'll stand up on the table here and publicly tell everyone what a royal prick I've been. How's that sound?"

"Pretty good," Annja said. "And I'll hold you to that." She picked up her tray. "See you guys down at the dig site later."

Annja put her tray back by the entrance and then zipped herself up. Outside, the weather seemed a little warmer today, but it was still brilliantly cold. Maybe she was starting to adjust to the harsh environment. She wondered how penguins endured this kind of weather when they marched deep into the interior to shelter their young.

Colonel Thomson's administration center lay ahead of her, and Annja headed straight for it. As she walked through the snow, she rehearsed what she intended to say to Thomson when she saw him.

She reached for the door and pulled it open.

"Colonel Thomson."

She stopped. The shelter was empty.

Annja frowned. She could see the bank of computers sitting on the back table. Each one of them had a screen saver blipping across the screen in random order.

Annja glanced back outside. All it would take was a few quick keystrokes to see if the report was on there. And if she

could get access to it and a printout, that might be all the proof she needed that something was going on here.

It was worth a shot, wasn't it?

She moved around the receptionist desk and toward the back of the shelter. She glanced back at the door and then turned toward the screen. As soon as she touched the first key, the screen blossomed into light.

A single prompt asked for a password.

Annja frowned. Great. Security even down here.

She paused and tried a number of entries. Each one produced no results. Worse, the prompt told her she had only two more tries before it locked itself down.

Annja thought and then typed "Thomson" into the computer and hit Enter.

The screen flashed and asked for another password. Annja typed the same string in and hit Enter.

The screen flashed red and then informed Annja that she was being frozen out of the system.

"Damn."

She heard a noise outside the door and hustled back around the table. The door opened and the young soldier she'd spoken with yesterday came in.

He took a look at Annja, then at the computer in the back, and then back at her. "Can I help you with something, Miss Creed?"

Annja smiled. "Sorry, I was just trying to access my e-mail."

The soldier typed a few keys and rebooted the computer Annja had frozen. He frowned at her. "Computers are off-limits to nonmilitary personnel."

"I didn't know," she said as innocently as she could manage.

"Some things we shouldn't have to tell you guys, for crying out loud. If the colonel gets wind of this, he's going to be pissed," the soldier said.

Annja flashed a smile again. "We don't have to bother him

with that, do we? I'm sure he's busy and all, and that kind of thing would probably just put him in a bad mood."

"You're damned right it would. He doesn't like anyone messing around with the system. It's not like we've got a tech unit to come in here and fix things if we get buggy. We need these things running in top condition all the time."

"I'm sorry. It won't happen again. I promise."

He looked at her and then grinned. "Yeah, all right. Don't worry about it. I get lonely for some e-mail myself. Stinks not being able to talk to my friends back home."

"You've been with the colonel for a long time?" Annja asked.

"Only a couple of months, actually. I graduated tech school and got assigned to him once I passed the security background check. That took the longest time."

"Must be nice working for him. I'll bet you know all his behavioral patterns and stuff like that."

He grinned. "I can tell when he's not happy. Like yesterday, he wasn't too nice to be around."

Annja leaned against the desk. "Oh? Why do you think that was?"

"I don't know. I thought I heard him saying something about incompetence, but I can't be sure. He spends a lot of his time in his shelter. He and Major Braden seem to have a lot to talk about."

Annja looked around the shelter. "So is this it for you? You just sit here all day and do nothing?"

"I file reports, take in reports, get stuff signed and send it on out. That kind of thing. It gets boring sometimes, but I like the job."

"How's the communication system? You're set up for satellite relays, right?" Annja asked.

"Yep. We've got times when we can get a clear stream of communication back to the States and other times we have

to bounce stuff around. That's when things are good. But during the blackout times, it sucks."

"Blackout?"

"When we don't have any satellite coverage. We're totally alone then. Hell, someone could come down here and wipe us out. If it's during that blackout window, no one would know anything about what had happened to us."

Annja frowned. "That's a bit scary."

"Tell me about it. I get the shakes just thinking about it."

"How often do you have blackout periods?" Annja asked, alarmed.

The solider shrugged. "Every day. One in the early morning and one toward the end of the day. They're like clockwork."

"And there's no way to get a message out during those times?"

"Well, if you've got a landline, sure you could. But there ain't no landlines down here. So you'd need your own sat phone on a different network—something that doesn't use a defense satellite to send through."

"That would take some doing," Annja said.

"Yep. Sure would."

Annja leaned closer to the soldier and smiled warmly at him. "I was hoping to see the colonel and ask him a few questions."

"About what?"

"The report from the laboratory about the nature of the artifacts that were found."

The soldier frowned. "What do you want to see that for?"

"I've got some questions about the carbon dating exactitude algorithm that I need cleared up." She smiled and hoped the line of technobabble would suffice. "It's pretty complicated stuff, but if I can see the report, it'll help me understand a little better about what it is we've got down here."

The soldier leaned closer to her. "I hear they're from outer space."

"Could be," Annja said. "But I won't know until I see the report. Is there any way you could see your way to helping me get a copy of it?"

"I would, sure, but I don't have access to it," he said.

Annja sighed. "Why not? I thought you were in charge of everything here."

"Well, most things, yeah. But not stuff like that. It's top secret stuff that gets read only by the colonel. Maybe Major Braden, too, but I'm not sure. Anyway, they get to read it and then I'm pretty sure it gets destroyed."

"Destroyed?"

"If it's a hard copy, they'll burn it. If it's an e-mail they'll delete the file and make sure it can't be undeleted."

"And they don't read the reports here?"

The soldier glanced around. "I'm not supposed to be telling you this or anyone else for that matter, but when a classified message comes in, I route it to the colonel's private terminal in his shelter."

"He's got a computer in his tent?"

"Yep."

"That must be nice, huh?"

The soldier grinned. "Rank has its privileges, ma'am."

"Indeed it does," Annja said. "Well, maybe I'd better go see the colonel then about getting a copy of the report for myself, huh?"

"You can try, but I don't think he'll let you see it."

"Why not?"

"It's classified stuff. Anything relating to this dig site has already been classified top secret. That means unless you have the proper security clearance, identification and a need-to-know, you aren't going to get a copy of it."

Annja frowned. "I don't suppose you can whip me up any of that stuff here, can you?"

"Afraid not, Miss Creed. I'd be glad to help you out but I

can't. Far as I know, the colonel doesn't show that stuff to anyone. He said something one time about things needing to be kept compartmentalized. Otherwise we'd have havoc back home if people knew we were looking at alien artifacts and whatnot."

"I suppose that makes sense," Annja said. "Do you know if the colonel is over at his shelter now?"

"I don't know. I think he's still at breakfast. He and Major Braden have been hanging out quite a bit, but I think that's because the colonel really enjoys talking with him about security and stuff."

Annja smiled. "Yes, that Major Braden certainly has an eye for security."

"Your best bet is to wander over and knock on his door. Who knows? He might just be there."

Annja smiled at him. "Thank you. I'll do that."

24

Outside in the dim light, the snow fell harder, coming at Annja in small, dry flakes that pelted the few bits of exposed skin she had. The frozen landscape was brutal and as the wind screamed in her ears; the entire environment seemed almost entirely…dead.

Colonel Thomson's shelter was several yards away from the admin shelter, and Annja moved quickly. Some people moved past her, but no one stopped to speak. Out here, it was always a matter of getting from point A to point B in the least amount of time possible.

And Annja wanted to get to Thomson's shelter soon before he came back to it and found her there.

The only way I'm going to be able to do this, she thought, is if I can sneak in and get access to his computer system. She frowned. There would be a security system of some sort on his laptop. She'd need a password and without knowing anything of his past, she'd have a hard time guessing it.

Still, there might be a way.

Instead of heading for the colonel's shelter, Annja turned and

headed for her own shelter. Inside, she flipped open her laptop and booted it up. She'd need some way to connect to the outside world, though. And she didn't have a satellite phone.

But Dave did. She'd seen him unpack it earlier in the trip when they first arrived. She hadn't thought much of it then, just figured it was something he always carried. A just-in-case solution in the event he needed it. Now, however, she found herself wondering why he had one.

Not that it mattered. At the moment, she needed its ability to reach out and touch someone. Annja peered out of the door but saw no one heading toward her shelter. She ducked back inside and went right for Dave's bag.

The sat phone was about twelve inches long, and Annja found a USB jack on the side of it that she could hook up to her laptop. She switched it on and found her way to the Internet dial-up connection. It was extremely slow working on dial-up rather than broadband, but at least she had a line out.

She headed right for the message board she knew her hacker friend Knightmare always hung out on. In the forum area, she posted a quick note:

K, it's Digger A. Drop me a line—got a project for you.

Then she sat back and waited. No sooner had she posted it than her e-mail indicator light turned green. She had a new e-mail waiting for her. Annja clicked over and saw it was from Knightmare.

Can you video? Go to Yahoo if you can.

Annja clicked on her Yahoo Instant Messenger video feed and peered into the camera on her laptop. An instant later, Knightmare's face popped up on her screen.

"Yo, Annja."

"What's up, Knight?"

"You rang?"

Annja smiled. Knightmare was a sixteen-year-old from Beverly Hills who enjoyed raiding all sorts of cryptic government files just for the fun of it. He certainly didn't need any money. Form what Annja knew, Knightmare's father was the head of a software company that had just gone public for billions of dollars.

"Guess where I am?"

"Someplace cold, judging from the parka."

"Antarctica."

His face lit up. "No shit?"

"Really. But I need your help."

He nodded, getting his game face on. "What gives?"

"I can't go into details right now, but suffice it to say I'm on a covert government job right now. I need to get access to a computer network that is linked up to a defense satellite communications system. Can you help out?"

Knightmare whistled. "That's a tall order, pretty lady. Defense networks alone are tough game, but via satellite is tougher still. Their sat systems have multilevel encryption systems designed to kick out the genuinely curious such as myself from pursuing truth and freedom wherever our cyber circuits take us."

"Very poetic. Can you or can't you help?" Annja asked.

He grinned. "I take it time is of the essence?"

"Yep."

"Can do, then. Gimme a sec."

Annja watched him rummage through some file cabinets near his desk. He pulled out a number of CDs and started flipping through them. "I've really got to start labeling my software," he said absently.

"Knight, I'm not sure how long I have this phone for. I didn't exactly ask to borrow it."

He nodded and slipped a CD into the computer. "Okay, what's the network protocol?"

"Uh…"

He sighed. "Annja, you're making this tougher than it has to be."

"I don't know what the protocol is. I'm on a classified government operation here. They don't exactly broadcast it, you know?"

"Fine, fine, where are you, then?"

"Horlick Mountain."

"Hang on, I have to find out the latitude and longitude and then overlay that with the geosynchronous orbits of all known defense satellites." He spent a few seconds typing something into the computer. "Okay, got it. Let's see, Navstar 5."

"Did you say Navstar?"

"Yeah."

Annja frowned. "Okay. Keep going."

Knight kept typing. His fingers seemed to fly over the keys, and his eyes never left the screen. It felt weird seeing him look at the computer with such intensity. He wasn't even looking at Annja, but it felt as if he was.

"Hang on, I have to route this through a number of cutouts so they can't trace it back to me. If they do, I'm screwed. My dad said he'd take my computer away."

"Not that," Annja said.

"Yeah, I'd be forced to hack through my PSP instead and that's no fun." He kept typing, rambling off a string of cities as he did so. "Rio, Dubai, Tokyo, Manila, Johannesburg, Stockholm, back to Capetown, over to Mumbai and then back to Wellington. That last one should give them pause." He chuckled and kept typing.

"How you doing?" Annja asked. At any moment, she figured Dave would definitely come through the door and see her on his sat phone. Then she'd have a lot of explaining to do.

"Hang on, I'm picking up the stream of communications now. This will give me the information I need to tap into it. It should be small. How many computers have you seen where you are?"

"Maybe five or six."

"So they can't have a lot of traffic flowing back and forth. That helps me narrow it down." He continued typing. "Okay, I think I've got it. Stand by."

Annja heard him clicking the keys and then saw the broad smile splash across his face. "I'm in."

"You can get into the computers?" Annja asked.

"No, I just hooked on to their network. Cracking the security will take me a little longer. But at least I've got access. You proud of me or what?"

"Excessively," Annja said. "But I need access to one particular computer terminal."

"Is it on the network?"

"I think so, yes. One of the people I spoke to said that he sent traffic and e-mails over to that terminal."

"Good, that means I can piggyback onto it." Knightmare continued typing. "You know where it would be?"

"Well, it wasn't grouped with the other five computers, if that's what you're asking."

He frowned. "Lemme try something…"

Annja glanced at the door. She needed to hurry this along or Dave would find out. And since she wasn't yet sure if he was entirely trustworthy, she didn't want him to know what was going on.

"Got it."

Annja looked up. "You found the computer?"

"Yep. Registered to a Colonel Thomson. Next time tell me, okay? That would have cut down on my time by like thirty seconds."

"Sorry."

"What do you need to know?"

"You're into his computer?"

"Working on it, Annja. I'm not Superman, you know." He typed a few more keys. "Looks like he's got a nice long alphanumeric string here. Time for me to step aside and let the Icebreaker do his thing."

"Icebreaker?"

"Little program I wrote some time back. It can crunch numbers and letters roughly ten thousand times faster than I can. In a single minute it can sometimes break a computer code. Cool, huh?"

"Very," Annja admitted.

Knightmare slapped a new CD into the computer. "Hold on just a second…"

Annja looked at the door. Did someone just walk by outside? She thought she could see a shadow in the light silhouetted against the wall of the shelter. Was it Dave? Or maybe Garin?

"Knight, any luck on that?" she asked urgently.

"I need another minute, Annja. I'm going as fast as I can."

"Go faster. My cover might be blown here at any second."

"Your cover?"

Annja sighed. "You know what I mean."

"Someone's been watching too many spy movies."

"Yeah," Annja said. "That's exactly right."

"Hold on, I think I got something."

Annja leaned closer to the computer, as if she wanted to be right there looking over Knight's shoulder as he read his screen.

"Yep, I think I've got it. I'm in his hard drive."

Annja rubbed her hands together. "I need a certain file."

"Which one, there are a lot of them here…looks like the colonel likes his pornography, too."

Annja shook her head. "I don't need that."

"What's the name of the file?"

She could hear laughing now. Someone was outside her shelter. "Look for something labeled something like Laboratory Report or something similar."

"Hang on."

The walls of the shelter kept the noise to a minimum and it was difficult trying to figure out if the voices she heard were of Dave and someone else talking or not. She couldn't afford to take the risk. She might need to use the sat phone again.

"Look, Knight, I need that file."

"There's nothing here, Annja. No files like that one."

"Nothing?"

"No."

"Can you send me any documents on the hard drive?"

Knight looked at her. "Well, yeah, but you're on a dial-up connection, right? It would take a while."

"Send me anything from the past week or so."

Knightmare typed a few keys. "That's much better. Just three files. I'm sending them to you now."

Annja hit Refresh and then after another grueling minute, saw her green light flash. She had mail.

"I think that's it, Annja. I've got to get off the line now. They've detected me on the system."

"They have?" Annja asked, alarmed.

"Yeah, be careful. There's a chance they could work it back to you if they know you've got a sat phone."

"They don't."

"Be careful anyway. I'm out."

Annja's screen went dark and she quickly unplugged the sat phone and put it back in Dave's backpack. She rushed back to her bed and sat down with her laptop as the door to the shelter opened and Dave walked in.

"Hey."

Annja looked up and smiled. "Hey yourself."

"Any luck with Thomson?"

Annja shook her head. "Nah, he wasn't in so I just left and came back here. I wanted to jot down a few ideas I had in my journal. Nothing too elaborate, but you know…"

Dave came closer to her. "Listen, sorry about how Zach and I got all over you at the cafeteria."

"It's all right."

He shook his head. "No, it's not. You've obviously got some thoughts on this and we didn't respect them. I'm sorry for my part and I hope you weren't too offended."

Annja smiled. "Thanks. I appreciate it."

Dave nodded. "You coming to the dig site? I was just on my way down there when I thought I'd stop by and see if you were here."

Annja glanced at her laptop. She wanted to read that file now. Badly.

But staying might look suspicious. Instead, she closed her laptop and smiled. "Yeah, I'm coming. Just let me get my stuff."

25

Dave and Annja walked through the wind toward the dig site. Dave kept his head down, trying to ward off the cold as much as possible. Annja followed in his wake, using his larger body as a shield.

When they reached the entrance, Dave held the door and Annja ducked inside. The warm air greeted them and she breathed easier now that they were out of the cold. "All this exposure to extremes of temperature can't be good for my health," Annja said. "Anyone ever do any research to see how that affects the human body?"

Dave shrugged. "I don't know. But I'd rather be warm than cold."

Annja smiled. "At this point, I think that's a rather foregone conclusion. Don't you?"

"Well, maybe." Dave pointed at the entrance to the caverns. "You going down?"

"Yeah." Annja showed her identification to the armed guards and then led the way down the sloping walkway to the tunnel. As she walked, she was aware of Dave behind her. He wasn't saying anything.

"You okay?" she asked.

"Huh? Yeah, fine. I was just thinking about something, that's all."

"What about?" Annja asked. "It's weird not hearing much of anything down here. It's like we could get lost and scream and no one would hear us."

"We are basically inside a mountain, if you think about it," Dave said. "Surrounded on all sides by rock and dirt. All that weight above and below us, pushing in on all sides like some giant vise."

Annja glanced back at him. "Are you trying to make me claustrophobic?"

"Is it working?"

Annja shook her head. "Remind me to tell you about the time I was locked in a coffin for several hours."

"Underground?"

"No, in a funeral home. But the effect was the same. I had to make peace with being in that tight spot. And those caskets are remarkably airtight. I barely made it out of there alive."

Dave chuckled. "That must have been one for the journal."

"The what?"

"Journal. What you were working on when I came back to the shelter."

Annja nodded quickly, "Well, yeah, it would have been, but I wasn't keeping a journal back then. That's only something I took up recently when my life started taking strange twists and turns that even I can't figure out."

"Like coming down to the bottom of the world?"

"Exactly."

Dave smiled and Annja turned back around. "What about you? Do you ever write things down?"

"Never."

"So secretive, huh?" Annja laughed. "Got all sorts of things no one should ever know about rattling around in your head?"

"Something like that. Turn here," Dave said.

Annja turned at the fork in the tunnel. Far off, she could hear the telltale clangs of shovels sinking into dirt, followed by the sound of dirt being thrown into piles. "Is Zach already down here?"

"Yeah. He said he was going straight from breakfast."

"Cool." Annja kept walking. Ahead of her she could see more light coming from stationary lamps set up at the dig site. She heard voices, as well.

When she walked through the cavern opening, she was surprised to see Colonel Thomson standing there. Garin stood nearby. Zach was in one of the holes still working his shovel furiously. Dirt and grime stained his face and his coveralls.

Colonel Thomson looked up. "Hello, Miss Creed. Nice of you to come on down at last."

"Sorry, I had to finish up a few things in my shelter."

"Oh?"

"Just some notes."

Colonel Thomson smiled. "I believe you know Major Braden?"

Annja looked at Garin and smiled. He nodded back. Thomson kept speaking. "So Zachary here tells me that you're a bit obsessed with the laboratory analysis report regarding the necklace."

"I wouldn't say I'm obsessed with it," Annja protested.

"But you think there might be something valuable to be gleaned from it, if you were allowed access to it," he said.

"I think so, yes."

Thomson smiled. "Well, I'm afraid you're not allowed to see that report. You see, it's classified. There are other things going on here besides your scientific study of this area and the dig for various artifacts."

"Such as?"

"Such as I'm not going to get into it with you at the

moment. Surely, you can appreciate the need for the strictest confidence in this regard," he said.

Annja frowned. "To some extent, yes. But it seems like the security of this place is stifling the search for the truth."

"It's doing no such thing," the colonel stated.

"Isn't it? That report might shed some light on where these relics come from. We can't fathom them being created here on Earth around the time the carbon dating stamp supposedly says they were made. Nor is the metal alloy apparently something that was created here. But all of that is secondhand information. You told the scientists that, rather than letting them see the report."

Thomson's expression darkened. "It seems to me that you might be implying that I lied about the analysis results," he said angrily.

"I'm not implying that. I'm merely pointing out how strange it seems that we wouldn't be allowed to see it," Annja said.

"I'm sure there are lots of things you haven't been privy to in the past, Miss Creed. Another report shouldn't make that much of a difference to you, should it?"

Annja glanced at Garin, who kept his eyes focused on the wall of the cavern. "It shouldn't, no. But it does. I want to know what I'm dealing with here. What we're dealing with. And not having all of the information makes it that much harder to come to a conclusion about this. Which is, I thought, why I'm down here in the first place," she said.

"You're down here," Thomson said, "because Zachary here wanted you with him. He said your expertise would be invaluable to the project."

"My expertise is in researching and knowledge of ancient cultures and texts and relics. Anyone can dig big holes in the side of a mountain. If you're not happy with my presence here, then you can always send me back home."

Thomson shook his head. "I wish it were that easy. But it's not. As you know, the winter is closing in on us."

"So call the flyboys back."

"The weather is far too dangerous for them to make the run again like they did a few days back to drop you off. If they flew in now, there's a very good chance we'd lose the entire plane and crew. We can't take those odds."

"I could go by ship, then," Annja said.

"Again, the winter is against you here. Ice packs are already threatening to close off the harbor port. We'll have to wait it out, I'm afraid."

Annja put her hands in her pockets. "So, what—we come to terms about how you're best able to use me?"

"If you stop pestering me about the report."

"Without that report," Annja said, "I won't be able to tell you what I think. I won't be able to give you my best informed decision about what these relics could possibly be."

Colonel Thomson looked at her and then smiled. "And yet, somehow, I think at the end of this we'll have a much better idea of where we stand."

"If you say so."

"Oh, I do, Miss Creed. Very definitely."

Annja looked again at Garin, but the man's face seemed utterly impassive. What's his place in all of this? Annja wondered once again. And why is he mixed up with Thomson? It didn't make sense.

"Well, we'll leave you to your work." Thomson looked at Garin. "Major."

Garin followed him out of the cavern, leaving Annja, Dave and Zach there by themselves.

Dave eyed Annja. "What was that all about?"

"I guess he doesn't want me to look for the report."

"Were you?"

"Was I what?"

"Looking for it?"

Annja sighed. "Dave, I did what you guys suggested I do. I went to his admin shelter, spoke to the soldier there about getting the report and he told me to take it up with Thomson himself. I went to his private shelter and he wasn't there so I went back to our shelter, and that's where you found me."

Dave nodded. "Okay."

Zach wiped his brow. "You guys didn't happen to bring any water with you, did you? I'm parched."

"I can get some," Dave said. "Be right back."

Annja watched him leave. Then she turned back to Zach. "How are you holding up?"

"Huh? I'm fine. Why?"

"Just wondering."

Zach stopped shoveling. "Annja, is everything all right with you? You seem further and further away every time I look at you. I'm worried."

Annja took a deep breath. "I'm concerned about what we're doing here. Things don't seem…right. And I can't get any answers from people. And no one seems willing to talk straight about what is up here."

"You heard the colonel, it's classified."

"Yeah, yeah, classified. Whatever. You and I aren't soldiers, Zach. We're scientists. And as such, our priority is the search for the truth."

Zach frowned. "Actually, Annja, my number-one priority right now is that paycheck I've been promised. I need that money to take care of my obligations and my children. As far as I'm concerned, the truth is going to have to take a backseat on this one."

Annja nodded. "I understand. Really, I do. But I can't begin to figure out how this is all fitting together."

"Maybe you're not supposed to figure it out. Maybe it's

supposed to be one big hodgepodge of junk that doesn't have a rational explanation."

"I hate that," Annja said.

Zach put his shovel down. "But don't you see? How many people go through life thinking they're going to figure out all the deepest, darkest mysteries? Probably a lot, right?"

"Yeah."

"But does anyone ever really do that? Is there really any rhyme or reason to why we're here? I haven't seen it yet. To me, life is just a series of random equations and variables. We were the end result of one of those equations. But trying to spend your time matching us up with other equations and theorems, it just doesn't work. It eats you up inside. In the end, we're all dead, anyway."

"So you think I should just live my life one day at a time?"

Zach sighed. "There's a lot to be said for that, Annja. Let me tell you. God knows, it's been my mantra recently what with all the divorce bullshit, kids being taken from me and my creditors lining up to eat me alive. One day at a time is about all I can handle."

Annja slid into the hole at the far corner, stripped her parka off and picked up her shovel. "Yeah, well, I'm not so sure I can follow that philosophy myself, but for your sake at least, I'll give it a try."

"Really?"

Annja smirked. "Well, for at least the next five minutes."

"Fair enough," Zach said.

Dave came back into the cavern and handed them each a bottle of water. "I miss anything while I was gone?"

Zach took a long pull on his water and shook his head. "Annja is thinking about trying a new approach to life."

Dave smiled. "Really?"

Annja waved him off. "It's temporary. I don't know how good I'd be at it, anyway."

"Yeah, well, apparently you made quite the impression on the colonel with your impassioned speech."

Annja put her water down. "Excuse me?"

"I just ran into him back up by the entrance. He asked me to tell you to report to his shelter later on when we're done here. Says he's got some things to talk over with you."

Annja raised her eyebrows and then took another sip of the water. "Well, perhaps there's something to be said for being a stubborn pain in the ass, after all, huh, Zach?"

"If he gives you the report, then I'll concede defeat." Zach wiped his face. "Until then, get back to digging, okay?"

26

Annja spent the next several hours digging her way through piles of dirt and rock. She found nothing for her efforts except chunks of coal, pyrite and granite. Gradually, the pile of dirt she dug out of the hole grew larger than most of the cavern.

Twice, she had tried to use her inner sense to see if she could detect the presence of more relics. Each time, the conclusion had been the same—nothing.

As far as she was concerned, this was becoming more and more of a ghost chase than an actual scientific exploration. She hadn't seen any more of the rest of the scientists, either, which struck her as equally odd. When she mentioned this fact to Zach and Dave, neither of them seemed particularly interested.

Finally, after another lunch of MREs, and another hour of digging, Annja decided to call it a day. "I need to go and get cleaned up before I see Thomson," she said.

Dave smirked. "Make sure you wear your Sunday best."

"Oh, and some perfume," Zach said. "I'm sure that will help your cause. Guy's a sucker for a hot chick."

Annja smirked. "I'm not trying to seduce him."

Dave held up his hand. "You want the report, right?"

"Of course."

"Well, all negotiations are a seduction. I recently read a book about it, and the author made a great case for using seductive strategies for getting your way in negotiations. Great read."

"Thanks for the tip. I'll be sure to remember that later when I'm putting on my thermal lace underwear," Annja said, laughing.

Zach shook his head. "Hey, I'm trying to work here. Don't go carbonizing my hormones with images of that stuff, okay?"

"Sorry." Annja waved goodbye. "See you guys at dinner."

She walked back up the slope toward the entrance of the dig site. As she walked, she listened to the sounds of Dave and Zach resuming their digging. She glanced back and smiled. At least she was out of there.

Parts of this dig made her feel as if she was involved in slave labor. Colonel Thomson had basically told her that they were trapped there for the winter and that digging for more relics was on the agenda every day.

That seemed vaguely fanatical to Annja. She was convinced there weren't any more to be found. And she was intensely curious as to whether the ones already found were of any special importance, anyway.

At the tunnel fork, she started heading back toward the surface, but then stopped. What was down the other fork? She realized she'd never seen anyone venture down there.

Annja paused and took a step toward the other branch. Could she hear something farther down? Were the other members of the research team digging down there at another site? Were there other relics down there? And if so, why were Dave, Zach and Annja wasting their time back at the other cavern?

Or was it something else entirely? Perhaps, as Colonel Thomson had said, there was more going on here than Annja was allowed to know about. The problem was, she wanted to know about it.

All of it.

Annja took another step down the tunnel and then kept walking. They hadn't strung lights along the roof of the tunnel as they had on the other side. Was there a reason why they kept this place in the dark?

Annja felt her way along, making sure she lifted her feet and didn't trip. The more quietly she moved, the better chance she had of actually seeing what might be going on down here.

She walked another thirty yards before she started hearing ambient noises. But unlike the sound of shovels, there was nothing loud about the noise down here. Everything came in small pops and pings.

Annja could see better now as some light spilled out of what must have been another large cavern.

She crept around the corner and then her eyes blinked in the sudden light. In front of her, she could see the other members of the research team. Each of them worked in a section of the cavern. Annja could see a wall of rock in front of them. In key places, small cylindrical holes had been bored deep into the rock.

Boring? Were they looking for oil?

Annja frowned. The little she knew about the oil industry, they usually drilled down, not horizontally into rock.

What was going on here?

She watched as another member of the team finished clearing out the holes, using a long pole to determine the depth of the hole. He seemed satisfied, got up and walked across the cavern to a metallic footlocker.

Annja frowned. The scientist reached into the footlocker and removed something. Annja watched him walk back to the hole he'd just finished and slide something down inside it.

When the scientist ran wires back out of the hole, she knew what was happening.

Blasting.

They were getting ready to demolish a whole section of the mountain. But if they did that, then wouldn't the section where Zach and Dave were working cave in?

Annja looked at the rest of the research team members. Each one of them seemed to have been assigned a different section of this particular cavern. And each one had his own hole to bore out, and then plug with explosives. Once that was done, they ran the wires back out of the hole.

Annja assumed they would all run to a master detonator switch. Once they were properly wired, they could run the wire back out of the dig site and explode the charges. Horlick Mountain might just fall apart at that point.

But why? Did they have information that they needed to blow up this part of the mountain to reach something more valuable? Were there other relics? Maybe there was an entire spaceship hidden in the mountain.

Annja smirked. Yeah, right, you're letting your imagination run wild.

Whatever was happening, this was far too dangerous not to let Zach and Dave know about it. They might be killed if those charges went off unexpectedly.

Why hadn't they been told? Why had Colonel Thomson been content to let them continue digging if he knew another team was getting ready to blow up the mountain?

Annja took a calming breath. Hang on a second, she thought, maybe the charges aren't all that big. Maybe they're doing a controlled explosion to open up part of that cavern. After all, she'd seen it was a rock face they were boring into. Maybe they were stymied by the rock and needed to get through it.

Still, Dave and Zach had to be warned. Any type of blasting could be extremely dangerous. Especially in an environment like this.

She moved back down the tunnel toward the fork. If she told Dave and Zach and it turned out they knew about it, then all was well and good. But if they had known about it, why hadn't they mentioned it to her?

She frowned. Maybe they hadn't wanted to give her something else to think about. They thought Annja had been acting a little weird about the whole report thing.

She still had to get back to her shelter and read it over. At least she didn't have to rely on Thomson for access to it when Knightmare had come through in spades for her.

She returned to the fork. The cavern behind her seemed far away and as she walked, she realized it might be possible to do a controlled blast without damage to the other cavern.

But her instincts told her that the situation was very dangerous.

Suddenly she had the sensation of tripping and falling through the dark space of the tunnel. She seemed to almost float in space as she went almost horizontal.

And then she fell.

Hard.

She put her hands out in front of her, hoping to brace herself as she made impact with the ground, but part of her hand caught on an outcropping while the other scraped the ground. She landed awkwardly and her head snapped forward, smacking her forehead against the rocky ground.

Annja moaned. The blow to her head had been square on and she felt darkness rushing at her as she lost consciousness.

THERE WERE SOUNDS from far off in the distance. But they were muted by the indescribable throbbing pain echoing through her skull. Annja raised a hand to her head and moaned.

"Ugh."

"Well, well, look who decided to come back to the land of the living."

Annja opened her eyes and instantly regretted it. The light was bright and it hurt her head. "Lights," she groaned.

"Huh? Oh, sorry about that."

She felt the lights dim and then opened her eyes again. She was in her shelter and there was a bandage around her head. "What happened to me?"

Zach's face swam into view. "You took a header in the tunnel. Smacked yourself right unconscious by the way the doctors tell it. They said it would have been like taking a straight shot from a heavyweight boxer at close range."

Annja felt as if her stomach were rolling on a stormy ocean and she tried to swallow to settle it.

"Nauseous?" Zach asked.

"Yeah. Bad."

He nodded. "They said that would be the end result. It should pass pretty soon. They want you to rest, but I told them that there was no way you'd do that." He frowned. "You want to tell me what happened?"

Annja looked at him. "Do you know about the other cavern?"

"Where the other part of the team is? Sure."

"You know what they're doing down there?"

Zach smiled. "I've been kind of busy in our little rat hole. I've heard a few things, but nothing much. Why?"

"I saw them, Zach. They were boring holes and putting explosives into them. I think they want to blow up the mountain."

Zach smiled. "I heard they ran into a serious problem with the granite. One of them requested permission to blow an entrance. Apparently, they've got some type of scanning equipment that tells them there's a cavern on the other side of that wall. They want to get through."

"But isn't it dangerous?" Annja asked.

"Well, sure, they're explosives, after all. But it's being controlled. The colonel has some of his guys helping out."

Annja took a deep breath. Everything hurt. She was sure she'd hurt other parts of her body, as well as her head. "When are they blasting?"

"Tomorrow morning, first thing. Before anyone goes down."

"Oh."

Zach smiled. "Let me guess—you thought it was some grand conspiracy that would end up killing Dave and me?"

Annja smiled weakly. "Guilty."

Zach sighed. "When did you get so conspiracy crazy? I don't think I've ever seen you like this. It's kind of weird."

Annja frowned. "Let's just say that I've run into a lot of people lately who haven't been what they say they are."

"Everyone has secrets," Zach said. "That doesn't make them assassins or spooks or some shadowy government outfit bent on world domination."

Annja nodded. "You're right. I've been off base."

Zach smirked. "Tomorrow should be a good day. Once that blasting is done, we might get a glimpse at something new and exciting. I'm looking forward to it."

Annja nodded. "Okay."

"Look, I'm going to get some grub. You want me to bring you back something? I hear it's lasagna night."

Annja held up her hand. "Not sure I could stomach it right now. But thanks."

"Okay. Dave and I will be back later." He stood and walked to the door. "Get some rest, okay? I'll let the colonel know you're okay."

"Why?"

"He seemed concerned about you earlier when he heard about your fall. Guess he respects you a little bit more after your back-and-forth earlier. I get the feeling he might just show you that report, after all."

"Even without the perfume?" Annja smiled.

"Yeah, even without. Talk to you in a little while." Zach disappeared outside.

Annja watched him go. Her head throbbed. After all of this, she thought, and I nearly end up killing myself before I could figure this out. She sighed and closed her eyes.

There'd be time to deal with Thomson in the morning.

27

"You're quite certain?"

The sergeant nodded. "We got confirmation midafternoon today of the security compromise."

Colonel Thomson frowned. "And you're certain it involved our communications network?"

"Without a doubt, sir. The initial hacker intrusion occurred on our Navstar satellite, which, as you know, is in a geosynchronous orbit that takes it into our area of operations throughout the day, except for the blackout periods."

Thomson nodded. "How on earth did a hacker know we were even operating down here? It's not like we advertised our presence."

The sergeant shook his head. "I don't know, sir. It could have come from another source when we moved through McMurdo. That's the problem with having to filter through there. There are a lot of people around and one of them might have mentioned our presence to someone else who then took it upon themselves to hack into the system."

"But it's not that easy, is it?" the colonel asked.

The sergeant shrugged. "Sir, nowadays these kids can type a few words into a search engine and come up with our satellite networks, corresponding protocols and all that stuff. Frankly, I'm surprised it didn't happen sooner."

Thomson glanced at Garin. "Major, what do you make of all of this stuff? Is it a serious compromise? Should I be concerned?"

Garin shrugged. "I'm not sure yet, sir. I think we need to ascertain the extent of the compromise before we start passing judgments."

"Agreed," Thomson said. He looked back at the sergeant. "So where did the hacker tap into us from?"

The sergeant looked uncomfortable. "Well, that's the problem, sir."

"Don't tell me there's a problem."

"I'm sorry, sir, but they used a sophisticated routing program that led our intercept teams all over the world. Mumbai, Tokyo, Wellington even."

"Wellington? You think it could be a compromise coming from New Zealand?" The colonel frowned. "If that's the case, it would make for a very bad diplomatic situation."

The sergeant shook his head. "I don't know that I believe it did come from New Zealand, sir. I think the hacker just wanted to make it look that way. But he wasn't on the line long enough for us to do a trace. He must have known we started the intercept program and at that point, he simply disconnected."

Thomson threw his hands in the air. "Great. Just great. So how in the hell am I supposed to accurately judge whether or not this installation is under some sort of threat or if our information has been pilfered?"

The sergeant handed him a sheet of paper. "We were able to figure out what the hacker was after, sir."

Thomson snatched the paper and started reading. After a

moment, he glanced at the sergeant. "You're dismissed. Good work."

"Thank you, sir." The sergeant turned and left the shelter.

Thomson watched him go and then handed the sheet of paper to Garin. "Well, Major, what do you think of this?"

Garin read the report and his eyes gleamed. "I would say that it seems like someone has gone through an awful lot of trouble to acquire some of your files."

"One in particular," the colonel said.

"Yes, sir."

Thomson nodded. "Very well. If that's how this is going to play out, at least I know who I'm dealing with now."

"We don't know for a fact it was Miss Creed, sir."

"No, we don't. But I myself have never trusted coincidences. To me, there are none. Just indicators that behavioral patterns are being adhered to."

"We should have some more proof before we accuse her, sir. Otherwise she will make it something of a rallying cry and possibly damage your work here," Garin said.

The colonel nodded. "Then we'll need to find some proof, won't we?"

"How, sir?"

"I have some thoughts on that matter. I must admit I'm a bit surprised she pursued it like this."

"She's very resourceful, sir," Garin said. "And she doesn't seem like the kind of woman to take no for an answer."

"Apparently not," the colonel muttered. He glanced at his watch. "She should be asleep right now, no doubt sleeping off that mild concussion she acquired earlier this afternoon."

"You want me to go and get her?"

Thomson shook his head. "Not just yet. I want her awake and alert when she has to answer questions."

"Very good."

"However, I do want to talk to my administrative aide. Bring him to me, would you?"

Garin nodded and left the shelter. Thomson looked down at the paper and saw the name of the file that had been liberated from his computer. It had to be her, he thought. Who else would want something like that? Annja Creed had been asking for the report for the past day or so and suddenly the computers were hacked and that exact file copied from his hard drive and presumably accessed.

No, coincidences didn't exist except as a convenient excuse for people who weren't willing to face facts. Thomson had a mole in his camp and he aimed to get rid of her through any means necessary.

In the morning, he would see exactly what Annja Creed had to say about the hacker intrusion and subsequent file copying.

The door to his shelter reopened and Garin walked in behind a nervous-looking soldier. The corporal marched to the front of the colonel's desk and stood at attention.

"Sir."

"Stand at ease, Corporal," Thomson said.

Garin cleared his throat. "You want me to go now, sir?"

The colonel shook his head. "No, actually, I want you to stay and listen to this so we can plan our next move better." He eyed the corporal. "Do you know why you're here, son?"

"No, sir."

"Earlier today this base experienced what can best be described as a hacker intrusion into our secure communication networks. Specifically, our computers were hacked. Mine in particular."

The corporal looked shocked. "How is that possible, sir?"

"Well, now, that's what we want to know. And that's why you're here, son. We've got a few questions for you, and you just be yourself and answer them honestly and I don't think we'll have any trouble. Understand?"

"Yes, sir."

The colonel nodded. "Excellent. Now, where were you this morning?"

"After I ate breakfast I reported to work right away. I was sitting in the admin shelter, sir. I had some reports to file and some routine maintenance work to perform, but otherwise, the day was pretty boring, frankly, sir."

Thomson glanced at Garin, who was looking at the corporal. "And did you do anything out of the ordinary while you were there?"

"No, sir."

"What about visitors?" Garin asked.

The colonel nodded. "Yes, did anyone stop by to say hello? Any of your friends who were on duty at the same time?"

The corporal shrugged. "I don't have any friends, sir. I only just joined the outfit and haven't had much of a chance to meet folks yet."

Thomson smiled. "Well, I'm sure you'll fit in here just fine, son. Eventually people will get to know you."

"Visitors?" Garin repeated.

"Just one, sir."

"Annja Creed?"

The corporal nodded. "Yes, sir. She stopped by looking for you, sir."

"Me?" The colonel smiled. "And what did she want with me?"

"Said she needed to talk to you about something. I told her you might be at your shelter and that she could look in on you there."

Thomson nodded. "Very good, son. Did she ask about anything else?"

The corporal frowned. "Well, funny thing was when I got there, she was already there and she'd tried to get on one of the computer terminals. Said she was going to check her e-mail."

"E-mail?"

The corporal nodded. "She said she was lonely and hadn't heard from anyone back home in some time. I told her she wouldn't be able to access e-mail while she was here because of our strict comms guidelines and all."

"Did she understand that?"

"Oh, yeah, she took it real well. Seemed concerned that if word got out she was trying to access e-mail on the computers, that she might get in trouble."

"Really." Thomson frowned. "And after that, you said you sent her to see me at my shelter?"

"Yes, sir. I don't know if she ever went there or not, of course, because by that time I was already back working on what I needed to be working on."

Thomson nodded. "Of course you were. That's why I brought you in here—because I know what a hard worker you are."

"Was that the only visitor you had this morning?" Garin asked.

The corporal looked at him. "Aside from Miss Creed, there was just you, sir."

Thomson glanced at Garin. "You, Major?"

Garin smiled. "I stopped by to see if you were there. Remember, we were supposed to go down to the dig site together, which we eventually did, once I found you."

"Yes, of course." Thomson looked at the young soldier. "All right, Corporal, you can go now. But make sure you don't tell anyone about this. What we've shared with you here is classified information and we don't need anyone finding out about it just yet. When the time comes to make judgments, then everyone can know. But for now…"

"I understand, sir."

The corporal turned and marched out of the shelter. Thomson looked at Garin. "So?"

Garin shrugged. "Seems like a few more dots got connected, sir. It's not conclusive, by any means, but it's leaning in that direction."

Thomson nodded. "I want more, Major. Find out from the communications people if there have been any calls made from this camp to the outside world."

"Phone calls, sir? I wasn't aware there was cell-phone coverage in this region."

"There isn't. But if someone has a sat phone, they can call out. And if they can call out of here, they can also access the Internet. And that might just lead us to our hacker."

Garin smiled. "I'll get started on it right away, sir." He turned to leave.

"Major?"

Garin turned. "Sir?"

"Find me something conclusive about this matter. I don't want to drag her in here tomorrow unless we're absolutely sure that she was behind the intrusion. The last thing any of us needs is bad publicity. For that matter, any publicity."

"I understand, sir."

Thomson watched him leave and then leaned back in his seat. The piece of paper on his desk lay there with the file name written in bold letters. How in the world could someone from across the world reach out and get access to the most secure communications networks the United States government could field?

It seemed impossible. And Thomson wasn't happy about the idea that a complete nobody could penetrate the secrecy of this mission. Given what was going on, he needed an absolute quarantine on all communications unless he approved them.

Yes, that was the answer.

He got up and pulled on his parka and hood before heading out into the snowy night. The wind stung his cheeks and he trudged toward the admin shelter. At the entrance, he pulled the door open and stomped inside.

The young corporal was still there, typing up a report. He snapped to attention until Colonel Thomson put him at ease.

"I need you to do something for me, Corporal."

"Yes, sir?"

"Because of the communications breach earlier today, I'm suspending any communications out of the camp unless they are routed through me first."

"Sir?"

"Yes, Corporal, you're understanding me correctly. We're going dark."

28

Annja's head felt a lot better when she woke up the next morning. Concussions, she'd found, were never the same twice. And after more than her share of them, she was of the opinion that enduring them was probably the least favorite aspect of her life. Sitting up, Annja was prepared for the head rush, but had none. She smiled. Maybe her head was getting harder after all the knocks it had taken.

She glanced around the shelter, but Dave and Zach were still snoozing away in the dawn darkness.

Annja rolled out of bed and checked herself over. She felt a little weak, but chalked that up to the fact that she hadn't had much to eat in the past twenty-four hours. Plus, she suspected she was a little dehydrated from the low humidity in the region. She needed to get herself topped off with food and drink and then she'd be able to face the day.

She dressed quickly and wandered over to the mess hall. The cook was alone behind the counter and smiled as she came in. "What can I get you?"

Annja looked around. No one else was up yet apparently. "Am I the first one here?"

"Early bird catches the worm." He grinned. "I hear there were some serious talks going on last night into the wee hours. Probably folks are sleeping in a few extra minutes."

Annja nodded. "Can I get a ham-and-cheese omelet?"

"Sure thing. It's powdered eggs, though. We're out of fresh until we get a resupply."

"That's fine." Annja leaned against the makeshift counter. "How often do you get resupplied?"

"Well, up until the winter started, I would have said every week. But seeing how we only just arrived a few short days ago and the weather's already making it tough on us, I'd say we have about two more days on what we've got before we have to pack up and move on back to McMurdo."

"Two days?" Annja couldn't believe it.

"Uh-huh." He stirred the powdered eggs with water and then whisked the mix in a bowl before pouring it into a hot griddle. "You said ham and cheese, right?"

"Yes." Annja frowned. Two days wasn't a lot of time. "Will you all be bunking back in McMurdo until the weather clears, then?"

The cook shrugged. "Don't know. I'd imagine so, but you never can tell with the colonel. He's got this way of planning things out so no one else knows what the deal is but him."

"Has he always been like that?"

"Again, I don't know. I've only been in this unit for a month or so, ever since the last guy put in to get his separation papers. He wanted to start his own restaurant, I think the colonel said. Anyway, he tapped me and said to come on over. He's a real food lover, the colonel is. It always makes it nicer to be cooking for someone who loves to eat."

"I'm sure it does," Annja said.

The cook slid a spatula under the cooking mix and then flipped it over before adding the chopped bit of ham and the strands of grated cheese to the egg. Then he carefully folded it in two, and let it cook a few minutes more.

"You don't have any orange juice, do you?" Annja asked.

"Only from concentrate. But it's the good stuff. Doesn't taste like freezer burn. It's over there. I just made a fresh batch a few minutes before you arrived."

Annja helped herself to a tall glass and poured the orange juice into it. The cook slid her omelet onto a plate and handed it over. "There you go. Enjoy it."

Annja smiled. "Thanks. I will."

He pointed. "Got some pastries over there on the table. Not bad for doing it myself, but they could use more work." He shrugged. "I have to make do with what I've got."

"I'll give them a try," Annja said. She headed over to the long table and sat down. When she bit into the omelet, it tasted exactly as if it had been made with fresh eggs. The cheese melted slowly in her mouth and with the ham produced a great swirl of flavors. Annja's mouth watered and she suddenly realized how hungry she was.

At least until Garin showed up.

Rather than walk over to the cook, he headed right for Annja's table. He sat down across from her and grinned. "Early breakfast for you today, huh?"

"In case you didn't hear, I had a rough day yesterday."

Garin nodded. "I did hear that, yeah. How's your head feeling today?"

Annja chewed another forkful of the omelet. "Pretty good, actually. Not a hundred percent, but then again you never should expect that the day after. Feels sort of like a mild hangover," she said.

Garin nodded. "Good."

Annja frowned. "You're up early."

"I don't sleep all that much unless I've had one of my flesh benders and the exertion lulls me into a dreamy world of post-lust headiness."

"Sometimes you're almost poetic with that stuff, you know that?" Annja said.

Garin leaned closer to Annja. "You're in trouble, sweetheart."

Annja leaned back. "First of all, don't call me sweetheart. I hate that. Secondly, why am I in trouble?"

Garin sighed. "It's not really the wisest thing you've ever done. I mean, did you honestly think they wouldn't find out?"

She knew he had to be talking about the hacker work Knightmare had done. Somehow they knew. Somehow they had traced it back to Annja. But how? Her mind raced at how they could know it was her.

"I don't know what you're talking about, Garin. And you're interrupting a perfectly good breakfast, I might add."

He laughed. "Thomson wants you hauled in for questioning. He seems mighty upset that someone actually hacked his computer, of all the ones here, and managed to get access to a specific file."

Annja looked him right in the eyes. "How in the world could I possibly manage to pull off something like that? I'm sitting here just like you. I don't have access to the Internet. I don't have e-mail. So how could I manage to do that?"

Garin shook his head. "I don't know. But you did. And it doesn't help your case that you were poking around in the admin shelter yesterday. That kid reported you to the colonel."

"It was an innocent occurrence. I went looking to use one of the terminals. Besides, he wasn't supposed to say anything."

Garin laughed louder. "Who do you think that kid's more scared of, you or the colonel? Of course he sold you out. God, Annja, don't be so naive."

Annja frowned. Her omelet was getting cold, so she plucked another forkful into her mouth. If the day was going to be as challenging as Garin seemed to be implying, she would at least need a solid meal in her stomach if she hoped to weather all the questions Thomson would lob at her.

"So why are you telling me all of this?" Annja smirked. "I would have thought you'd be enjoying seeing me possibly get myself into hot water."

Garin shook his head. "Contrary to what you might believe about me, Annja, I'm not the enemy here. I'm simply trying to understand what's going on down here, just like you are."

"And what have you found out?"

"Nothing."

Annja sneered. "Come on. With all your high and mighty power you can't determine what's up? I find that a little hard to believe."

"Maybe I just don't trust you," Garin said.

Annja nodded. "Fair enough. I don't trust you much, either."

Garin leaned closer to her again. "So, then, why don't you come clean? Tell me about the hacker you hired to do your dirty work. Maybe we can use him again to crack the system. I've got a few questions I'd like answered myself."

Annja drank some of the orange juice. Was Garin really suggesting they team up and work together? She tried to remember the last time she'd done that and not ended up screwed in the process.

She couldn't remember any.

"There's nothing to tell, Garin. It wasn't me that hacked that computer. Maybe some lonely fourteen-year-old in Des Moines got lucky and tripped his way onto the network. You know there are kids out there that groove on that stuff."

"Adults, too."

"Yeah, but not this one," Annja said.

Garin smiled. "I've never known you to turn down an opportunity to learn something new even if means using a questionable method."

"I have standards. There are some things I won't do. Like torture people. I find that distasteful."

"No doubt," Garin said. "You've always had far more faith in humanity than I have."

"True," Annja said.

Annja finished her omelet and slid the plate away. "Are you going to get any of the food?"

"Was your omelet good?"

"Delicious, even with present company included."

Garin smirked. "Fair enough. I'll try it." He got up and wandered over to the cook. Annja watched him go and shook her head. Sure, she could always team up with him, but how smart was that? For all she knew, Garin had a wire on transmitting everything they spoke about. Hell, he'd sell her out faster than the kid in the admin shelter.

Annja got up and got herself a pastry. The icing was still warm and the sweetness of it made her mouth water even more. She was feeling, on the whole, pretty good physically.

Except for the ever-present ache in her gut.

Something bad was going to happen today. She knew this. Expected it. And it was all she could do to simply down a decent breakfast and get on with it.

Garin returned with his omelet and sat down. After two forkfuls, he nodded. "For the limits of this place, the cook does a very respectable job."

Annja smiled. "A compliment from you? I'm amazed."

"Well, it's not Maison Robert, certainly, but one must adapt one's standards given one's environment."

"Indeed."

Annja ate the pastry in silence, occasionally sipping her juice. Garin seemed preoccupied with his breakfast.

Annja felt very unsettled.

Garin glanced at her. "You feeling all right?"

Annja frowned. "My stomach hurts."

"Really?"

"Yeah."

Garin continued eating. Annja glanced around the mess hall. Everything seemed still. Quiet.

Too quiet.

Annja stopped eating her roll and put it down on her plate. Then she wiped her hands calmly on her napkin.

Garin watched her. "You're all finished?"

"I think so, yeah."

Annja leaned back in her seat and got her feet under her. She looked over at Garin, who had slowed down on his chewing. He was watching her closely.

Slowly, a smile spread across his face. "Your instincts really have become much more intense since you found the sword," he said quietly.

"The sword found me," Annja said. "And what are you playing at right now?"

"Me?"

Annja looked at the door. "Yeah, you."

Garin shook his head. "Can't be helped, Annja. It's too late to get out of this. Best to just go along with what happens and see where it takes you."

Annja glared at him. "You bastard. You sold me out."

"I did no such thing."

"You kept me here. You kept me from leaving—"

The door flew open and five armed men rushed in with their weapons drawn. Annja faced them. The automatic rifles would tear her apart if she tried to do anything at all.

Garin rose and wiped his mouth on a napkin while Annja stood still. He leaned over and whispered in her ear, "I had to do it."

Then he turned and addressed the men. "Take Miss Creed into custody. She's under military arrest for espionage."

29

"This is absolutely ridiculous."

Annja sat inside Thomson's personal shelter surrounded by two armed guards and facing the colonel himself. He'd said nothing for the past five minutes, ever since he had arrived shortly after Annja had been detained. Annja wondered where he was during that time, since it certainly seemed as if breakfast had been temporarily put on hold until Annja could be taken into custody.

The metal handcuffs she wore brought back painful memories of other times and places. None of which cheered her up. Trying to extricate herself from handcuffs was always a challenge.

Thomson stared at her hard. She could see no pupil dilation in his eyes and there wasn't a nervous facial tick to be seen anywhere. He was definitely used to exerting control over a situation and she suspected he didn't usually get very many people who defied him.

Finally, after another three minutes of no one saying anything, Annja cleared her throat. "I know this tactic, Colonel.

You're trying to make me uncomfortable. You're hoping that I will start babbling about something as a way of filling the silence."

He continued to stare at her.

She frowned. "The truth is, I'm already uncomfortable. Your soldiers applied these handcuffs a little too zealously. They're cutting off circulation to my hands, and if I don't get some relief soon, you'll have to cut them off because I'll have gotten gangrene."

She saw the colonel barely nod and then one of the soldiers moved behind her and removed the handcuffs. Annja rubbed her wrists. "Thank you. That's a huge improvement."

Thomson removed a pipe from his desk drawer, packed it with tobacco and then lit it. He puffed away for several seconds and then leaned back, chomping on the stem.

Annja coughed slightly. "I thought the military frowned on smoking."

"I'm grandfathered," the colonel said. "Something about you can't teach an old dog new tricks." He blew out a smoke ring and then fixed his eyes on Annja again. "We've got quite a situation here."

"I don't see it. I'm not guilty of the charges Major Braden accused me of. Espionage? You've got to be kidding me," Annja said.

"Nevertheless, we had an incident yesterday and the trail leads back to you, Miss Creed."

"What kind of incident?"

"I believe Major Braden already informed you about it. The hacker intrusion into our secure network system. Someone gained access illegally. They poked about in our computers and even gained access to a certain highly classified file."

The file that Annja hadn't been able to read yet. She cursed herself inwardly for tripping and knocking herself out. If she hadn't been so clumsy, she could have spent last evening reading it over and convincing Dave and Zach that there was really something odd going on here.

Instead, the colonel had her in a bind. But did he know she hadn't read it yet? Probably not. Annja knew she had to bide her time and hope that he would reveal how much he knew.

"What was in the file?" she asked.

The colonel smiled. "Why, Miss Creed, don't you know? It was the selfsame file that you've been obsessing over."

"Oh, the lab analysis?"

"Indeed."

Annja frowned. "I don't think *obsessing* is the right word in this case. Sure, I've been curious, but obsessing? That's not entirely accurate."

Colonel Thomson leaned forward. "Let me ask you a question."

"Shoot."

"Do you believe in coincidences?"

Annja shrugged. "Well, I don't know. I mean, there have been times in the past when things just sort of hooked up in time and space. No real rhyme or reason to it. Other times, it definitely seemed like it was a deliberate kind of thing, you know?"

"No. I don't know. What I do believe, however, is that there are no such things as coincidences. None at all."

"Don't you think that perspective is a bit…limiting?" Annja asked.

The colonel ignored her and continued. "So when a scientist like yourself comes around asking to see a classified file and is told that she won't be given access to it and then a little later on, a hacker infiltrates our supposedly secure system and goes right after that very file, I have to ask myself a question—are they connected?"

Annja tried to grin, but it felt forced. "The answer is no."

"Actually, the answer is yes. Most definitely, in fact."

Annja shook her head. "You've got no way of connecting

me to any hacker operating on his or her own in the outside world."

Thomson smoked his pipe. "You know, as a matter of fact, we do have a way of connecting you."

"And how might that be?" Annja asked.

"A phone call went out from this very camp yesterday, shortly before the hacker infiltrated our system."

"So what? You've got plenty of people with cell phones here, don't you?"

Thomson laughed. "Miss Creed, you don't expect me to believe that you're really stupid enough to suggest that a cell phone would work out in this remote wilderness, do you? I mean, come on now…"

Annja almost grinned again. "So how did they make the call?"

"A satellite phone."

"Ah, well, I don't have one of those," she said.

"Of course you don't. Your gear was searched. However, someone in this camp does have one."

"Don't a few people? I mean, in case of an emergency, I'd certainly want a way to reach out to some help."

"Satellite phones are banned in this camp," Thomson said. "They're compromising to our security."

"Really? I'm afraid I don't see how that would happen."

"A call made at the right time of day might give the enemy the chance to pinpoint our position. They could discover what it is we're up to down here and then threaten our security here."

Annja shrugged. "Well, what exactly are we up to down here and who is the enemy?" Annja asked.

"There's no *we* anymore, Miss Creed. You are no longer a member of the scientific research team assigned to this unit."

"Great. Send me on home, then," Annja said.

"We've already gone over that."

"Yeah, well, I thought I'd try again." Annja sighed. "So where's the big bad evidence you have that proves beyond a shadow of a doubt that I was responsible for yesterday's intrusion?"

Colonel Thomson looked beyond her to the soldiers standing behind Annja. "Bring it in."

One of the soldiers walked outside. Annja waited, her heart beating a little bit faster. Surely they wouldn't have found Dave's phone. Wasn't he one of them anyway?

Thomson continued staring at her through the smoky haze. He kept puffing on his pipe, generating more smoke and making Annja extremely uncomfortable. Her eyes hurt from the smoke.

The door reopened and Thomson looked up. "Did you get it?"

"Yes, sir."

The soldier walked over and handed Thomson a satellite phone. It was the exact model that she'd used yesterday to connect to the Internet. She couldn't tell if it was really Dave's, but it sure looked like it.

"This is the satellite phone you used to make a call to an Internet service provider yesterday morning."

"I've never seen that before in my life."

Thomson nodded. "We thought for sure you would say that, so we took the liberty of having it dusted for fingerprints."

"And?"

"We also took the liberty of taking your fingerprints last night while you slept that nasty concussion off."

Annja frowned. She thought her hands had smelled odd this morning. But she'd chalked it up as part of the medical evaluation she'd undergone as a result of her misfortune in the cave.

"Did you get a match?"

Thomson smiled. "A partial, actually."

Annja wanted to laugh at him. Of course they'd only gotten a partial. Annja had wrapped the sat phone back up the way Dave had hidden it. The friction would have destroyed much of her prints.

"Partials aren't enough to convict, Colonel. You're grasping at straws here and you know it," Annja said, hoping her bluff would work.

But the colonel seemed unfazed. And Annja's stomach continued to ache.

What does he have? she wondered. What does he have that he can use to pin this on me? Her laptop? Had they cracked her personal security codes?

She frowned. They had Dave's phone. And they might know about her laptop. Was Dave working with them, after all? Or was he something else entirely?

"Are you all right, Miss Creed?"

She glanced up. Thomson was looking at her with a renewed sense of interest.

"I'm fine."

"Forgive me for saying so, but you don't seem fine. In fact, I'd even go so far as to suggest you're feeling a bit nervous right now."

"Nonsense."

"Could it be that you're wondering what else we have to connect you with yesterday's crime?"

"I'm wondering how soon I can get out of here and go back to work."

"Ah, but I've already told you there will be no more work for you. You're off the team. Permanently."

Annja sighed. Zach was going to kill her.

"The time to come clean is now, Miss Creed. If you want to tell me everything about your conspiracy, I might be inclined to be more lenient on you than if you continue to cling to the notion that you are an innocent in all of this."

Annja eyed him. "More lenient?"

"It's going to be a very long winter. Temperatures, as you know, dip well into the negative fifties at night. All this darkness, this isolation, anything can happen. And if we have no way of getting you back to the authorities at McMurdo, we'll just have to dispense our own justice out here."

So that was it. He was going to kill her? For hacking his computer? Talk about a little baby, she thought. "That seems a bit extreme for a crime like this. I mean, what happens if someone steals your lunch around here?"

Thomson didn't rise to the bait. "The compromising of security is a very serious offense. People's lives are at stake here, and hard decisions have to be made regarding the operational security of this establishment. If that means severe punishments for violators, I am granted that authority by virtue of my rank and position within the United States armed forces."

"I wouldn't think the hacker would want anyone to get hurt, Thomson. That's being a bit far-fetched," Annja said.

"I take my job very seriously. And the lives of my men depend on that fact. I want to bring them all home alive. That won't be possible if we've got people who insist on sabotaging our efforts."

"Well, as I said before, you've got the wrong woman, I'm not guilty of hacking your system. I don't care if you've got a partial print match or not—it wasn't me."

The colonel smiled and then leaned forward again. The air was thick now. Annja coughed and tried to take a deep breath.

"So that's it, then?" the colonel said.

"What?"

"You're going to insist that you're innocent?"

"Absolutely," Annja said.

Thomson sighed. "Very well. You leave me no choice."

Annja looked up. "No choice?"

Thomson nodded at the soldiers. "Do it."

The doors behind her opened, blowing a fresh stream of frigid air into the shelter. Fortunately it cleared out some of the smoke. Annja heard footsteps behind her and looked up.

Garin walked in.

Thomson smiled. "Major Braden. You have something for me?"

"Yes, sir."

Annja saw the movement and then looked as Garin slid Annja's laptop computer onto the colonel's desk.

Colonel Thomson looked at Annja. "This, I believe, is yours."

30

For a few seconds, Annja said nothing. Her laptop sat on Thomson's desk looking vulnerable. Thomson stared at Annja as if expecting she might break down and cry.

She frowned. "That's my personal property."

"You're upset," the colonel said. "As you should be. After all, one has certain expectations when it comes to private property—be it actual physical or more in the realm of, shall we say, intellectual property?"

Annja wanted to kill Garin for betraying her like this. What was he playing at, handing her over on a plate to the colonel? He'd already stymied her earlier and now he'd sealed her fate by giving her laptop to Thomson.

Thomson smiled. "Not going to say anything? Have I finally got you to the point where you realize how futile it is to keep insisting you had nothing to do with yesterday's intrusion?"

Annja glared at him. "You took my laptop. So what?"

Thomson gestured to one of the armed guards. "Open it," he ordered.

"I wouldn't do that if I were you," Annja said.

"Why not?"

Annja frowned. "In the short time you've known me, do I really strike you as being foolish enough to leave my laptop unprotected?"

"What—you've got a password?"

"Nothing so pedestrian as that," Annja said with a smile. "I took some more, shall we say, extreme methods to ensure its protection."

Thomson steepled his fingers. "And I should believe you—why? I'm not sure you've told us anything even remotely truthful since you got here."

"You don't have to believe me," Annja said. "In fact, go ahead and open it. See if I care. All I ask is that you move me away from it when you do it. Would you mind if I sat over by the door?"

Thomson glanced at Garin. "Major?"

Garin cleared his throat. "It was sitting right out in the open. I have to admit it struck me as being a little odd it would simply be so exposed if she was really trying to hide something."

"What—you've never heard of hiding in plain sight? It's an old trick."

"If you say so, sir," Garin said. "But I think she might be capable of a little more than we've thought so far."

Thomson took a deep breath and put his pipe down. Then he leveled a finger at Annja. "You're going to open that laptop."

"No. I'm not," she stated flatly.

"You are. If you don't, then—"

"Then what? You'll shoot me? On what grounds? You've got to remember that anything you do here will have a lot of repercussions. Even if you killed me, there would always be someone around who is willing to talk. Unless, of course, you're planning on killing everyone in the camp."

"Open the laptop, Annja," the colonel said.

Annja smiled. "We're on first names now? That's not fair. I don't even know yours."

Thomson frowned and spoke to one of his soldiers. "Get me someone over from the demolitions team." He stared at Annja. "We'll see how complex it will be to disarm your laptop."

Annja smiled and sat waiting. She'd gained herself a little time, but it would be over soon enough if the demolition guy saw through the charade. How could she make it more convincing? Annja racked her brain for any stories she'd heard about laptops being converted to bombs.

The door opened and a man walked in. "Sir?"

"You're Hawk, right?"

"Yes, sir."

"Good. Sergeant Hawk, this woman has booby-trapped her laptop and is refusing to open it. I want it opened."

Hawk looked at the colonel. "I'm assuming, sir, that you want the laptop intact as much as possible?"

He nodded. "We need access to her hard drive. There's a file on there that we need to see."

Hawk bent over the laptop and then looked at Annja. "What'd you use?"

Annja batted her eyes. "Now, if I'm not telling him anything, then what makes you think that I would be any more forthcoming with you?"

"My sparkling personality?" the sergeant said.

Annja smirked. "Sorry."

He nodded. "Had to ask." He turned to Thomson. "Has it been moved?"

"I brought it in," Garin said. "It seemed safe enough."

Hawk nodded and moved the laptop around. As he peered at it from a variety of angles, he kept talking to Thomson. "You should know, sir, that my specialty, as with all of my team, lies with planting demolitions. Not disarming them."

"Yes, but you and your men can disarm what charges you've set, isn't that right?"

"Sure, but that's because we planted them. We know what we're dealing with. But this is someone else's work. And to be honest, it's a real risk. If I guess wrong, the thing could blow."

"You're telling me there's a good chance she's telling the truth?"

"Would she lie?"

Thomson sputtered. "Of course she would. She's trying to protect herself and cover up the fact that she has one of my files on her laptop."

"Look, sir, if I try to do this, then it's going to have to be on my terms, okay?" Hawk said.

"What do you need?"

"Everyone out, for starters. It's too dangerous for people to stay here while I work. If I screw up, then there will be some badly injured folks here."

Thomson frowned. He waved the two armed guards out. "You're dismissed." He looked at Garin. "Major, you may leave also, if you wish."

Garin shook his head. "Actually, sir, I'd like to stay."

"Very well." Thomson stared at Annja. "And you will stay, as well. We'll see if there's any truth to your claims. When the sergeant cracks your laptop, the game will be up."

"You might get injured in the blast," Annja said. "I made sure to pack a big wallop."

Hawk looked at her. "I take it you didn't put it in the battery compartment?"

Annja smiled. "Now, what good would that do? All you'd have to do is turn it upside down, pop the cover and take it out. Not much good in that, is there?"

"Like I said before, I have to ask."

Hawk went back to looking at the laptop, specifically where the lid latched to the bottom assembly. After several minutes, he shook his head. "I can't see anything there that would trigger a detonation."

"So that means it's safe?" Thomson asked. "Good, go ahead and open it right now."

"I didn't say that, sir." Hawk stood up and stretched his back. "Fact is, she could have rigged any number of trip actions here and I wouldn't know until they detonated. It's way too risky."

"Sergeant, we're running out of time," Thomson said. "I need some results here and I need them now."

Hawk looked at him. "There's no way I can guarantee this isn't going to be messy when I pop the lid. There's plenty of metal and plastic here to turn into some nasty shrapnel. Any of us could be maimed or worse by an explosion in this confined area."

"I think that is a risk we are going to have to take, Sergeant. You see, I don't believe that she has wired this laptop to explode. I don't believe it at all. I think it's a last-ditch effort to keep us from discovering that she was behind yesterday's hacker intrusion."

Annja said nothing. She simply sat there and let the smile on her face do all the work for her.

"She knows she's out of time and is playing this one last card in the hope we fall for it," Thomson said.

Hawk chewed his lip. "If you want me to pop the lid, sir, I'll do it, but I really have to stress that I don't agree with the decision."

"Your position is noted, Sergeant. However, I am hereby ordering you to proceed with opening the computer."

He nodded. "All right. But first things first." He went back outside and returned with several flak jackets. He handed one to Thomson, one to Garin and one to Annja.

"She doesn't get one," Thomson said.

Hawk frowned. "I'm not going to watch a civilian die because she wasn't given a flak jacket."

"She's being held on the charge of espionage, Sergeant," Thomson said angrily.

"Excuse me, sir, but she hasn't been tried yet, which makes her innocent until proved guilty."

"I thought your specialty was in demolitions, Sergeant?"

"It is, sir."

"Then leave the legalities to me."

Hawk frowned. "Sir—"

"Oh, very well, give her the jacket and be done with it already. We're wasting time," Thomson shouted.

Hawk handed Annja the flak jacket and she strapped it on. "Thanks."

"You're welcome."

Hawk strapped his own on and then looked at Thomson. "Last time I'll ask, sir. Are you sure you want to proceed?"

"Absolutely."

Hawk nodded. "All right, then. Here we go."

Annja watched as he bent lower and reexamined the laptop from all angles. Then he eased back the lid release.

The lid sprang up a millimeter and Annja heard everyone's breath catch. She was surprised at how involved she was in the situation, even though she knew there were no explosives inside. The tension in the room was incredible.

Hawk grinned. "So far so good."

He eased the lid up. Nothing happened.

"There now, you see?" Thomson said. "I told you there was nothing inside that would explode. She's been lying the entire time and now she has to finally accept—"

"Sir?" Hawk looked at the colonel. "We're not done here yet."

"We're not?"

"No, sir. I still have to power it up. If she knows what she's doing, she could have rigged it to explode when the power is switched on."

"Can you gain access to the interior of the computer without switching it on?" Thomson asked.

Hawk shook his head. "If I had the proper tools to do so, yeah, but this is a complicated piece of machinery. If I go poking in there and happen to trip something, it's as good as just switching it on."

"Switch it on, then."

"Sir?"

"Do it, Sergeant. I'm tired of this."

Hawk took a breath and pressed the power button. Annja heard the computer click and then the opening melody as the operating system booted up. Again, it seemed as if everyone was holding their breath.

But nothing happened.

"There. Now it's been powered up and still no explosion. Would you go so far as to deem this computer safe for me to poke around in, Sergeant?"

Hawk shrugged. "I don't know that I would, sir. But you seem determined to go rooting through there, so I don't know that anything I say would make a difference."

"There are bigger things at stake here, Sergeant. You're dismissed."

"Very good, sir." Hawk started to leave and then turned back around. "If you can all return the flak jackets later on, I'd appreciate it."

Thomson waved him out. Only Annja and Garin remained with him in the office. Thomson leaned across the desk and grabbed the laptop. "Now, then, I believe this is when the bell starts tolling for you, Annja."

Annja sat perfectly still, trying to quell her hammering heart. "I guess we'll see, Colonel."

She sensed that Garin had moved behind her. She frowned. "Get away from me."

Thomson started using the mouse to examine the hard

drive. After a minute of searching, his face suddenly lit up. "Ah. Here it is."

"You found it?" Garin asked.

Thomson nodded. "The date stamp matches perfectly. And the title of the file hasn't even been changed." He looked over the top of the computer at Annja. "Any last words?"

"Boom?"

Thomson chuckled. "Too late for that, my dear." He double-clicked the mouse.

The laptop exploded.

31

The blast blew Annja backward in her chair, tumbling over onto the floor as bits of plastic and metal sprayed the air. She felt a pair of hands grab her from behind and drag her out the door into the cold darkness.

"What the hell—"

"Shut up," Garin said. "Don't say anything and just do as I say. Is that going to be too much to ask?"

Annja shook her head. "No."

"Good." Garin looked around as soldiers came running. "There's been an explosion! Check on the colonel!" he ordered.

Hawk came running. "What the hell happened?"

Garin shook his head. "I have no idea. The colonel clicked a file open and the damned thing blew itself up."

Hawk frowned. "That's some pretty sophisticated work." He glanced at Annja. "You don't strike me as the type to do such things."

Annja smiled but said nothing.

Garin pointed at the tent. "I don't know the extent of the damage in there, but it looked pretty bad."

Hawk hurried away to help with the recovery efforts. Garin kept a firm hand on Annja's shoulder. In her ear, she heard him whisper, "Just keep quiet and everything will work out fine. Trust me."

"Do I have a choice?"

"Not really. Right now, you look like a terrorist."

"Swell."

"Like I said, trust me and it will all work out fine. But you've got to play the part for a little while longer. Okay?"

Annja nodded.

A medical team came running out of one of the nearby shelters. They hurried into the colonel's shelter, and Annja could hear a lot of noise coming from within. Garin called two soldiers over.

"Watch her. Make sure she doesn't escape."

Garin strode toward the shelter and ducked through the blown door. Annja craned her head, trying to see what was going on inside. She could hear people moving bits of furniture and Garin shouting commands at them. Annja shook her head. How much explosive had been in her laptop?

And who had placed it there?

She smirked. Well, she thought she knew the answer to that question. Obviously Garin knew something about it. And that probably meant that he had wired her system. Annja marveled at his ability to know how to do such a thing given that he wasn't gone all that long while Thomson had interrogated her earlier.

But, she thought, he has had a long time to learn how to build explosives and use them. Probably this was a simple task for him. And with the availability of explosives in the dig sites, it wouldn't have been hard for him to fabricate something.

The medical team emerged carrying Thomson on an improvised litter. One of them was holding an intravenous bag high above him as someone else was doing chest compressions.

Hawk came out of the shelter and looked at Annja. "Jesus Christ, woman, how much explosive did you use in there? And why the hell weren't you or Major Braden injured by the blast?"

Annja said nothing, figuring that if she kept mum, it would simply make her look all the worse. And until she knew what Garin was up to, she had to do as he said and play it the best she could.

Hawk walked away muttering something. A few seconds later, Garin emerged, pocketing something that Annja couldn't see. He waved the two guards off.

"I'll take responsibility for her now."

The guards moved away and Garin took Annja by the arm and steered her back toward his shelter.

"What the hell is going on here?"

Garin squeezed harder. "Just wait until we get back where we can actually talk about this, all right?"

"Fine."

The wind was kicking up snow as they walked, but Annja tried her best to ignore it. She'd left her jacket unzipped and the wind caught the flaps, slapping them back and forth.

At his shelter, Garin held the door. "Inside."

She stepped in and found a place to sit down. Garin stepped in after her and nodded. "All right, let's have all the cards on the table, shall we?"

Annja smiled. "You know, you've been speaking in a lot of clichés lately."

Garin frowned. "I'm trying to blend in with people who have no appreciation for language. Of course I'm cliché."

"Well, as long as you know."

"Annja, we may not have much time. Thomson was pretty badly injured by that blast and he may not survive."

"Well, why did you pack my laptop with that kind of explosive?" she asked.

Garin looked at her. "Annja, I didn't do that."

"You didn't?"

Garin frowned. "I know some basic skills when dealing with things that go boom, but in order to alter your laptop, I would have needed a lot of time and patience. I have neither. Whoever did that to your computer knew exactly what they were doing. More to the point, they had plenty of time to work on it."

"How long would something like that take to do?" Annja asked.

Garin shook his head. "Judging from the expression of that guy Hawk, a good couple of hours at the very least. And to rig it to explode when a particular file was opened? That took a knowledge of computers, as well. Again, not exactly my forte."

Annja shook her head. "I thought you did it when you went and got my computer."

"Your computer was lying on your bed. All I had to do was scoop it up off the bed and go."

"It was on my bed?"

Garin nodded. "Like I said when I came back, not exactly hidden from sight. I thought it a bit weird."

"I'll say."

Garin sat down opposite from her. "Look, Annja, let's be honest here, okay? If someone is going around wiring things to explode at the drop of a hat, then we should probably consider working together, despite our past differences."

Annja frowned. "I'm not crazy about it."

Garin sighed. "Well, look at it from this perspective—if Thomson dies, you're a murderer. If he doesn't die, he's going to be incapacitated for a while. He might need an emergency evacuation out of here."

"Wouldn't that leave you in charge?"

Garin smiled. "Don't start celebrating just yet. I'll only be in charge until they do some checking back home and see that Major Braden died in an airplane crash late last year. And then you and I will both be persona non grata around these parts."

Annja nodded. "I guess that wouldn't be a good thing."

"Not at all." Garin paused. "So did you have anything to do with yesterday's communication system hacking?"

Annja took a deep breath. What the hell, she thought. They were both screwed anyway. "A guy I know. Back in the States. He's quite good at penetrating government systems."

"Apparently."

"He was quick and we thought he'd gotten away with it. And then, of course, you nailed me at breakfast today."

Garin nodded. "Sorry about that. I'm sure you understand the need to keep up appearances. If it hadn't been me, we might not have gotten any time to talk about things prior to Thomson giving you the once-over."

"Not that it helped."

Garin shrugged. "Well, you never know. At least we know we're both on the same team here."

Annja stood. "Are we really? I mean, you're here telling me all of this and I'm still finding it difficult to trust you."

"I think that's because of our past."

Annja shook her head. "Maybe. But you moved behind my chair right before the laptop exploded. What was that about? Did you know?"

Garin eyed her. "No. I didn't. But of more importance is how come you didn't know it was going to explode. Aren't your instincts more fine-tuned now on account of the sword?"

Annja sighed. "Garin, I've got more questions now than I ever did before. The sword has done a lot for me, but it's also a loaded gun of sorts. Half the time I don't understand what I can do or what I'm capable of with the sword around. It's extremely frustrating."

Garin smiled. "You could always give it to me."

"Not a chance."

Garin nodded. "So there is some loyalty there, after all. Interesting."

"I'm loyal to what I believe the sword represents—helping thwart evil."

Garin walked to the door and peered out quickly. "Listen to me. I took the hard drive out of your laptop back at Thomson's tent. I don't know what's on this thing or what was on that file you wanted so badly—"

"The lab analysis."

"Of course." He frowned. "Do you really think this is all a fake?"

"I don't know. But I think it's odd he wouldn't let me see it and he seemed to be going to extraordinary lengths to ensure no one sees it."

Garin handed her the singed hard drive. "Well, here it is. Maybe you should go and try to hook it up somewhere. See if you can get access to that file after all. Considering Thomson was injured by the blast and all."

Annja took the hard drive. "I don't have another computer. How can I get access to what's on here?"

Garin walked to his bag and removed a case. "Here's another one. Go back to your shelter and get started on it. I'm not exactly happy there's something going on in this camp. It's upsetting my plans."

"And what plans would those be exactly? I mean, now that we're on the same team and all."

Garin smiled. "If these relics are extraterrestrial, I want them. It's that simple."

Annja nodded. "You think there's something inherent in their properties that you can use?"

"Perhaps. But I do know that with my money and resources, I can get them examined faster than the bureaucrats in charge elsewhere. And if there's power to be had, then I want it for myself, yes."

"Such a humanitarian," Annja said.

"Not a chance. Five hundred years can do a lot to make

you rather self-centered, Annja. I'm horribly selfish, I admit it."

Annja smiled. "I didn't want to say anything, but—"

Garin held up his hand. "Get back to your shelter and stay there. If anyone stops you, tell them I said you're to stay in your shelter until I say it's okay to come out."

"So, I'm grounded?"

Garin frowned. "Get to work, Annja. Lives just might depend on it."

Annja turned for the door and then stopped. She looked back at Garin. "Say, something just occurred to me."

"What's that?"

"When the laptop exploded, we weren't injured. Why not?"

Garin shook his head. "The blast blew us both back."

"That was the concussion wave, though."

Garin frowned. "You think it was a shaped charge? Designed to only blow out in one direction with effect?"

"Maybe."

"That would mean that the laptop was designed to injure only the person who triggered the blast."

"Which would also mean the person we're looking for is even more skilled than we thought," Annja said. "And who was the target? Thomson—or me?"

Garin nodded. "This just keeps getting better."

Annja opened the door. As she did, one of the medical team soldiers came in and reported to Garin.

"What is it?"

The medic shook his head. "We did all we could."

Annja felt her stomach turn.

Garin frowned. "Is he—"

The medic nodded. "Yes, sir. Colonel Thomson is dead."

32

Annja made it back to her shelter without being harassed by the soldiers surrounding the area. Garin had informed everyone that she was allowed to move around the camp. His argument was simple—where could she go in this environment? If she left camp, she would die from exposure.

Sitting on her bed, she looked around the shelter. There was no way of knowing who had come in and rooted through her stuff, although apparently someone had. Her poor laptop was fried. And it had taken Colonel Thomson with it.

Annja looked down at the singed hard drive and wondered if the file would still be intact. Only one way to find out, she reasoned, and she placed the laptop that Garin had given her onto the small table nearby.

Annja used the screwdriver blade on her Swiss Army knife to unscrew the back of the laptop case and gain access to the interior. She picked out the hard drive right away and unclipped the wires leading to it before reconnecting them to her hard drive. Once that was done, she closed everything back up and switched on the computer.

She heard the drive start up and, fortunately, it seemed to work. Annja had no clue how someone could wire explosives so that when a file was opened, the laptop would explode but still keep the hard drive intact. To her, it seemed impossible. But then again, it wasn't the first time she'd wondered about stuff like this.

Annja clicked open the various file directories and started looking for the file that Knightmare had stolen from Thomson's computer.

She spotted the file name and clicked it open.

A new screen blossomed into view, and Annja could see the letterhead from the laboratory where the colonel had sent the necklace. She quickly scanned down the report and then saw what she needed to see.

Object in question composed of aluminum and lead. Carbon dating estimates that the object was made in the past year.

Annja looked at the screen. There it was. Proof that the relics weren't relics at all. Nor were they from some far-off planet in the solar system. They might have just as easily been made in someone's basement in Duluth.

She shook her head. Who would go all this way and through all this trouble to create such a fraud? Obviously, Thomson knew about it. Was he behind this fraud? Or was there some other reason for wanting to keep it such a secret?

Annja frowned and closed the file. Not good. Now, with Thomson dead, she had more questions and the only source of answers was lying in an improvised morgue until his body could be transported back to McMurdo.

What the hell is going on here? she wondered.

There was a knock at her shelter door. "Come in."

Garin poked his head in. "Did you have any luck?"

"Sure did."

Garin closed the door behind him. "And? What'd you find out?"

"The things we've dug up are fakes. Aluminum and lead counterfeits by the look of it. Someone is playing an awful big trick here."

Garin frowned. "But why? To what purpose? I can't figure out why someone would want to stage something like this. Can you?"

"I've been sitting here thinking about the same questions."

Garin sat down. "You think Thomson was behind it?"

Annja shook her head. "I don't know. Part of me wants to say yes. But then again, maybe I'm hoping he was a true patriot after all who stumbled upon this fraud and decided to let it play out so he could get to the bottom of it."

"Dangerous game," Garin said. "We're trapped here until the thaw. And now we've got a killer on the loose? Talk about playing with fire."

"What's the mood in camp?"

Garin sighed. "Well, a lot of them want your head. Can't say I blame them. Thomson was the kind of officer who seemed to engender a lot of respect from his troops. Some of them have been with him for years."

Annja frowned. "Would that give him the time to plan something this elaborate?"

"I don't know. He's only a colonel, after all. But then again, there really is no way of accurately gauging the extent people will go to do what they feel they have to do."

"So you think he could be behind it?" Annja asked.

"I don't know what I think," Garin said. "But if there's no value to the relics, then there's got to be something else of value here that we haven't looked at yet. After all, whoever is behind this is apparently perfectly willing to kill."

"Scary thought."

Garin smiled. "At least you've got the sword to protect you."

Annja frowned. "Well, yeah. If my instincts are right."

"What do you mean?"

"I mean, I'm more than a little concerned that my gut didn't tell me that damned laptop was about to explode. I've been in plenty of hairy situations and known that trouble was coming."

"All the time?" Garin asked.

"Well, maybe not all the time…"

He shrugged. "Maybe your instincts knew that the laptop was only going to take out the good colonel."

"How is that possible?"

Garin smirked. "Annja, how is you having a sword that once belonged to Joan of Arc possible? And how is it possible that you apparently carry it everywhere but aren't weighed down by it? How many other things in your life right now border on the unexplainable?"

"Plenty," Annja admitted.

"But they're still a part of your life. My advice is to make peace with the fact that you may never be able to explain everything, and just move on from there. We've obviously got a lot more to worry about right now."

Annja sighed. "You're right."

Garin stood and began pacing. "Who would have had access to your stuff?"

"Anyone. I don't think we're walking around locking our doors. Well, except for the colonel. His place and yours were the only ones that I've tried and found locked. Our door has always been unlocked."

"That doesn't exactly limit our suspects."

"No." Annja frowned. "But I suppose we would have to start with my roommates."

"You've known Zach for a long time?"

"Long enough. I trust him, if that's what you're getting at. I've never had reason not to."

"He's going through a horrible time right now, yes?"

"Divorce, separation from his children. It's one of the reasons he took this job. He said the paycheck would enable him to get himself out from under a mountain of debt."

"Motivation?" Garin asked.

"For what, though? So the relics aren't real. He'll probably be the one who is most devastated by that news. I think part of him dearly wants them to be real. It might restore his faith in the mysteries of life."

Garin sighed. "God, another dreamer."

"You're just a five-hundred-year-old cynic."

He smiled. "I am at that."

"Not everyone is," Annja reminded him.

"What about the other guy—Dave?"

Annja shook her head. "He's something of a mystery. He claims to be a geologist, but there's a part of him that seems to be anything but a scientist. I get the feeling he's worked in covert operations before."

"He's a spy?"

"Maybe not a spy, but he knows that world. I'm pretty sure of it," Annja said.

Garin crossed his arms. "So why's he here?"

"He told me his job was to look after Zach. Help him out on the dig site and make sure that things got on okay."

"You believe him?"

"He was the first person I met when I got down here. Picked me up at the landing strip."

"You didn't have the typical in-briefing with the marshal like I did?"

Annja shook her head. "Dave told me Zach asked him to pick me up and get me squared away before we saw the marshal. As it turned out, I met the marshal that night anyway after my near-death encounter with the Sno-Cat."

"Dave seems a bit off the mark. I don't know what he

would be up to, though. That's the thing. If we can figure out why there'd be such an interest in being down here, we could reverse engineer the plot and find out who is in command."

Annja pointed outside. "What about the mountain itself?"

"What about it?"

"Is there anything of value to it? I saw large chunks of coal. Lots of fool's gold, as well. Are there any other mineral deposits there that could make someone rich?"

Garin frowned. "Does it make sense for all of this to be about a mountain of rocks? I just think there's got to be something else. Something probably right in front of us. We just aren't seeing it."

"We're too close," Annja said.

"Undoubtedly."

"So what's our next step?"

Garin sat down and ran his hand through his hair. "All right, let's assume for a moment that everything is proceeding according to whatever plan is in place. That means that someone wanted Thomson dead for some reason. I say we sit back and wait and see what happens next."

"Sit back?" Annja was appalled.

"Think about it. If they wanted Thomson out of the way, they must be getting ready to put another part of the plan into action. That's the only way we'll know what they're up to."

Annja shook her head. "Yeah, but what if the next part of their plan involves killing everyone else who isn't in on it? Or Thomson wasn't the target?"

Garin smiled. "Well, I'd suggest sleeping with your sword. I know I'll have my gun under my pillow—that's for sure."

Annja sighed. "It's not much of a plan, Garin."

"I'm open to suggestions, Annja. I just don't think we have very many of them at this point. We can do nothing and see what transpires. Or we can try to force their hand by doing something drastic."

"Like what?"

"I don't know. How about announcing to the entire camp that Thomson was murdered by someone who is, as of yet, unknown?" Garin said.

"Yeah, that would just spread paranoia throughout the entire camp. I might end up dead anyway."

Garin nodded. "Hence my suggestion that we keep quiet for now."

"What about my role as the terrorist? I can't very well stay in the shelter here and not get any food or water."

"I'll pass the order that you're to be allowed access and without harassment. I don't think anyone will mess around with you."

Annja nodded. It wasn't a good plan, but it was the only plan that seemed open to them at the moment. And perhaps Garin was right. Maybe the people behind this would make their next move and reveal themselves when they did.

"How much longer do you think your cover will hold up?" she asked.

Garin shrugged. "Thomson's last order was that the camp go into blackout mode. No communications in or out. So we're pretty isolated right now."

"That could work to our favor."

"For right now. But it could also work to the enemy's benefit, as well. They'll know we don't have any help coming."

"Great."

"Our job," Garin said, "is to keep our eyes and ears open and see who makes the first move. As soon as we see that, we'll need a plan of action."

"How about stopping them from destroying the camp and everyone in it?" Annja said.

Garin shook his head. "You're assuming that's their goal. It might not be. We need to keep ourselves open to the possibility that there could be something else at play here. Otherwise, we'll miss seeing it when it happens."

"You're right."

Garin headed to the door. "I should get going. People will expect me to be visible for the next few hours at least. I'll let the camp know you're free to move about. Let me know immediately if you learn anything new."

"Okay, good luck."

"You, too."

Garin pushed his way out of the door and Annja leaned back on her bed. She hated waiting. But Garin's plan seemed most logical. At least for right now.

The door opened and Zach and Dave rushed in. Zach was covered in dirt and grime. Dave looked less harsh for the day's work.

"Are you okay?" Zach asked. "We just heard."

Dave smiled. "You look okay for having been in a bomb blast."

"Shaped charge, apparently," Annja said. "But I could have easily been killed. And given everything that's gone on so far on this trip, I'm a little amazed I wasn't."

Dave smiled. "Well, we're glad you're okay."

Annja nodded.

But inside, she wondered if that was true.

33

The next couple of hours passed uneventfully. Annja could see that the camp was in a bit of turmoil with a lot of soldiers wondering whether they should call in for help or stay where they were. Garin was quite visible, reassuring the soldiers that he had the situation well in hand. He played the part well, and Annja found herself admiring his leadership skills.

She went to dinner with Zach and Dave. The mood in the mess hall was grim. Annja got a lot of nasty looks. It was all she could do to not stand on the table and scream her innocence. Garin sat with them toward the end of the meal, asked a few questions and then left them alone.

For his part, Zach still seemed convinced that there were more relics to be found in Horlick Mountain. Annja watched him going on and on about where he wanted to dig next and felt pity.

Look at how devoted he is, she thought. This dig is a life raft for him. It's the only thing keeping him above water and I know that it's all fake. When he finds out, it's going to devastate him.

"And, Annja, if the major will let you come with us, Dave

and I were talking about trying a new spot tomorrow, once the blasting is done," Zach said.

"I thought the blasting was scheduled for this morning?" Annja said.

Dave frowned. "Well, it was. Until the colonel ordered everything put on hold while he solved the mystery of who broke into the communications systems yesterday."

Annja frowned. "So the other team hasn't broken through the granite yet?"

"Nope."

"Do you know what they expect to find on the other side of that wall?"

Zach shrugged. "Apparently, there's a cavern of sorts. Who knows, it could be like opening an extraterrestrial tomb of the pharaohs."

If only, Annja thought. But she smiled and nodded. "That would be an incredible find."

Dave was looking at her. "You don't seem convinced, Annja. Something bothering you?"

"Just everything. I mean, I've been accused of espionage. Then someone obviously broke into our shelter and wired my laptop with a bomb. I narrowly avoided being killed and everyone thinks I killed the colonel." She sighed. "I'm happy for you guys, believe me, but it's hard getting upbeat when the entire camp wants my head stuck on the business end of a pike."

Dave smiled. "Well, for what it's worth, I don't think you killed Thomson."

"Thanks for the vote of confidence. Any chance you'll be my campaign manager?"

"I'll paint a sign and everything."

Annja smiled. "Great. That'll help a lot."

Zach looked at her. "So did you hack into the computer systems?"

Annja smiled. "I wanted to see the report. What can I say? I'm stubborn when it comes to that kind of thing."

"How did you do it?" Dave asked. He seemed to be concentrating on his mashed potatoes.

Annja realized too late what she'd done. He must have known they took his satellite phone. Was it better to deny it or just get it out of the way? Then she remembered that the phone had been in Thomson's shelter when the bomb went off. Was it still operational? Or had it been destroyed? She'd have to check with Garin.

She sighed. "I'm not proud of it, Dave, but I used your satellite phone."

"I don't recall ever showing it to you," he said.

"I saw it when you were unpacking." Annja smiled. "Anyway, at least no one thinks you hacked the system."

He nodded and swallowed some of his food.

Zach smiled. "Hey, at least we know we have a way out of here if it turns out this thing blows up in our faces." He grimaced. "Ugh, bad choice of words. Sorry."

"Forget it," Annja said. "I'm ready to move on if you guys are. I just honestly want to get back to digging and finding these relics. It's been hard keeping my mind on it with everything else going on."

Dave looked up. "Well, that sounds good to me."

Annja held her breath for a moment. Did he buy it? Would it have been better to deny that she had used the phone? She didn't think so. Dave would have figured it out. Besides, once it had been confiscated, the game was up. Annja was sure she would have done more harm than good by saying she hadn't used it.

"I'll find out if it's still in operational shape," she told Dave.

He shook his head. "It's okay. I'll check in with Major Braden after dinner. See if it was recovered from Thomson's shelter."

"Send them the bill if it's not. That blast was powerful and I'm not sure anything would have survived," Annja said feebly.

Dave smiled. "Well, you did."

"By luck or chance or design, I don't know," Annja said. "It was pretty scary stuff. I don't know that I've ever been so close to an explosion like that."

"Any hairs singed?" Zach said, smiling.

"None that I could find."

Dave nodded. "Well, whoever stole your laptop and rigged it to explode obviously knew what they were doing."

"You think?"

"Without a doubt. From the sounds of it, it wasn't an easy thing to pull off in the first place. You should be grateful they may not have rigged it properly. Maybe it was supposed to blow up in all directions or something."

Annja frowned. "Thanks, Dave, that makes me feel a whole lot better about the day."

"I'm just saying."

"Well, don't. The fact is someone is dead now because of my computer, and even though I didn't have anything to do with that, everyone thinks I did. My name is mud around here and I have to live with it. You guys don't."

Zach frowned. "I thought we were moving on from this?"

"I was all set to until Mr. Optimism showed up," Annja said.

Dave put up his hands. "Okay, okay, that was a bad choice of wording on my part. I'm just trying to make sense of all of this. And it seems so strange to me."

"Yeah, well, I'm pretty sure I've got a monopoly on the strangeness," Annja said. "It's all been happening to me since I arrived in Antarctica. It's not a very comfortable feeling, let me tell you."

Zach leaned back in his chair. "Annja, I hate to bring this up, but I want to ask you something."

"What?"

"Have you considered the possibility that the computer was supposed to kill you?"

"I thought we just discussed this?" Annja frowned. All she wanted to do was go back to their shelter and sleep.

"Yeah, but only in one context."

Dave leaned closer. "Explain, Zach."

"What if the computer wasn't meant to be detonated by Thomson? What if it was supposed to explode when Annja clicked to open the file? After all, the person who rigged it might have had no idea that Major Braden would grab it and take it to Colonel Thomson."

"You're saying that shaped charge was meant to kill Annja and not Thomson?" Dave asked.

"Why not? Annja was the one who was presumably going to open the file and read it, right?"

Annja nodded. "That was the plan, yeah."

Zach spread his hands. "Well, then…?"

Dave took a breath. "He's got a pretty good point, Annja. You might want to look into getting some protection. If you take Zach's theory and apply it to the rest of your trip here, you seem to be a marked woman."

"I've noticed," Annja said.

"I'm being serious." Dave frowned. "You could be in real danger. And not for nothing, but the people around you could be, too. Thomson might simply have been a case of mistaken identity."

She took a breath. "Well, that about seals this day as being one of the crappiest in my life. Guess I'll go off to bed and hope I wake up in the morning."

Dave started to stand. "Annja—"

She stopped him. "No, no, you guys stay here and enjoy dessert. I'm out of here. Maybe I'll check in with Major Braden and make sure it's okay to sleep tonight."

She walked away from the table and heard Dave telling Zach what an idiot he was for bringing that up. Zach retorted with something about how Annja deserved to know the possibility existed. Annja wanted to hear no more of it and pushed out into the Antarctic night.

She stood outside the mess hall for a moment, letting the frigid wind wash over her. If only it was that easy to wipe her fears away, she thought.

But it wasn't. And like it or not, she was stuck here for the duration. This had to play itself out with her as a participant. If she tried to stay away from it, she'd likely just end up dead.

And that wasn't an option she wanted to consider.

She could see the light on in Garin's tent. She could wander over and tell him about the conversation she'd just had, but was any of it really news to him?

Everyone thinks I'm responsible for this, and yet I might be the most innocent person here.

Another stiff breeze threw snow at her from the side. She turned away and saw the line of Sno-Cats parked under a frozen tarp.

I could just grab one of them, get it fueled up and head back to McMurdo, she thought. With the GPS system, it wouldn't be that difficult finding her way back. Once there, she could tell the marshal about everything that had happened. If nothing else, he might be able to protect her.

She smirked. Whom was she kidding? Traveling alone in the darkness on a remote continent with no real idea of where she was going? It was a recipe for disaster.

It might also make her an easier target.

She turned and walked through the snow toward Garin's shelter. Love him or hate him, he was at least a connection back to the outside world.

Her boots trudged through the snow as the wind blew harder. Annja bent lower, trying to take herself out of the direct path of the gusts. It was brutal out. Annja wondered why anyone would come down here to put up with these conditions. She was thankful they at least had the generator going to provide them with warmth and electricity.

If the generator was gone, they'd all be dead.

She stopped.

The generator. It was nuclear powered. The first of its kind. Small, compact and powerful.

It had to be worth a lot of money to someone, especially nations that were desperately trying to acquire nuclear power. She hurried through the snow. Could it be the target?

Had someone orchestrated this entire thing knowing that the military would use the new generator to power their camp? Had they come down and faked the dig sites, the mineral deposits and more—all for a chance to steal the nuclear generator?

It would have taken an awesome amount of planning. It would also take a devious mind that knew how to manipulate events and people to the extent that it could work.

She frowned. But where did she fit into the picture? Why was she being targeted for death?

That question still remained unanswered.

Annja stopped in front of Garin's door and knocked.

"Who is it?"

"Annja."

"Come in."

She opened the door and stepped inside. Garin sat there behind his desk. "Got something to tell me?"

Annja nodded. "I think I know what this is all about."

34

Garin looked at her. "I'm listening."

"It's the nuclear generator," Annja said. "That's what they're after."

"Who?"

Annja shook her head. "I don't know that yet."

"Well, according to what Thomson said, the generator is cutting-edge technology. I suppose it might be of some value," Garin said.

"It's definitely valuable," Annja said. "Think of what emerging nations would pay to get their hands on something like that. Nuclear power, portable, and they could probably copy it so they could then produce others. It would solve their energy needs, and at the same time put them at the table of the other nuclear powers."

Garin stroked his chin. "Interesting. And not exactly comforting since my shelter actually backs up to it." He reached into his parka and withdrew a large-caliber pistol. "Guess I'll be keeping this handy for the next couple of days." He smiled at Annja. "So this entire thing was designed to get the Americans to bring one of their new supersecret nuke generators here?"

Annja sat down in a chair. "I think it's the only thing that makes sense. The relics are fake. The mountain, while it might contain plenty of minerals and deposits, wouldn't be something that someone would be able to swoop in and make a quick buck off. That leaves the generator."

"Unless, of course, we're still not seeing something else that's right here," Garin said. "But I don't know what that could be."

"Neither do I," Annja said. "I really think this is it. And it's a big one."

Garin frowned. "I wonder what the plan is. I mean, are they simply going to drive it out of here? It's not exactly the kind of thing you could just up and take. The effects would be too immediate. Everyone would know the instant we lost power. Obviously, it's protecting us. Lose that protection and people will die."

Annja looked around. Garin must have been lying on his bed when she knocked because the blanket was ruffled. "And where would they take it? McMurdo's still a long haul," she said.

"Worse, the weather is dire. The generator is portable, yes, but it's not something you wouldn't need a plane or a ship to ferry out of here." Garin frowned. "Still too many questions left unanswered."

"But at least we know."

Garin nodded. "True, but in this case, that might harm us more than protect us."

"How do you figure that?"

"If the people plotting this find out that we know, then we'll naturally be the first ones they seek to eliminate. Someone's wanted you dead from the start. And now it looks like they have an even better reason to want it so."

Annja sighed. "Your suggestion about sleeping with my sword? I just might do that. I don't care what my roommates think."

Garin smiled. "Well, at least you always have that weapon. It's not as though it ever leaves you. Does it?"

"Not so far. I've had trouble using it in cramped places, but otherwise, it's always there when I need it."

"Good," Garin said. "At least I don't need to give you a weapon now. I tend to think people might mutiny if they saw that."

Annja nodded. "You should have seen everyone at dinner after you left. They hate me here."

"They think you killed their commanding officer. A man who was well liked by his troops. Of course they hate you."

"Speaking of which," Annja said, "did the satellite phone that you took from Dave's pack survive the explosion in Thomson's shelter? I think he's pretty steamed that I used it to make contact with my hacker friend."

Garin shook his head. "It was pretty mangled. I don't think you'll be using that to call for help, if that's what you're after."

"I just wanted to return it to him. But if it's gone, then I guess he'll have to manage without it."

Garin got up and walked over to his bed. "All right, then. If that's all you've got, I should get some sleep. Unless, of course, you'd like to spend the night with me?"

Annja smiled. "I don't think we're at the point where we need to keep watch over each other by sleeping in the same bed."

Garin lay on his back. "Perhaps not, but it would certainly make for some entertaining times. We might both wake up tomorrow dead. Did you ever think about that?"

"You're going to use end-of-the-world lines on me now? Garin, you must be losing your touch if you think that will work on me. Besides, it's not like you can die. Even if I do, I imagine you'll still be around kicking."

Garin sighed. "Most likely."

Annja moved to the door. "Good night, then."

"Be careful, Annja. Someone is obviously gunning for you."

She pushed the door open and walked back out into the cold. The winds howled through the camp, sliding snow all over the place. Bits of it pelted her parka and face, and she blinked, trying to get her goggles and mask back in place before her exposed skin froze. In conditions like this, it was no wonder people lost skin after only a minute of exposure.

She moved through the night and headed back to her shelter. Sleep would be a welcome relief for her. She dreaded telling Dave about his satellite phone, however. If she got out of this alive, she'd buy him a replacement as soon as they managed to get home.

If she got home.

The thought that someone was so actively seeking to kill her made her feel awful. It couldn't be the two guys back from Gallagher's, could it? Why would they expose themselves so early on? The best way to kill someone was to not announce your intentions and then simply erase the target one day out of the blue. No one would ever see it coming.

Yet there'd been at least two very clear attempts made on her life.

She passed the entrance to the dig site and paused. *I wonder if the research team really did wait to blow that wall.*

She smiled. *She would have heard the explosion, wouldn't she?*

Why not just peek down there and see if it was still wired and ready to go?

She looked around but could make out no one watching her in the darkness. The snow blew hard, blinding her as it flew in horizontally.

Annja ducked into the shelter.

The guards who had been stationed there were absent.

Annja shook her head. Once the commanding officer is gone, discipline apparently starts to slip in this unit, she thought.

Poor Thomson would be disappointed.

Annja unzipped her hood and parka and walked down the long sloping tunnel toward the fork. The lights overhead seemed to move of their own accord, probably from the ambient breeze that Annja had let into the shelter when she entered.

The light was fair and she could make out more pockets of coal in the dirt and rock of the mountain base. She picked up a lump and smiled. Some day this might even turn into a diamond, she thought. If I could just crush these all up by hand, I'd be a rich girl.

Her boots skidded along the path as loose gravel plagued her steps. She stumbled once and had to caution herself to slow down or risk repeating the concussion she'd given herself the other day.

At the fork in the tunnel, Annja turned left and headed down into the darkness. There still weren't any lights strung up in this part of the dig site and it bothered her. Why hadn't the other team arranged for lights? Wouldn't they want to be able to see as they made their way down to the cavern?

Like a lot of other things going on here, that didn't make sense, either.

So what else is new? she thought.

Annja picked her way carefully down the path. Ahead of her, she could make out ambient light coming out of the second dig site cavern. She could start to make out the features of the tunnel and it helped her avoid a nasty depression in the ground.

That's probably where I stumbled and fell yesterday, she thought.

Annja reached the entrance to the cavern and stopped.

Was someone there?

She waited, squinting to try to make out anyone who might

be moving around. The cavern was large but not nearly large enough that she wouldn't be able to see someone sneaking about.

And yet something felt weird.

In front of her, she could see the massive wall of granite. It would take a lot of explosive to blow that apart, she thought. And it was strange that she could only make out a few of the bored holes that she'd seen them putting explosives into yesterday.

Had they changed the wiring since then?

Annja stepped into the cavern, her feet grinding a bit of loose rock underfoot. The sound of it echoed throughout the chamber.

So much for staying quiet, she thought.

But did she need to? There was no one here in the cavern.

Annja took a quick glance around to reassure herself she was alone. Then she closed her eyes and saw the sword hovering, ready for use. Annja opened her eyes again, already feeling much better. Peace of mind was a precious commodity lately.

She walked around the cavern to the boxes of high explosives. Opening one of the crates, she was surprised to find it empty.

Where was the rest of it?

She glanced at the granite wall. It seemed utterly impenetrable. How in the world would they blow that in such a way that they could gain access to the other side? Wouldn't they have to dig out all the rubble before they could do so?

Annja walked over to the granite and stared at it. Nooks and crannies of the tough rock stared back at her. Annja could feel the weightiness of the wall looming before her, a giant block in the way of progress.

She ran her hands over the cool rock.

She froze.

Annja felt the rock in other places. Her heart rate kicked up a notch.

She placed both her hands on it and what she felt on her skin didn't feel like rock at all.

She pushed. Part of the granite wall gave in.

Annja pushed harder and the wall gave in more. It felt like a combination of papier mache and cardboard.

The granite wall was fake.

Annja moved closer to where the wall seemed to vanish into the side of the cavern. Find the edge, she told herself. Find the place where the wall meets the real rock and dirt of the mountain.

She ran her hands over the surface of the wall quickly. What was behind this? What was it that someone was trying so hard to hide from view?

And even more concerning, how many people were involved in this from the start? She'd seen at least four people in here yesterday. All of them were busy planting explosives.

Was the entire camp planning to steal the nuclear generator? Was it an entire team of traitors?

Annja thought she found the end point of the fake wall. She felt farther down toward the ground and found a little bit of purchase. She tried crushing the wall inward, but it held, so instead she pulled back on the bit she had and a large piece came away in her hands.

Annja got down on her hands and knees and looked through to the other side.

What she saw scared her.

Piles of explosives sat from the floor to the ceiling of the cavern.

Whoever had planted them wasn't trying to take out a wall. They were trying to demolish an entire mountain.

And everything around it.

35

She had to get out and tell Garin, she thought.

Annja turned and found herself staring into the barrel of a gun. Behind the gun, she saw a face she hadn't seen since her first night at Gallagher's bar. He wore a broad smile across his face. "Remember me?"

Annja brought her hands up. "Yeah. I remember you. You're the jerk who hassled Zach. And then later on you tried to kill me."

He shrugged. "Guilty as charged."

"You got a name?"

He smirked. "You can call me Mitch. That'll do for now. You know, at least until you die."

Annja looked around. "Where's your partner in crime? The smaller guy you were with."

"Right here."

Annja turned and saw the second guy from the bar entering the cavern. "Nice to see you again, Annja. Sorry about that elbow blast to your ribs that night. I hope they've been causing you a great deal of pain."

"Not too much, actually," Annja said. "I guess you just aren't the man you thought you were."

He scowled and then looked at Mitch. "Coast is clear. No one saw us come in after her. We should be good to go. Let's get this finished up and then get the hell out of here. Things that go bang make me nervous."

Annja frowned. "And what's your name?"

"Chuck," he said.

"Mitch and Chuck. The two chaos brothers. Is that it?" Annja smiled. "And you guys are behind this whole operation? Somehow I just can't see that."

Mitch glared at her. "Shut up, Annja."

She nodded. "Yeah, this was far too well planned to be orchestrated by you clowns. Someone else has to be pulling the strings."

Chuck frowned. "Can't we just kill her now?"

Mitch shook his head. "You know what the orders are. It has to look like an accident."

Annja smirked. "Uh, yeah. You guys might want to rethink subtlety when it comes to wiring my laptop to explode. That wasn't going to look like an accident."

Mitch smiled. "Nice piece of work, huh?"

"Oh, that was you, Einstein? Yeah, real nice the way it was shaped to blow in only one direction," Annja said.

"Had to make sure we got the target."

Annja shook her head. "Well, you missed, didn't you? I'm still here."

Chuck laughed. "She thinks we wanted to take her out. She doesn't know a damned thing, does she? And here we were, concerned that she'd be able to figure it out and ruin the whole thing. Waste of worry."

Annja couldn't conceal her surprise. "You wanted Colonel Thomson dead? Why?"

Mitch sighed. "Because you'd be out of the way, that's

why. If it looked like you'd rigged your own laptop to explode, then we hoped that fool Major Braden would have you locked up for murdering Thomson."

"But he didn't," Chuck said. "Not that it matters anymore." He busied himself with positioning a small black box in the center of the explosive bundles. "He'll die soon enough, anyway."

That's what you think, Annja thought. She knew Garin might be able to survive the explosion, but she wouldn't. She had to get out and she had to warn Zach.

But Dave?

Annja knew now. He had to be behind this whole thing. She thought back to Gallagher's and how quiet he was when Mitch and Chuck came to the table to harass Zach. Dave hadn't done much of anything. He was content to let them rile up Zach and Annja.

Mitch hadn't moved the gun barrel and he was far enough away that making a move on him would have been extremely dangerous. She had to find some way to close the space or she'd be shot several times before she could reach him.

"So where's Dave, then?" she asked.

Mitch shook his head. "What are you talking about?"

"Dave, the guy behind this whole thing. Where is he now? If he's hurting Zach, I'll kill you all."

Mitch laughed. "I don't know what's funnier—the fact that she has no clue or that she thinks she's going to be able to kill us."

Chuck joined in. "You've really been in the dark here, huh? I almost feel sorry for you. Almost, but not quite."

Annja saw some movement from somewhere behind Mitch. Someone was coming. All she had to do was keep Mitch and Chuck occupied and then they'd be surprised when they saw the new person show up. Annja could use that to her advantage and jump Mitch and his gun.

Annja's heart sank.

"Hey, Annja," Dave said.

She couldn't figure out what was happening. None of it made any sense. Someone was pushing Dave into the cavern.

"Zach?" she whispered.

He poked Dave in the back with another gun. "Get over there next to her and don't try anything."

Annja shook her head. "What the hell is going on here?" she asked angrily.

Mitch greeted Zach. "You were right—she doesn't have a clue. She's been spouting off her theories and none of them have been close to correct so far."

Zach nodded. "It's a shame, really. I so hate for this to have to end this way, but that's how it comes down sometimes, huh?"

"Wait a minute," Annja said. "How did you get mixed up in all of this? I thought these guys hated you."

"Yeah, well, that's the way we wanted it to look," Zach said. "We figured if you were so preoccupied with the thought of Mitch and Chuck here gunning for you, you'd miss seeing what was really going on right in front of you. Apparently, it worked like a charm."

Annja felt herself getting angry. "Why did you bring me down here? I mean, if you're just going to kill me, then what's the point of asking for me in the first place?"

Zach shrugged. "I never thought they'd actually go and get you, to be honest. The winter was coming down and when I made my request, I figured it was a given they'd tell me no. Instead, they got you down here in record time and I suddenly had a big problem. I needed you out of the way, Annja. There's too much at stake here to let you interfere with it."

"The relics are fakes," Annja said.

"Obviously," Zach replied. "We planted them."

"You did?"

He sighed. "Absolutely."

"But you've been digging your heart out. Every day. For what? Just to sell the appearance of being obsessed with this?"

Zach smiled. "Pretty good, huh? I never knew I had it in me. I'd give myself an Oscar for it, but I suppose I'm a bit biased."

Annja shook her head. "What about the divorce? And the kids?"

"Oh, hell, they left me a long time ago." Zach smiled. "Annja, it's been years since we last spoke. That little bit of trickery was easy to pull off. It's the truth, after all, just with the time line altered. I've been dead to them for years."

"So you staged all this?" she asked.

He nodded. "Sure. This payoff is huge."

"What payoff?"

Zach sat down on a nearby cluster of rocks. "It's twofold, really. We take the nuke generator and sell it to the highest bidder on the black market. Should fetch us a cool two billion, at the very least. At the same time, when we blow the mountain, the assumption will be that this is an environmental-disaster area. They'll send in a cleanup crew that will discover that this mountain is actually filled with tons upon tons of valuable minerals and chemical deposits. Navstar will come in as the contractor to clean it up and when they 'discover' the deposits, they'll remove them, as well."

"Meaning even more money," Annja said.

Zach smiled. "Lots more, in fact. Easily enough to make the three of us set for life."

Annja stared at him. She felt sick. "What happened to you? I would never have thought you could dream of doing something like this."

He frowned. "I grew up, Annja. I got tired of life handing me the short end of the stick. I was sick of hearing about how everyone I knew was getting success handed to them without any work to speak of. You know what that's like? Day after day of getting news about so-and-so buying a new vacation home or investing in the next great dot-com? Meanwhile, your family hates you and you've got a crummy two-bedroom bungalow outside Tampa where you spend the majority of time praying there's not a bad hurricane season. Day after day of that is enough to make anyone a bit twisted."

"But to go so far as murder?"

Zach shrugged. "I recognized early on I wasn't necessarily cut out to be the triggerman. But finding capable talent is never that hard. You just have to know where to look. Mitch and Chuck here are experts. Former military with combat under their belts. Not to mention the all-important explosives work."

Annja looked at Dave. "And where does he come into play?"

Zach sighed. "Well, Dave here is a bona fide special agent with the Federal Bureau of Investigation."

Annja stared at Dave and he shrugged. "You thought I was the bad guy. Sorry about that," he said.

She shrugged. She'd gotten everything so wrong. She looked back at Zach. "So what, he was sent to dismantle your operation?"

"We had a tough time figuring him out. He played the geologist part well. But when you went and used his satellite phone, that kind of made us a little nervous. You see, he's not the only one with a sat phone. I've got one, too."

Annja frowned. "You're full of surprises."

Zach nodded. "You bet."

Mitch still hadn't done much in the way of moving closer to her. And Zach seemed perfectly at ease. Chuck was still rigging the explosives.

"And now you're going to kill us?" Annja asked.

Zach got up from his seat. "Definitely. I'm afraid your

deaths are necessary to ensure that our plan comes off without another hitch."

"And the three of you will be the only survivors? How suspicious is that going to look?"

"Not suspicious at all. You see, we're bringing the colonel's body back to McMurdo. We're on a mission of mercy. How could we ever know that this entire camp and its inhabitants were about to die?"

"Poor you," Annja said.

"Money is a perfect grief counselor," Zach said. Chuck laughed and Mitch smiled.

Annja frowned. "Wait a minute, there's one thing I don't understand—"

"Just one thing?" Zach said mockingly.

"Yesterday, I saw members of the other research team planting explosives in here. But that wall is fake. Anyone would be able to see that if they felt it. Why didn't they know?"

Zach nodded at Chuck. "Show her."

Chuck walked over to a section of the cavern she hadn't explored. She heard him switch a button on, and instantly the area was filled with people. And they were doing the exact same actions Annja had witnessed yesterday.

"A hologram?" The whole scene was getting crazier.

Zach smiled. "Tripped by a motion sensor at the entrance to the cavern as you came in and snooped yesterday. Nice, huh?"

"And what about the real team? Where are they?"

Mitch smiled. "Buried farther down another tunnel that we dug and covered up."

"I saw them in the chow hall the other night," Annja said.

Mitch nodded. "And then the next day they had a tragic accident."

"You're sick. All of you."

Zach sighed. "I wish you'd try to understand that I don't want to kill you. But unfortunately, it's just one of the things that has to be dealt with. And I've suffered far too long to have anyone interrupt my plans now."

Zach looked at Chuck. "How much longer?"

"Two minutes."

Zach nodded and then looked back at Annja. "So this is it, then. Goodbye. I hope you can forgive me."

"No chance in hell of that," Annja said.

Zach shrugged. "Fair enough. All right, let's see your hands. I've got to tie you up so we can get out of here." Zach spoke to Mitch. "Keep them covered."

He nodded. "No sweat."

Zach approached Dave first.

But as he came in, Dave suddenly exploded, lashing out with a punch and a kick that caught Zach right in the stomach. "Run, Annja!" he shouted.

As Annja moved she heard a gunshot. She felt something hard slam into the back of her head.

And everything went dark.

36

"Wake up, Annja."

She opened her eyes and squinted at the light. Her head throbbed. Again. If this keeps up, she thought, I'm going to have to get steel plates embedded over my skull.

Her hands were bound behind her. She was also tied down to a number of wooden crates that reduced her mobility even more. Annja took a few shallow breaths and looked around.

Dave's body lay nearby, a large pool of blood spreading out and seeping into the dark ground. "You killed him?" she cried.

Zach shrugged. "He left us no choice. If it's any consolation, he was going to die anyway, soon enough. Maybe it's better he went this way."

"So you've added killing a federal agent to your list of crimes now. Very impressive," Annja spit out.

"Actually, it was me," Mitch said, "but whatever."

Zach checked the ropes holding Annja down. "Chuck does such good work with knots. I don't imagine you'll be escaping from these anytime soon. Certainly not before this whole mountain explodes and comes down on top of you."

Annja frowned. "I never thought I'd have to kill a friend before, Zach. But you've certainly proved yourself worthy of being the first."

Mitch chuckled. "She's got quite the mouth, doesn't she?"

Zach stepped away from Annja. "If you can somehow manage to free yourself in the next few minutes, I'll be more than happy to hand myself over without complaint. How's that sound?"

"Like you're lying again," Annja said.

Zach smiled. "Well, you're right. But I do have a responsibility to spend all of my newfound money. So forgive me for not following through."

Chuck stood and came walking over. "It's done," he said.

"All of it?" Zach asked.

"Yeah. How much time do you want to put on the clock?"

Zach checked his watch. "It'll take us some time to get the Sno-Cats started up. And I don't want to risk any problems given this damned weather."

"What about the colonel's body?" Mitch asked.

"It's being stored out behind the mess shelter. There's no security on it, so it shouldn't be a problem just getting it right onto the back of a cat."

Mitch stowed his pistol. "I can get that and head over to the cats. Once I get one primed, it shouldn't take but a minute to roll on out of here."

"We'll need two," Zach said. "Plus the tow hitch for the generator."

Annja laughed bitterly. "Yeah, you guys are going to be low profile towing that thing back to McMurdo. You going to kill everyone who happens to see you pulling that thing behind your convoy?"

"Only if we have to," Zach said. "But once we get to the harbor, it won't matter. It's going on board a freighter registered out of Liberia and no one will even know about it once it's safely stowed."

Annja shook her head. "What about the ice floes blocking the harbor?"

Mitch paused before leaving. "Nothing that a good couple of portable charges can't break up."

"Somehow, I doubt the marshal will appreciate you mining the harbor."

Mitch grinned. "Oh, didn't you hear? Poor Marshal Dunning and his deputy are dead. Terrible accident, really. Guess they weren't paying attention to things and wound up dead from carbon-monoxide poisoning. I hear some replacements are flying in when weather permits. Of course, we'll be long gone by then."

Annja watched him leave and then turned to Zach. She had to find a way to stop him. "It's not too late, you know. You can still change this," she said gently.

"And why would I want to?" he asked.

"To do the right thing?"

Zach laughed. "Doing the right thing is exactly why I'm in this position right now. You ever notice how the worst people in the world—the liars, crooks and cheats—are always the ones that gain the most? And that the naïve fools who try to live an honorable life are the ones who have to skimp and save and live paycheck to paycheck. Why is that?"

"I don't know," Annja said.

"Exactly. All around there are these idiots telling you to have faith that things will work out in the end. Wrong. Things don't work out in the end. You die a miserable fool who spent his whole life wishing and hoping—all for nothing. That's not how I'm going to spend my life. Not a chance. I'm doing this because I can get away with it and live to spend a god-awful amount of money."

Annja tried her hands, but the knots were indeed tight.

"Were you ever promised an easy path, Zach? Did God come down and tell you it was going to be easy? Did he renege on that promise?"

"If there was a God, why would he make so many people struggle and suffer? You ever think of that? Why would he permit these other scumbags to have all the money they needed and more and yet never see fit to give some to the good folks who actually deserve an easier life?"

Annja shook her head. "I don't know."

"Two for two," Zach said. "You aren't exactly convincing me to give up my plan here."

"You're going to kill an awful lot of people," she said.

"Yes. I am."

Chuck walked past Annja. "You're wasting your breath. If I were you, I'd spend more time trying to find God and see if he's going to help you get out of those knots."

Annja eyed him. "You're not nearly as funny as you think you are."

"Nothing comedic about it,' he said. "You're dying soon. I was actually trying to redirect your focus so you could make peace with that fact."

Annja tried to head-butt him but he jumped back out of the way, laughing. "Wow, she is a tough one."

Annja smirked. "A killer who does public-service announcements. That's refreshing."

Chuck glanced at Zach. "How much time?"

Zach chewed his lip. "Thirty minutes. That should be enough time."

"You sure?"

Zach nodded. "Do it."

Chuck walked to the detonator and Annja watched him as he punched in the time until the explosives detonated. Annja needed them to clear out if she was going to get out of this and warn the camp.

"So that's it, then," she said to Zach.

He nodded. "I wish it could have been different, Annja. But I won't lose sleep over this."

"I know it," she said sadly.

"Goodbye." He turned to Chuck. "Let's go."

Annja watched them leave the cavern. As soon as they cleared the entrance, she immediately closed her eyes. It was tough reaching the sword with her hands bound.

But she was sure she could do it.

In her mind's eye, she reached out with her hands and wrapped them around the hilt. She visualized the sword being in her hands so strongly that she could feel it against her skin even before she opened her eyes again.

The sword was behind her, its blade touching the first of the knots. It cleaved through them easily and Annja had to be careful she didn't drop the sword by accident. The sound of that could carry and bring Zach and Chuck back.

She leaned forward and cut the ropes binding her to the boxes.

She took a breath and rushed to the detonator near the explosives. The digital readout blinked as the scrolling numbers flew past as it counted down from thirty minutes.

She knew nothing about deactivating bombs. She had only basic skill with making them, and that had come from long talks with friends over lots of beer. Her mind was hazy when it came to actually doing it for real. Someone in camp would have to know how to deal with this.

Hawk!

The demolitions guy who had attempted to disarm Annja's computer might be able to handle the job. If she could get to him without being seen.

She had to try.

Annja turned and raced out of the cavern. With the sword

held before her, its energy rushed through her, making her feel powerful and capable of stopping Zach and his goons.

At the fork, she turned and kept going. Ahead of her, she could see the lit shelter by the entrance. She had no doubt that if Zach, Chuck or Mitch saw her, they would simply open fire on her and then try to escape.

Annja knew she needed Garin. No one would listen to her unless Major Braden ordered it.

She paused by the door leading outside and waited until she felt it was safe to proceed. She ducked out and instantly felt the blast of frigid wind slam into her. At the same time, all the lights in the camp were extinguished.

Annja rushed through the snow toward Garin's shelter. At the door, she banged on it and then tore it open. An emergency lantern hung near the door, and Annja turned it on.

Garin lay slumped on his bed, a giant welt on the side of his head. His shelter had been thoroughly ransacked.

Annja slapped his face. "Wake up!" she urged him.

He moved sluggishly, groaning as he did so. "Annja?"

"You've got to pull it together. It's Zach who is behind this. Dave's dead down in the caves and he's not the only one."

Garin's eyes fluttered open.

"There's a bomb rigged to explode in less than thirty minutes It's going to bring down the entire mountain on top of us unless we can get it deactivated. But I don't know how to do that."

Garin was mumbling. "They came in here. Too many of them to stop them. They nailed me before I knew what hit me. Hard hit, that guy. Bastard."

"Garin. You've got to pull it together," Annja said.

Garin frowned and tried to sit up. Annja helped him into a sitting position and he pointed. "You really think you should be running around here with that thing? Some of those soldiers might shoot you just for seeing that."

Annja nodded. "All right, fine." She closed her eyes and

willed the sword back to the other where. When she opened them, Garin was smiling at her.

"I never get tired of seeing that," he said.

"We don't have time for this, Garin. I need Hawk," she said.

"Right. The demolitions guy."

"Yes. He can dismantle the bomb," Annja said.

Garin shook his head. "He couldn't do squat with your computer. What makes you think he can deactivate the bomb?"

"He's the only one. You've got to make him try. He won't listen to me if I ask him."

Garin nodded. "Help me to my feet."

Annja got her arms around him and helped him up. Garin struggled into his parka and then led them outdoors. As they came outside, Annja looked behind his shelter. "They've already got the generator," she said. "That's why all the lights are out."

Garin looked. "How did they manage that so fast?"

"Zach had a plan. And two capable men with him. They knew what they were doing and how long it would take to carry it out. We've got to stop them."

Annja nudged him through the cold night. "We need Hawk first, though. We can always catch up with Zach. Right now, the lives of everyone in camp depend on us stopping that bomb."

Garin pointed. "Steer me over there to that shelter."

Annja helped him walk. The wind tore at them both, and Annja had to grunt and push her way through the bitter blasts to reach the shelter. She yanked on the door and then Garin stepped through to the other side, which was illuminated by several emergency lanterns. Annja could see they were in a barracks. Garin removed his hood. "Where's Sergeant Hawk?" he called out.

"Here."

Garin nodded. "Get your gear and your crew, Sergeant. I've got a job for you."

"A job, sir?"

"Yes. Earlier today, you weren't able to disarm the laptop bomb."

"That's right, sir. Bombs aren't my specialty."

Garin laid a hand on his shoulder. "Well, they are now. Because there's a bomb down at the dig site. And if you can't figure out how to deactivate it, the mountain is coming down on top of all of us in this camp. We'll all be dead."

37

Annja stepped out of the shelter and watched as Hawk and his team ran toward the entrance to the dig site wearing headlamps. She wished them luck. They were going to need it.

Garin came up behind her. "How much time do they have?"

"No more than twenty minutes. At the most. Then this whole place is going to be leveled."

"Look!"

Annja spun and looked in the direction that Garin pointed. She saw the bright headlights of Sno-Cats coming out of the parking area. One of them had a tow platform on its back, and she could make out the tarp covering what must have been the nuclear generator.

"They're already leaving!"

Garin put a hand on her shoulder. "Forget them for right now. Let's make sure everyone gets out of here first."

"You're right, we've got to get people out of here."

Annja moved from shelter to shelter telling the soldiers to get packed. Most of them didn't believe her until Garin addressed them and told them it was not a drill. They started moving quickly after that.

"Forget anything that is not immediately necessary for your survival," Garin said. "Team up on the Sno-Cats and plot your course back to McMurdo. We need to evacuate the area as soon as possible."

There wasn't a lot left to do. Garin looked at Annja. "We need to reserve a few Sno-Cats for us and for Hawk and his team."

"You take care of that and I'll head down to see how they're doing," Annja said.

Garin nodded and rushed off.

Annja checked her watch.

Fifteen minutes.

Maybe.

She hustled back to the entrance to the dig site, grabbed a headlamp and ran down to the cavern. Operating with the light from emergency lanterns and their headlamps, Hawk and two of his men had the detonator box open, but they didn't look happy at all.

"What's the matter?" she asked.

Hawk frowned. "What the hell are you doing here?"

Annja sighed. "This wasn't done by me. Or the bomb earlier today. I'm telling you guys I have nothing to do with this. You've got to believe me!"

Hawk looked at her intently. "Yeah, all right. That job on the computer wasn't the kind of thing I'd expect you to be able to do anyway. No offense."

"None taken," Annja said.

"Come here and look at this," the soldier said.

Annja walked over and knelt next to him. Hawk had an insulated set of tools with him that he used to prod several parts of the detonator. "Here's the problem. Whoever built this knew what they were doing. It's got three redundant backup switches. If we clip one of them, the others will fire anyway. We'll be blown apart."

"Can't you cut them all?" she asked.

"We'd have to cut them at the same time," Hawk said. "And we don't have enough people."

"You do now," Annja said. "I can be one of the cutters."

Hawk eyed her. "You understand what you're saying? If we screw this up, the bomb will blow even if the countdown hasn't reached zero yet."

Annja took a breath. "Hang on. Let me run back and make sure the camp is as evacuated as it's going to get. Don't touch anything until I get back."

Hawk smirked. "Like we would."

Annja ran back and found Garin standing by the entrance directing Sno-Cats out of the parking area. "How long until everyone's gone?"

He shrugged. "Five minutes. I've got two Sno-Cats held in reserve for us to go as soon as you give the word."

Annja nodded. "You'd better go, then."

"What?"

"I'm staying to help Hawk and his team. The bomb has three redundant switches or something. They have to be cut at the same time or else the bomb will blow."

Garin shook his head. "Don't be ridiculous, Annja. You can't stay."

"I have to."

"You could die."

She nodded. "Maybe."

Garin frowned. "And you're willing to do it anyway?"

Annja tried to smile, but somehow it didn't come out the way she hoped it would. "I feel like I owe it to Colonel Thomson and Dave. So their deaths aren't in vain."

Garn shook his head. "You weren't responsible for their deaths, Annja."

"We're running out of time," she said. "Take the Sno-Cat and go. You've got to catch up with Zach and stop him from selling that nuclear generator."

Garin shook his head. "No. You go. I'll stay behind."

Annja looked at him. "What are you talking about? I just said that I was fine with it."

"Annja." Garin stared at her. "I won't die."

"You don't know that you can take a blast like that. There's enough explosive down there to demolish a mountain. I'm not so sure even you could survive that. And I don't believe you want to take a chance."

"What about you? What about what you have yet to accomplish with the sword?"

Annja frowned. "What do you mean?"

Garin had to shout over the roar of the howling wind now. "Haven't you ever thought about it? Don't you realize this is why your life keeps plunging you into these crazy situations?"

Annja shrugged. "What are you getting at?"

"This is why the sword picked you, Annja. Your sense of self-sacrifice. It knew you'd be the only one willing to die so others could live. This is why you get wrapped up in these adventures. You're supposed to. There's evil in the world and you're one of the few who has the courage to face it. And defeat it."

Annja thought about what Garin was saying. Maybe he was right.

"But that doesn't give me the right to back out now just because there's a chance I might die," she reasoned.

Garin shook his head. "No, you're not supposed to die here. But maybe I am."

"Garin, if what you just told me is true, then if I leave now, I'll be shirking that responsibility. I'll be proving that I don't have the courage to see this through to the end. And I might lose the sword. What would happen then?"

"But if you die—"

"I won't," Annja said. "Now, go."

Garin looked at her for another moment. "I'll never forgive myself if you die in that mountain, Annja."

She smiled and then did something she never thought she would. She leaned forward and kissed him lightly on his lips. "You know, you're pretty cool when you show that you actually care about someone other than yourself."

Garin looked shocked. "I don't know what will happen to the sword if you die," he said.

Annja smiled. "I've got to go."

She turned and hurried back into the entrance before she thought twice about it. The last thing she wanted to do was run back toward the danger. Toward what might be her death.

But she had no choice.

She hurried down the tunnel passageway, back into the cavern.

Hawk looked at her. "What kept you?"

"We had to get everyone out."

"Everyone?"

"We're the only ones left," she said.

Hawk nodded. "I'm an eternal optimist. You made sure we've got a Sno-Cat, right?"

"Absolutely."

He smiled. "All right. Let's do this."

Annja knelt next to him. "You'll have to explain to me exactly what I'm supposed to do."

Hawk used a pair of wire cutters to point out the wire in question. "This one is yours. Tony's got that one, Don has the one next to it and I have this one here. That puppy is all yours."

The guy Hawk had called Tony cleared his throat. "Hawk, we've got another problem here."

Hawk looked up. "What now?"

Tony held up two more wire cutters. "Only two left. And there are three that need cutting."

"Shit. None of you has a knife or something?"

Don brought out a Swiss Army knife. "I've only got a blade on it and there's no guarantee it would cut in time as the others were cut."

Hawk shook his head. "We can't risk it."

Annja looked at him. "What does that mean?"

"It means we get the hell out of here and put some distance between us and this mountain before this entire places goes up."

Annja frowned. There had to be another way. "Wait," she said.

Hawk turned back. "What?"

"I've got something that can cut the wire."

"You do?"

Annja nodded. "Yeah, but you guys won't believe it. So I'm going to ask you to not ask any questions. Just accept the fact that I can cut the wire and let's move on from there."

Hawk frowned. "Yeah, okay. No sweat."

Tony and Don nodded. "Let's get it done," Tony said. "I've got three minutes on the clock here. Time's ticking down."

Annja raced into the tunnel out of the men's field of vision. She closed her eyes and unsheathed the sword. As she rushed back into the cavern, she heard the sharp intakes of breath

"What the hell?" Tony said.

Hawk pointed at her. "You said not to ask, but damn—"

"No questions," Annja said firmly.

Hawk looked at Tony and Don and they simply shrugged. "Let's get in position," he said.

Hawk backed off to allow Annja room to get in with the very point of her sword. He turned to her. "You absolutely positive that thing will cut?"

"It's razor sharp," she said.

"Okay," Hawk said. "Positions." He placed his wire cutters over his wire. Tony got his into position and Don did the same.

Annja waited until they were set and then she carefully placed the tip of her sword next to her wire. "I'll cut upward to sever it, just so you guys know which direction the blade will be moving."

"Thanks," Hawk said. "It would suck to get beheaded right after we deactivated this thing."

Tony smirked. "Don't make me laugh, man."

"You guys ready?" Hawk asked.

Don and Tony nodded. Hawk looked at Annja. "Annja?"

"I'm ready."

Hawk looked at the detonator clock. "One minute to go."

Tony took a breath. "What's the count?"

"On three," Hawk said.

Annja looked at him. "I always get confused by that. Do we do it one-two-three-cut or one-two-cut?"

"One-two-cut," Hawk said. He glanced around. "Clear?"

"Clear," everyone said in unison.

Everyone took a breath and readied themselves. Annja looked at the tip of her sword. She closed her eyes. Please let this work, she thought to herself. These people don't deserve to die.

Hawk cleared his throat. "Here we go."

Annja tensed.

"One."

Annja gripped the sword.

"Two."

Annja took another breath.

"Cut."

38

Nothing happened.

Hawk exhaled in a rush. "Tony, check the clock."

"It's stopped."

Annja stepped away from the bomb. "Did we do it?"

Hawk nodded. "Sure looks that way."

Don pointed. "Holy shit, was that close. Look at the clock."

Annja peered at the digital readout display and saw that there were eight seconds left on the countdown. "Oh, my God," she said weakly.

Hawk smiled. "Better early than late, I guess." He looked at Annja. "Thanks for your help. And I'm sorry that no one believed you earlier about killing Colonel Thomson."

"Forget it. I'm just glad that we were able to stop the detonation." Annja pointed at the piles of explosives. "But what happens now? Is it safe to just leave this stuff here?"

Hawk frowned. "I didn't even think about that. I mean, I suppose we could stay—"

"No, you can't. They stole the generator. That's what this whole thing was about. There's no power left in camp. No lights, no heat. You'd never survive out here," Annja said.

Hawk frowned. "I thought this whole mission was to uncover relics that might have been from another planet."

"That's what we all thought," Annja said. "But it was all a setup to get their hands on the latest technology from the government and then sell it on the black market to anyone with the right amount of cash."

"And there'd be plenty of people willing to play a lot of money for that, as well," Tony said. "Non-nuclear powers in particular. Cripes, can you imagine what that would do? They'd have the ability to make more of them and become a nuclear power."

Annja nodded. "We know they're on their way back to McMurdo. Major Braden is tracking them and we hope to stop them before they get away with it."

Hawk stood. "In that case, we'd better get going. I don't think there's much chance of someone coming by and stumbling on a huge cache of explosives, especially since the generator is gone."

Annja led the way. "There's one Sno-Cat left. It won't be comfortable, but it will get us all back to McMurdo."

Hawk nodded. "Well, let's get back on the hunt for those guys. I don't want to hear about some place like the Sudan getting their hands on a nuclear generator just because we were too busy defusing a bomb."

Annja led them out of the cavern and back up the tunnel. "You sure the explosives will be okay?"

Hawk nodded. "As soon as we can get another team mounted, we'll come back and retrieve them. That way, there won't be any danger to anyone. But for now, I think the priority is getting back to McMurdo."

They walked back up the tunnel and out of the shelter. Annja pointed at the Sno-Cat sitting by the parking area. Its engine was already idling and the wipers kept the snow from collecting on the windshield.

Garin must have left it running, Annja thought. That was optimistic.

Hawk and his men climbed in and then Annja climbed into the shotgun seat. As soon as she got the door closed, Hawk put the gear into Drive and the Sno-Cat ground its way out of the parking area. In no time, they were leaving the camp behind.

Annja keyed the radio. "Major Braden, come in, please."

She heard nothing but static. Outside, the wind was blowing even harder, kicking up fearsome snow squalls and drifting snow.

Hawk pointed. "Look at that storm. You may not get any kind of transmission right now."

"You think the other Sno-Cats are okay?" she asked.

He nodded. "The GPS units will work regardless. They should be fine with finding their way back to McMurdo. It's just a question of how long it will take us to get there. These things max out at about twenty-five miles per hour. And you can bet the bad guys are pushing the pedal to the metal right now."

"But," Annja said, "they're weighed down with the generator. There's a chance we might overtake them. Or rather, Major Braden might overtake them."

"Possibly," Hawk said. "I wouldn't count on it, though. I think the best thing to do is get back and try to catch them before they leave McMurdo."

Snow pounded the windshield, and Hawk switched the wipers on to full force. "We're driving right into the brunt of the storm now," he said. "It's going to be tough going from here on out."

Annja glanced back at Tony and Don. "Did you guys happen to bring any weapons with you?"

Tony smiled. "What, like maybe large broadswords?"

Annja frowned. "Funny."

Tony smiled. "We have pistols. That's it."

"It'll have to be enough," Annja said. "You're going to need them because these guys we're going after are not going to play nice when we catch up with them."

"There's something else," Hawk said.

"What?"

"They may not be alone, either. They might have a whole bunch of friends there just waiting to help them smuggle that generator off the continent."

No one said anything for a moment.

And then Annja cleared her throat. "We'll have to take it as it comes. And if there are other people, we'll have to deal with them, too."

39

The Sno-Cat took another left turn. Annja watched the map on the screen and frowned. "Where are they going?" she asked.

Hawk shook his head. "I thought you said they were heading straight for McMurdo."

Annja studied the map, trying to pick out a route and wondering how Zach intended to get the generator out of Antarctica. Going to McMurdo didn't make sense. Her instincts were screaming that Zach had some other plan than the one he'd told her about. She tried to put herself in Zach's mind. Where would he go? Could she figure it out? "Look at this. Is it possible to put a boat into shore here?" she asked after some time.

Hawk peered closer. "Between Berkner Island and that cover?" He frowned. "I don't know. I think there's a huge ice sheet that makes that part of the coast completely blocked this time of year."

Annja looked closer. She felt sure she was on the right track. "Yes, but what if they traversed the ice sheet? Would it be strong enough yet to hold the weight they're carrying?"

"Theoretically. But it would still be a huge risk," Hawk said.

Annja nodded. "He's already taking a giant risk doing what he's doing. I don't know how much he'd mind taking another."

"You think that's his plan?"

Annja thought about it. "I think he'll traverse the ice sheet and rendezvous with a ship somewhere around here. If they can put in just offshore, they should be able to transport the generator and get in on board without anyone knowing about it."

Hawk sighed. "That's a long haul. We'll never make it unless we get some more fuel into our tank."

They drove in silence for some time as Annja formulated a plan. She glanced out of the windshield. Something about the area seemed familiar. She snapped her fingers. "Pull over there," she suddenly told Hawk.

"Huh?" Hawk looked at her. "Why are we stopping?"

"Gas station," she said as she zipped up her parka and hopped out. The wind tore at her, and she had to stoop low to avoid being swept off her feet. Snow and ice particles bit into her and pelted her parka from every angle.

But there it was. It all made sense now.

Just across the way, partially buried in the snow, was Zach's original Sno-Cat. She knew she'd find some jerricans filled with fuel. Did he cause the snowslide for just this purpose? Luckily, it looked as if Zach had drastically overestimated the amount of gas he would need, and there was plenty left.

Hawk jumped out to help her load up and they took a bunch more of the cans along, stowing them in the back of their vehicle. When they hopped back into the cab, the tanks were full and Annja felt a surge of confidence that they could catch up with Zach. She tried reaching Garin on the radio but still got nothing but static. At least if he got to McMurdo he could head off Zach if her instincts were steering them in the wrong direction.

"He'll be moving slower because of what they're towing. We can catch up with him," she said.

Hawk gunned the engine. "Let's see if you're right."

ZACH STUDIED the GPS display and sighed. The worst part of this barren land was the incredible amount of time it took to get anywhere. The Sno-Cats lumbered along at a slow pace, and the miles between anything remotely civilized stretched like years.

He checked his watch. Horlick Mountain should have exploded by now, reducing the entire area to a pile of rubble. He frowned. It really was too bad about Annja.

He cared little about the soldiers he'd just killed. They were an acceptable amount of collateral damage. And it was a sacrifice for the greater good—his greater good.

He tried to picture the reaction of the U.S. government. At first, they'd be horrified that there'd been a disaster of that scale down here. And not knowing right away what had happened to their precious generator, they'd have to assume it was also a casualty of the explosion. They'd send in nuclear-emergency specialists to try to contain the nuclear waste that would damage the environment.

Eventually, they'd discover that the generator wasn't there. And then they'd panic.

Zach allowed himself a smile. The plan had been incredibly expensive and elaborate to produce, but it had worked. Since he'd first heard whispers about the generator, he'd spent nights lying awake thinking about how he could get his hands on it.

Now, it was his. Soon he'd have wealth beyond belief.

His radio crackled and Mitch broke the silence. "You okay back there?"

Zach smiled and grabbed the microphone. "I'm fine. A little sleepy, but it's been a long haul."

"Yeah. Hey, the explosives should have detonated by now, huh? I'm surprised we didn't feel anything."

"I guess we got far enough away," Zach said.

"Sorry about your friend," Mitch said insincerely.

Zach chuckled. "Don't be. Just the cost of doing business. And the money will help me forget all about her."

"I think it will help us all."

"Absolutely. Have you both settled on a country with no extradition policy to the United States?"

"We were thinking about someplace nice and warm."

Zach understood that. After this jaunt, the last thing he ever wanted to see again was a snowflake. "Agreed. A beach resort with those fruity drinks and umbrellas?"

"And chicks with thongs," Mitch said.

Zach laughed. "Another few hours and we'll be on our way. We can celebrate by cracking open a bottle of champagne. You made arrangements with the freighter to have some stocked, I assume?"

"You know it," Mitch said.

"We'll talk soon, then. We shouldn't have more than fifty miles left to travel before we start seeing landmarks for it." He disconnected and continued driving. The biggest danger had always been getting out intact. There'd been no way they could go back through McMurdo. Killing the marshal had been a simple ruse and he expected it would work flawlessly. Investigators would search for signs they'd gone back that way, when in reality, they'd done the opposite, traveling across the barren land that skirted the South Pole to drive toward a more isolated section of the coast.

Once at their rendezvous area, they could stop, prepare for the meet and take a breath.

Soon, he thought, as the Sno-Cat's tracks churned through the snow and ice. Soon, I'll be able to relax.

ANNJA PEERED out of the windshield. The wind seemed to be dying down. Less snow pelted the windshield and the outside-temperature gauge was rising.

"Is it getting warmer outside?" she asked.

Hawk looked at the gauge. "Seems to be. Weird, huh? You can never tell what it will be like down here."

"It's still freaking cold," Tony said. "That's a constant."

Annja smiled. "Yes, it's still cold, but the storm seems to be dying. And that's a good thing."

"We might make better time, huh?" Tony said.

"Yes," Annja agreed. "Zach should be surprised when we show up. And we'll need every advantage we can get."

Don leaned in from the backseat. "How many guys do you think Zach will have with him?"

"I don't know. We know he already has two with him. I suppose it depends on what he has planned and how close they can get to the coast."

Hawk glanced at her. "You're convinced it's a ship, right?"

"How could it be anything else this time of year?" she asked.

"Yeah, you're right. I just had a strange feeling, that's all."

Annja nodded. "I've had a few of those."

ZACH KEYED the microphone. "Okay, we should be there soon."

Mitch's voice came back. "How long once we're there before we can expect our pickup?"

"The rendezvous is set for just over an hour from now. We'll have to wait it out. We made better time than I thought."

"I don't like waiting," Mitch said.

"Neither do I, but we don't have any choice. This was the best I could do given everything we had to accomplish back at that camp."

"And they'll be there, right?"

Zach sighed. "Yes, Mitch, they'll be there. Offer people a lot of money, and you'd be surprised what they're willing to do for you."

"As long as they show. We're dead if these guys aren't there to pick us up."

"They will be," Zack said. He looked out of the windshield. The sky seemed to be brightening a little. "I think it's going to be a great day."

THE SNO-CAT JERKED and changed direction. Annja studied the map and hoped she was right to follow her instincts. Stop doubting yourself, she thought. They'd be on Zach soon enough and then that would be that. She expected him not to survive their next meeting.

She hated that realization. She'd known him for a long time. But his refusal to give up his quest had angered her. Possession of the generator was a dangerous and evil thing, and Zach had embraced it.

He didn't care about what was right anymore.

The next time they met would be in battle.

Annja glanced around the cramped cabin of the Sno-Cat. She knew what she had to do. She just hoped Hawk and his men were up to the challenge.

"Look," Hawk said, breaking into Annja's thoughts. "The GPS is signaling that we're approaching our destination."

"What does that mean?" Don asked.

Annja felt her adrenaline starting to flow. "It means," she said, "that they're out here somewhere."

ZACH CLAMBERED OUT of the cab of the Sno-Cat and stretched his legs. It felt marvelous to be able to move again after that long drive. Mitch and Chuck joined him from across the way.

Mitch shielded his eyes and looked at the sky overhead. "You were right—it looks like it might be a good day, huh?"

"I think so," Zach agreed.

"How long once we get aboard before you can contact the potential buyers?"

Zach smiled. "Our auction will be held while we're on

board. I've got a secure communications system set up, and we'll have the luxury of reclining and drinking our champagne while they all try to outbid each other. I expect it will be a marvelous feeling knowing that with each passing minute we'll be exponentially richer."

Mitch smiled. "If we had glasses, I'd toast you right now."

Zach nodded. "Well, let's get this done and then we can toast each other for the rest of our lives."

ANNJA FELT her heart beating faster. "We must be close."

In the backseat, Tony and Don chambered rounds into their pistols. The metallic slides clicked into place and Annja realized how strange it felt to be riding into battle. She'd never get used to it, she decided. Something about knowing you were a few moments away from possibly killing another human being never felt like the right thing to do to her.

But she learned that sometimes it was the only way.

"There," Hawk said. "I see them."

Annja followed his direction and just a few miles away across the icy plain, she could make out the two Sno-Cats.

"You guys ready?" she asked.

"Absolutely."

"Then let's do this."

40

"Who the hell is that?"

Zach spun and frowned. "It's not our rendezvous, that's for damned sure."

Mitch pulled out his pistol and chambered a round. "Well, then, it's someone who isn't going to be happy they stumbled across us."

Chuck pulled a pistol, as well. "There's no way anyone stumbled on us. Somehow they found us." He turned to Zach. "How did this happen? Did you give us up? Not too keen on splitting the money with us, you cheap bastard?"

"You think I let them know where we were going? Don't be ridiculous! I've got more to lose on this than either of you and there's no way I'd ever sell us out." How had they found them? he wondered. And who were they?

"Yeah, well, if I find out you sold us out, I'm going to take a lot of pleasure in killing you," Chuck said menacingly.

"Enough of this," Mitch said. "Set up a cross fire. Chuck, get on the other side. As they come toward us, we'll press them with fire and see if we can't stop them."

Chuck grumbled but moved into position. Zach watched

the two men maneuver and eased himself back. He had a pistol under his parka but didn't really want to use it unless he absolutely had to.

He looked at the approaching Sno-Cat. Who was it? And how in the world had they found them?

"DID YOU SEE THAT?"

Hawk nodded. "They'll flank us on either side, hoping to catch us in a cross fire. They can direct fire and disable the cat, hopefully kill us before we can climb out."

"Right," Tony said. "Well, we know how to deal with that. Slow down."

Annja looked back. "What are you going to do?"

Don smiled. "Jump out and flank the flankers. No sense letting them have all the fun."

Annja nodded. "Be careful, guys."

Tony glanced at Don. "I'll take the right."

"Roger that. See you on the other side."

"I can't slow it down too much or they'll see the action," Hawk said. "I'm going to stutter-step it and then change direction to draw their eyes away from where you guys are."

"We're ready," Tony said.

"Stand by," Hawk said.

Annja clutched her seat as Hawk suddenly jerked the wheel and turned the Sno-Cat to the right. As he did, Tony opened his door and fell out. Hawk then jerked the cat left and Don did the same.

Hawk straightened the vehicle and then started aiming it in on a slight angle.

Behind them in the snow, Tony and Don were completely exposed. But Annja hoped they could maneuver and get an edge over Zach's men.

"WHAT THE HELL WAS THAT?"

Mitch frowned. "Maybe they skidded on a patch of ice."

Chuck shook his head. "I don't like it."

Zach pointed. "It's coming straight on us now, so whatever, right?"

"It's angling," Mitch said. "It might be trying to disrupt our positioning." He called out to Chuck. "Keep an eye on the ground it just left. I've got a bad feeling about this."

Zach fidgeted with his own pistol. He decided he might need it after all. "You think they've got something planned?" he called out.

"If I knew I was about to confront an enemy, I'd certainly make it my business to have a plan. Wouldn't you?" Mitch said.

"I guess."

"All right, then. How about this? You take over watching Chuck's flank. Shoot anyone who comes at us from that direction. I'll handle this side, and Chuck will make sure we don't get ambushed."

Zach looked at his pistol and sighed. "All right."

HAWK FROWNED. "Is that Zach I see? Looks like he's armed."

Annja nodded. "I guess there was no way he was going to give up without a fight. Makes me a little sad, though."

"You guys were close," Hawk said.

"I thought we were. Friends only, but you know, you've got that trust level there. And now I find out he was lying the whole time."

"Maybe not the whole time," Hawk said. "But he sure did when it counted, huh?"

"Yeah," Annja said sadly.

Hawk rested his pistol on his lap. "This is going to get messy real quick. I don't have an extra gun for you."

"I don't need one," Annja said.

Hawk looked surprised. "Oh? You have another sword tucked away somewhere like the one you hid in the tunnel?"

Annja laughed. "That would be nice, wouldn't it?"

Hawk gripped his pistol. "Well, let's make sure you don't get hurt doing this job, huh?"

"That'd be nice."

Hawk gunned the Sno-Cat.

And Annja closed her eyes and visualized her sword.

"I SEE SOMEONE over there!"

Zach looked to where Chuck was pointing. He caught a glimpse of something moving in the dim light.

"Shoot it," Mitch said.

"I can't. He's out of range," Chuck said.

Zach looked at Mitch. "What are they trying to do?"

"Outflank us, you idiot. They know we won't give up this position because we've got the benefit of cover with the Sno-Cats. So all they can do is try to come at us from the sides where we're exposed."

"What about the generator?" Zach asked.

Mitch glanced at him. "Is it bulletproof?"

"How should I know?" Zach said.

"Well, I guess we'd all better hope that it is or else we might just start glowing in the dark."

Zach looked at his watch. There wasn't much time left before the rendezvous. "If we can hold them off, our connection will be here soon!"

Mitch nodded. "Then that's what we'll have to do."

"YOU READY?" Hawk asked.

Annja nodded. "Yes," she said as she placed a jerrican on the gas pedal of the Sno-Cat.

Hawk lifted his foot and the Sno-Cat kept going. "Foot's clear," he said.

Annja gripped her door handle. "You sure you've got it aimed properly?"

Hawk nodded. "It shouldn't hit the tow hitch carrying the generator."

"Okay."

Hawk gripped his pistol and his door handle. "Remember to exhale when you land and roll," he advised.

"Got it."

"See you out there," he said. "Go!"

Annja pushed the door open and leaped out into the frozen air, her sword already held in hand.

ZACH HEARD THE GUNSHOTS. Chuck was firing at someone moving off to the left. Someone rose to a crouch and then fell forward. It all seemed to happen in slow motion.

The Sno-Cat continued rumbling toward them. Mitch was shouting something at Zach. Then he turned back and fired two rounds at the cat's windshield, spidering the glass.

The Sno-Cat kept coming.

"It's gonna hit!" Mitch shouted.

Zach turned and ran as the approaching cat crashed into the cat Mitch was using for cover. There was a violent sound of metal twisting and gears grinding as the tracks literally tried to crawl up the side of the stationary cat it had just impacted. Parts of the cab compressed as the weight of the cat settled on it. He wondered if it would explode, but then the cat stopped moving, its gears burned out.

Chuck kept firing at someone.

Zach heard a bullet fly past his ear and ricochet off the other Sno-Cat.

He heard something else, too. Somewhere off in the distance.

Rescue.

ANNJA ROLLED when she landed, exhaling hard as her body made contact with the frozen ground. It wasn't nearly as powdery as she'd thought and the blow to her body rattled her somewhat.

She came up to her feet and charged into the opening. She saw the smaller of the two men from Gallagher's. What had Zach called him? Chuck.

He saw Annja coming and tried to turn to point his pistol at her.

But Annja swung up diagonally from her right side, slicing into Chuck's arm. Blood sprayed and he dropped to the ground clutching at his limb as it pumped blood into the icy ground where it froze almost instantly.

Chuck fell back, already entering severe shock.

Annja spun and looked for Zach.

But her ears picked up a noise.

Reinforcements were arriving.

ZACH AIMED HIS PISTOL at the man who had suddenly appeared right out of the very snow they stood on. The gun bucked in his hand as Zach jerked the trigger back. He used too much pressure and the gun jumped, its bullet flying off at an angle.

The man in front of him smiled and leveled his gun at Zach.

Zach's stomach twisted.

He was a dead man.

When the gunshot came, Zach felt nothing.

He looked down but saw no blood. Then he looked back and saw the man in front of him fall. Behind him Mitch stood, his gun's barrel still smoking.

"Is that our rescue I hear?" Mitch asked.

"Just in time," Zach replied.

Mitch sounded angry. "Hold your own here, Zach. In a few minutes this'll all be over."

ANNJA SAW Hawk fall and two men standing together looking at him. She ran full speed toward them.

Mitch wheeled and brought up his gun.

She batted his hands away with the pommel of the sword. And then cracked him hard with the flat of the blade.

Mitch staggered back, clutching at his face. Blood streamed out of his nose, steaming in the frigid air.

Annja drove him back, swiping at him. But Mitch managed to evade the cuts somehow.

Annja caught some movement out of the corner of her eye. Zach.

Annja dropped. Spun. She threw the sword.

Zach fired his pistol.

The sword pierced the center of Zach's chest, puncturing the thick parka, driving through bone, muscle and arteries.

Annja heard Zach gasp.

He looked down in shock and then slumped to his knees.

His body fell over in the snow.

Annja stared at him in sorrow.

"Don't move, Annja," she heard Mitch growl.

She heard the sound of the trigger and froze. With a sidelong glance she could see Mitch was holding the pistol on her. His face mask was a bloody mess.

"I'm going to enjoy killing you," he said.

"Well, get on with it, then," Annja said angrily.

She heard a series of gunshots.

Mitch fell over dead.

Annja turned. Don stood, still aiming his gun at Mitch's back. He called out to her. "You okay?"

"Yeah," she said, shaking.

He nodded and moved away from Mitch. "Check on Hawk. I'll tend to Tony."

Annja scrambled over to Hawk's body. His eyes fluttered

vaguely, but his pupils were wide, darkness already settling in them. The cold was too much.

Annja looked at the front of his parka and knew it wasn't good. "Hang on, Hawk," she said futilely.

He coughed a little. "Hell, you mean this isn't the afterlife?" he whispered.

Annja smiled. "Not yet."

"Thanks," he said to her. "Thanks for helping make things right." A little bit of pinkish foam sputtered out of his lips. Annja could see darker blood inside his mouth.

"Don't thank me," she said.

"Someone should," Hawk said, before falling quiet.

Annja picked up Hawk's pistol and stood in the snow as Don came back. "Tony's gone."

"Hawk, too," she said.

"Shit."

Annja nodded. "I don't think that's the end, either."

Don looked at her. "What are you talking about?"

"You hear that?"

Don stared off in the distance. "Is that what I think it is?"

Annja sighed. "Yep. It's a helicopter."

41

Annja watched as the massive cargo helicopter came flying in, its rotors beating the ground in a giant swell of ice and snow. As the helicopter flared, the side doors opened and a voice blared out over a speaker.

"Stand where you are! If you move, you will be shot!"

Don looked at Annja. "I don't think these guys are playing around."

"Doesn't look like it. We'd better be cool."

She saw four ropes drop down and then four men in black shimmied down out of the helicopter. They spun and trained automatic weapons on Annja and Don.

"Drop your weapons!" someone shouted.

Don eyed Annja. "Do we do as they say?"

Annja frowned. "They'll shoot us before we can move an inch. We'd better play it their way."

Don dropped his gun. Annja closed her eyes and willed the sword away from Zach's body. She dropped her gun.

"Think they'll kill us?" Don asked.

Annja shrugged. "No idea."

The speaker called out again. "Move back away from the tracked vehicles. Do it now or you will be shot."

Annja and Don walked about forty feet away from the scene of battle. The wind kicked up a little bit and Annja saw the helicopter spin a bit in the updraft. It's got to be hellish trying to keep that bird steady, she thought. Whoever these guys are, they are really good.

The four men moved in on the vehicles. As soon as they reached the tow hitch, they waved the chopper closer. As it came in, a new set of ropes came down and Annja could see they were much thicker.

"They're not interested in us," she said to Don.

"What do you mean? Those guns certainly look interested enough."

"They want the generator. Not us."

"We can't let them get it," Don said. "Not after all of this."

But Annja didn't sense any imminent danger. And she didn't feel as if they had to do anything just now.

"Wait," she said. Something strange was happening. Again.

"Wait?"

"Don, just follow my lead here, okay?" she said.

"Fine," he agreed reluctantly.

Three of the men worked feverishly, securing the new ropes to the sides of the crate that housed the nuclear generator. They employed a series of special locks and cables to make sure everything was tight and unable to move in the wind.

Finally, the men stood back and waved the crate up.

The helicopter strained and then lifted up slightly. The crate moved slowly and then cleared the trailer, aloft about ten feet in the air. Each of the men then attached himself to the rope he'd come down on. As Annja watched, the ropes were drawn back up into the helicopter by a winch.

As quickly as they'd come down, the men were back in the helicopter.

The chopper strained and then lifted higher into the air, taking the nuclear generator with it.

Next to her, Don sighed. "Well, so much for that recovery mission."

"We did the best we could," she said.

"Yeah. But now we have no idea where it's going. That thing could end up in Sierra Leone for all we know."

Annja watched the chopper hover and then turn back toward them. "I hope this isn't the part where they machine-gun us," she said.

"Me, too."

Annja saw the pilot's window open a crack. His hand appeared and dropped something to the ground. It was too light to be a grenade.

As she watched, the chopper turned and sailed back the way it had come. In seconds, even the sound of its rotors beating the Antarctic air was a fading memory.

"What was that they threw down?" Don asked.

Annja shook her head. "I don't know."

She ran over to the small package and picked it up. It was a wooden box sealed with tape. She unsealed it, slid it open, and inside there was a piece of paper. Annja took it out and unfolded it.

Annja—my apologies for making you go through this charade. Zach wasn't the only one skilled at creating a living lie. The generator is, in my opinion, far too potent to be allowed on the black market. There's no telling the destruction it could bring about if it were allowed into the wrong hands. Therefore, I have done the responsible thing and taken possession of it myself. I will arrange for the U.S. government to buy it back from me at a modest profit for my time and troubles. I'm sure I can find a good use for the money. And hopefully, they will learn a vital lesson in the process. Someday, I'll explain how this all went down. Perhaps over a nice bottle of wine. By the time you read this, I'll have left McMurdo. Don't waste your time trying to track me down. You know we'll bump into each other again. It's inevitable. When you get back to McMurdo, think you'll find that there's an airplane inbound to extract the soldiers and yourself. Get some sun when you get home.

Fondly,
Major Braden

Annja laughed. "Unbelievable!" she shouted.

Don took the note from her and read it. When he finished, he looked at her. "What does this mean? Major Braden was a traitor? He set this whole thing up?"

Annja shrugged. "I think Major Braden is a concerned patriot who is keen on keeping that technology away from people who shouldn't have it. And when he figured out that Zach intended to steal it, he took steps to make sure that didn't happen."

"It's too weird. We'll have to show this to the higher-ups when we got back to McMurdo," Don said.

Annja held out her hand and Don gave her the note. Annja ripped it into small pieces. "I don't think that will be necessary. Major Braden will be in touch with them soon enough, anyway."

Don frowned. "Are you sure?"

"Absolutely." She looked back at the battle scene. "Help me collect Tony and Hawk. We'll take them back with us."

"What about Mitch and Zach?" Don asked.

Annja frowned. "Part of me thinks they ought to be left here. But I suppose that wouldn't be right. They deserve a proper burial if nothing else."

"We've got the room if we tie them on the trailer."

"And the gas?"

Don shrugged. "We can salvage enough from the other vehicles to get us home. I'm sure of it."

"All right." She took a moment to kneel down next to Zach's body. I wish it could have been different, she thought. But you made your choice. And I made mine.

"Annja, I need some help," Don said.

She walked over to where Don was already strapping Hawk's body on the trailer. As the wind picked up, Annja looked out over the Antarctic horizon.

"It really is strangely beautiful here," she said.

"And cold as all get-out," Don added.

Annja smiled. "I don't know. After a while, you kind of almost get used to it."

Don regarded her. "I don't know you all that well, but I have to say, your life seems pretty damned crazy. This kind of thing would put other people into therapy for life. And you're standing here enjoying the scenery."

Annja nodded at the other bodies. "Let's get the others strapped down and get going. I want a window seat on the plane ride out of here."

"Yeah, that sounds good."

Annja tucked her hood in a bit tighter. Her life was crazy. No doubt about it.

But at least it was her own.

Annja took a deep breath. Somehow, the frozen Antarctic air didn't seem quite so cold anymore. How Garin had arranged for the freighter to be one of his own, Annja had no clue. Perhaps he'd set the entire thing up when he'd heard about the dig through his network of spies. Garin had plenty of resources he could call upon, and finding moles working for him in the government wasn't nearly as surprising as it once might have been.

Perhaps, he'd wanted the generator himself all along with the intent of holding it for ransom.

Either way, she thought, he's proved himself a far more cunning man than I've given him credit for being. I'll have to remember that in the future. Someday, he just might fool me long enough to steal the sword.

She didn't think there was any way the sword would work for him. But the thought of his trying to wile it out of her didn't repel her quite as much as she once might have thought.

A smile played across her face. This one goes to you, Garin, she thought.

But the next time?

That's up for grabs.

ROOM 59

CLIFF RYDER

BLACK WIDOW

An isolated international incident turns into mass murder....

Young women widowed in Chechnya's bloody conflict with Russia are now willing suicide bombers. Room 59 wants an agent to go undercover as one of the Black Widows—and they recruit MI-6 operative Ajza Manaev. In a world where loyalties and the playing field are often shifting, Ajza is inducted by hellfire into Room 59's hard and fast rule. She's on her own.

Available April 2009
wherever books are sold.

GOLD EAGLE®